GORGEOUS WHITE FEMALE

Adam Zameenzad was born in Pakistan and brought up in East Africa. He went to university in Lahore, and subsequently became a lecturer there. Adam Zameenzad's other novels include: *The Thirteenth House* (winner of the David Higham Prize) and *Cyrus, Cyrus*.

Gorgeous White Female

THE COMIC ADVENTURES OF
A DEMENTED NONAGER
~ OR ~
A CHRONICLE OF
WISDOM AND ENLIGHTENMENT
~ OR ~
THE STORY OF A LOVE

Adam Zameenzad

FOURTH ESTATE • *London*

This paperback edition first published 1996
First published in Great Britain in 1995 by
Fourth Estate Limited
6 Salem Road
London
W2 4BU

A catalogue record for this book is available from the
British Library

ISBN 1–85702–406–0

1 3 5 7 9 8 6 4 2

Printed in Great Britain by
Clays Ltd, St Ives plc

with great affection

for
petter jacobsson

without
whose friendship kindness and apartment
this book
would not have been possible

i shall be always grateful

AND

for
the streets and avenues of manhattan
where i grew up

at long last!

all characters and situations
in this book
are the product of a sick mind
and
a putrid imagination

any
resemblance
to any
real person or event
should be reported
to the department of health and sanitation
forthwith

*the author dissociates himself completely and entirely from the opinions
and attitudes of the divine narrator of this book, either about venice,
new york, or anything or anyone.*

Contents

PART I

Venice

(once upon a long long ago)

I

Lahya was halfway up the stridently pungent stairs of the stridently pungent Hotel Romano when he felt this urge to kill himself. The reasons for that urge were unreasonable; but then, he was just eleven something, and stupid. Under twelve, under stress and under-brained, as his favourite teacher in his first year at his first comprehensive used to say at the drop of a chalk.

His right hand was holding tight to Mumsy's pink paw, his left surrendered reluctantly to dadso's murky grasp. He did not really like calling his mother Mumsy, but she liked to be called Mumsy, and went into bouts of the most spirited silence this side of a Quaker meeting if not called Mumsy. His father hated being called dadso. Lahya liked calling him dadso, so did his mother. She denied liking it, so did he.

The time was eleven something on a sunny morning in April. The city was Venice.

If he ran up the stairs, he thought, to the very top of that odoriferen, he thought, and jumped straight down into the fungi-vorous canal, he thought, that should do it, he thought. How I laugh when I think about it now. It wasn't funny then, not to him, once upon a long long ago. High tragedy, was how he saw it.

Only it wouldn't have worked. There was no canal below their stinkotel, just the crowded street contorting its narrow way to the railway station from where they had just got here, or should I say there. Being splattered on a stony street between the hairy legs of American tourists of various sexes was not his idea of a superior situation-tragedy. Nor a drop between the legs of anyone, hairy or not, tourist or not, American or not. I say this to avoid accusations of anti-tourism, anti-Americanism or anti-hirsutism. I do plead

~ 3 ~

guilty to sexism. I am not partial to the adult human male. Neither was Lahya, dadso being one.

He was a boy; and the wise of their neighbourhood back home in Gravesend, upon Thames, were of the solemn opinion that one day, with a little indifference from God and the social services, he too might grow up to be an adult human male. He was determined to resist such a gruesome future, even if he had to take the ultimate decision of not growing up at all. Hence the urge to dive from somewhere up on high in the manner of high tragedy. But not splattered between the hairy legs . . . I've already said that.

Floating face up alongside the gondolas was acceptable. Even desirable. In death, the unworthy world and its operatically inclined inhabitants would witness the grand and poetic resignation of his in-life querulous and prosaic features. However, with his luck he was more likely to be found mooning the moon. Or sink in a disturbed onion manner, and stay sunk. That is if there had been any waters below their stinkotel, he thought.

To be honest, I cannot say he actually thought all this at the time, perishing with pre-adolescent despair; or now, rocking with mature laughter, I think that he thought then; but there it is, for those with discernment to discern, and those with none, to discover.

However, there is no doubt about the one thought that rode all his thoughts. He did not want to be stretched out into a man, like dadso; much less a black man, like dadso, like a lightning-struck tree, all charred and spindly and dead. Not that dadso considered himself black. 'Indian,' he'd say, 'Indian, my boy. *Not* black! Indian.' That may well be, but he was the blackest Indian Lahya had ever seen. 'Indian,' he'd continue after a heavy sigh, 'Indian, and proud to be. And so should you!' Poor Lahya absolutely *died* of shame every time his father raised his head with pride.

At least the father had a halfway decent name, thought Lahya – Raj. *He* was called Lahyayani; yes, Lahyayani, long for Lahya. dadso found the name in the Upanishads, and nothing and no-one could make him change his mind. Not even Mumsy. Pity that he wasn't a witness to that lone triumph of dadso; or if he was, his memory did not run that far.

Mumsy did insist on Brendon as his middle name, and got it. Or rather, he got it; ending up as Lahyayani Brendon Cenna. Initials

LBC, which begot the lengthiest nickname in infant school: Little Black Courgette, a play on Prince's hit song at the time, 'Little Red Corvette'. The name stuck and carried through the junior to the comprehensive. He was not amused, even though he admitted to looking like a little black courgette in more places than one. Not that it helped matters, as the compassionate of Gravesend understood; as would understand the compassionate of other parts of the world with more vibrant names.

He wanted to leave all that behind him. He did not want to remain a little black courgette for the rest of his life. He wanted to be a white woman. A gorgeous white woman. After all, Mumsy was one. And when . . . if . . . he did become a gorgeous white woman, he would call himself Sigourney. Here he parted company with Mumsy. Marilyn may have been good enough for her time, but it was Sigourney for him. Either that or nothing. Not even life. Especially not life.

II

'Thank God that's settled,' said Marilyn, throwing herself upon the bed and kicking her red court shoes up in the air so that they landed any old how on the floor. Lahya loved it when she did that. Imelda could have held an election to secure the styles, colours and numbers of shoes that Mumsy possessed. *If the shoe fits, buy it*, was among the foremost principles of her life. dadso owned three lefts and three rights that did not quite match. Two almost brown ones; two blacker than his feet, one more so than the other; and two tatty old trainers at the height of fashion seven years and eleven months ago, once white, now of no noticeable hue.

'At least we'll be out of this stink-pot before the weekend,' continued Mumsy, eyeing her nails after an apprehensive floorwards glance at her shoes and thinking about the nice young night clerk at the hotel. He was the only attractive thing about the place, and she would miss him. Fervently she hoped that he hadn't noticed that the bright red of her nails was not quite the same shade as the bright red of her shoes when she went down that morning to see if there was anything to see. Before the day man took over.

Lahya glowed with delight. His mother had called the hotel a stink-pot! That was the name he'd given it. Ions of positive electrical energy charged through his ego, diffused into the subconscious labyrinths of his superego, some descending to the very roots of his id.

'It's not that bad,' said dadso, fidgeting with his tie, his mind still bound to the earthy spatiality of the stink-pot hotel while Lahya's was levitating on higher planes.

'Nothing is bad enough for you!' growled Mumsy, puffing up the pillows beneath her back and frowning with her voice. Frowns on the forehead leave frowns on the forehead was another principle of her life.

Lahya rushed towards his father as quickly yet as casually as he could, and bent over as if to remove a spot from his Nikes. He always did something of the sort to hear what dadso would mutter back whenever there was an occasion which called for his muttering back. 'Nothing is good enough for you,' he muttered. It wasn't a particularly interesting mutter, as far as mutters go, but still, Lahya would rather have heard it than not.

Marilyn did not often hear the mutterings of Raj, or, if she did, considered them unworthy of comment. This time she heard – the room was too small not to – and commented, 'Nothing you can do.' She shut her eyes gently as if not to disturb the imaginary slices of cucumber resting on the lids.

'I thought you wanted to come to Venice. I had to cancel so many . . .'

'I wanted to come to Venice. I did not want to come to this . . . this . . . shit-hole.'

More ions of positive electrical energy. His mother had used another of his favourite terms. It was turning out to be quite an ace-of-hearts day for him, after a two-of-clubs start. Who would have thought so. Perhaps it was true what Grandma Savitri said. Perhaps there *was* no telling what life would bring. It could even bring joy.

He raised himself up from his flicking-a-spot-off-the-shoe position, stretched to his full four feet four in front of the wardrobe mirror, and tried to look sensuous, like Mother did, like the gorgeous Sigourney would, when he'd be her: tall, blonde, white, and sexy enough to turn an eighty-three-year-old Jesuit into a salivating slave at her feet. Though he had heard that some eighty-three-year-old Jesuits were otherwise inclined. This in his second multi-faith class in his newly acquired comprehensive.

'What on earth do you think you are doing, Lahya!' said dadso with a strong hint of querulous worry in his voice, staring at Lahya in the mirror as he pranced in front of it. 'Just like him to put me down when I am feeling good about myself!' thought Lahya. And how he hated that note of querulous worry in his father's voice.

'Nothing. I am doing nothing. What do you think I am doing?' All set to deny any knowledge of prancing, much less practice of it, if accused, Lahya composed his limbs in as solid a state of masculine rigidity as he could, and spoke in his aggressive-boy voice, looking his father straight in the nostrils. That usually shut him up. It did so this time, but a hint of querulous worry remained in his eyes. How Lahya hated that hint of querulous worry in his father's eyes.

'Leave the poor boy alone,' said Mumsy, 'no point in ruining *his* holiday as well. If there is any *real* problem, let me know and I will talk to him. You know I always do. He listens to me.'

'No wonder he is the wonderboy he is,' muttered Raj, picking up his wife's red shoes from the floor and stacking them neatly along with the others on the opposite side of the bed, beneath the window overlooking the crowded street contorting its way to the station, upon which Lahya would have splattered between the hairy legs of American tourists of various sexes had he run up to the top of that odoriferen and jumped straight down. Or between some legs, hairy or not, American or not, tourist or not. He wondered if it was worth a try after all.

Might as well wait till they get to their new, improved hotel and see how things shape up. Mumsy was happy about it; and if Mumsy was happy, life may not be so bad after all.

III

Lahya was flying low over Lido when he developed engine trouble. Strapped and suspended beneath the aerodynamic centre of the hang-glider wings of the microlight, there was not a lot that he could do.

But he was able to steer. He could choose where and when to crash.

When I say when, I speak relatively. There wasn't that much time. He had to make a decision, and fast. The speed at which he was going, and the direction of the flight path, not to mention the angle, indicated that the San Marco Canal would be the best bet. It was wide enough, almost like the open sea. With some skill and a little luck he could miss the big boats travelling between the islands; there were no gondolas to sink, unfortunately; and he would come out of it alive, if wet. A little further to the left was the Grand Canal, narrow, and getting narrower, the alimentary canal of the city with much too much traffic both ways. Straight ahead lay the Piazza San Marco, the bursting gut of Venice, full of tourists, restaurants, gift shops and musicians, all doing grievous damage to pockets, palates, good taste and ears.

If he wasn't careful, if he teetered on the brink of indecisiveness for more than a sigh or two, he'd be upon the Bridge of Sighs; then crash wallop bang, dead him, splattered between the hairy legs . . .

Only this time it could be worse. He could end up setting fire to the Palace of Doges, if not the Basilica of St Mark itself. Upon violent and unnecessary contact with the Venetian landscape his microlight would burst forth into throbbing flames of Martian orange and mercurial blue in the descending shades of the starry starry night. Or so he imagined. Unless he got impaled on the Bell

Tower. He would not like to get impaled on the Bell Tower. Nor on any of the many crosses on the Basilica itself, however holy.

On the positive side, he could incinerate a million tourists and stop Venice sinking. Or six or seven tourists and stop the bands playing. Anything to get away from their way of 'My Way'. If he had to go, that was not a bad way to go. Not bad at all.

Yes, he would kill many birds with one stone. Himself and the band players with one microlight. Not to mention a million tourists, or a fraction thereof. And if in the process the Basilica or the Palace had to go, then so be it. Nothing worthwhile is ever achieved without sacrifice, his favourite teacher used to say on his way to the toilets. In truth, the wilful combusting of the Basilica and the Palace might well be an act of grace. No Basilica, no Palace, no tourists. His legacy to the future. Even if he wouldn't be there to relish the honours bestowed upon him, posthumously, for laying down his life to stop Venice sinking.

'What on earth do you think you are doing Lahyayani?' said Raj when the bed started to rattle violently as Lahya violently rattled the knob on the left upper bedpost – his side of the bed – in order to steer his microlight towards the centre of the Piazza San Marco.

How he hated being called Lahyayani.

'Nothing. I'm doing nothing. What do you think I'm doing!' he shouted back, coming to a halt in midflight, and nearly wrenching the knob off the post.

'Leave my poor boy alone,' said Mumsy from the adjoining bed, a frown in her voice. Frowns on the forehead leave frowns on the forehead was definitely one of her principles in life.

'I'd leave your poor boy alone if you'd leave your poor man alone,' muttered dadso.

'If you jump into the sea, Raj, dear,' cooed Mumsy with a sugar-in-her-throat voice from the depths of her pillow, 'I promise I will.'

Venice was beginning to have a good effect on his parents' love life. Marilyn had begun to take notice of Raj's mutterings. They had begun to communicate.

'Are there any top-class women mircolight fliers?' asked Lahya.

The question was addressed to neither parent in particular, and neither parent answered. Stupid question, he knew. But he only asked it to further the flow of affection between parent and parent.

It might bring them closer if they *both* believed he was an idiot . . . Stupid thought. It would only make matters worse, each blaming the other for his brainlessness. As indeed they already did. However, and there was a thought, if he had an accident and died, in such a way that neither could accuse the other, when flying a microlight . . .

He should have framed his question more precisely, 'Were there any cool, female microlight pilots, white and named Sigourney, preferably but not necessarily blonde – gingers and reds would count – who gave their life to save a country from tourism?' And then added, 'If not, there will be one soon.' That would have made them sit up and think.

He knew that deep down somewhere in his black heart, father loved Mother. If Lahya was like her, dadso would mourn his death with a true grief. If Mother knew that her husband was mourning her son's death with a true grief because he was a gorgeous white woman, like her, she'd be pleased with him. Then they'd live happily ever after. It wouldn't matter if he had to die for it. *And* he would have saved Venice from tourism.

But then, he only wanted to die to spare himself the pain of growing up to be a man; any man, much less a black man; skinny, ugly, old, like a lightning-struck tree, like dadso. Not that dadso liked him for being like him. Even Mumsy only took notice of him when he was pitted against the dreaded dadso. If he was a gorgeous white woman, like his mother, he wouldn't *want* to die, nor *need* to. His parents would be happy anyway, proud of him, instead of having to squabble over him all the time. In fact, if he was a gorgeous white woman, then his death would cast a pall over their lives and ruin their marriage.

What was an under twelve, under stress, under-brained person supposed to think, much less do?

IV

'Back, back a bit. A little to the left,' said Raj. Lahya thought of 'that dead man on TV, in old films, Peter Buyer or Seller or Something'.

'No, no, no; to the right; *my* left, *your* right, right! Yes, right, that's right,' continued dadso, now sounding more and more like Peter Whateverish, 'Just a little more, yes, yes, yes . . . little left, little left, yours, yes, yes, yes . . . wonderful . . .' His 'd' of wonderful hit a final dong on Lahya's brain after his 'ts' had battered his eardrums with the subtlety of Megadeath Rock.

Lahya waited for the right moment. Just before Raj clicked his camera he dashed into the frame and squashed himself against Mumsy, grinning widely, excited at the prospect of a 'surprise' picture hugging his gorgeous white mother.

He could feel dadso's mud-black face turning cyanic blue under the azure Venetian sky. But his glee turned to horror when it was not his father, but mother who hissed, 'You have gone and spoilt it all, stupid. You can be really mean sometimes. It took your father ten minutes to . . .' She saw Lahya's face drop on the street, and stopped, but the damage was done. She'd even called him 'your father'! instead of dadso. The betrayal was too much.

dadso decided it would be a wonderful opportunity to lure Lahya to his side now that chance had offered him that rare gift of a rift between mother and son.

'Come, come, Lahya, never mind. *You* and I can have our picture taken together. That would be fun, won't it now!'

About as much fun as sex with a hedgehog, thought Lahya. 'No it will not,' he muttered dadso-style and sulked away to the other end of the bridge. To get some joy out of his miserable life he spat into the slimy canal and watched his copious saliva sparkling in the springtime sun as it flew like a shooting star across the piss-coloured waters. Tall houses rose from either side of this unnatural fluid as it crawled along with the elegance of a spastic snake towards the relatively less odious and more open stretches of the sea. The brickwork of the surrounding buildings was eaten by the hack-honoured time and tide; the walls discoloured, corroded and pock-marked, trying their level best to create a spectrum of dignity around their crumbling facade while cargoes of hypermetropic beings blinked at them in myopic wonder.

On the stony arch of the bridge itself, bosoms with bouncy boobs bouncing upon them and thighs with bouncy balls bouncing between them rushed past Lahya this way and that with the unbounded enthusiasm of the permanently deranged. The most moving part of both the boob parade and the balls brigade was the mouth. Moving as it proclaimed and declaimed and acclaimed and chortled and giggled and trickled and expanded and expounded upon the myriad and manifold marvels of Venice. Moving as it ate and ate and ate, or pontificated upon eating, what it had eaten, was eating, or going to eat, and where.

There were static mouths too. Some drooping, some pouting, some just open and hanging about. Some were smiling, either without reason and with brain-flattening turpitude, or because they, too, had cameras focused on them by mouth owners giving flat-brained instructions to their willing victims. As dadso had done to Mumsy, and was now doing to Lahya. 'Come, come here and stand beside me, and we'll ask your Mum, Mumsy, to . . .' But Lahya had stopped listening.

This place, this bridge, this very spot where he had been so crucially humiliated by his own mother, his gorgeous mother, his white mother, that was where he would kill himself. Then she'll be sorry. They'll both be sorry.

'I'd rather die than have a picture with you,' he screamed at dadso and stamped his foot on the ground with a vicious force born of a double-edged rejection: being rejected by his mother, and rejecting his father. However, his tantrum took a different turn as his flimsy beach sandal hit a sharp flint on the stony street and an unpremeditated yell of the high note variety rose from his guts, tore through the dense atmospheric pollution and reached far out into the skies successfully expanding the ozone hole with its rampant carbon dioxide.

Raj's face was stunned by the ferocity of Lahya's words and scream as if hit by a wall, and he stopped his advance towards him in mid-stride. Marilyn on the other hand reacted with mercurial mobility, rushing towards her son, while addressing her husband, 'Look what you have gone and done, dadso.' As she spoke she turned and gave one of her 'looks' to Raj, a look reserved for the lowest of the low, 'dadso'.

'I, what have I done? I've done nothing, it was you . . .'

'Yes, yes, I know, save your voice. You never do anything wrong. You are the Pope. It's always someone else's fault. Usually mine . . . *We* know that, don't we?' she added this last bit as she put her arms round Lahya and began to ruffle his hair.

But for once Lahya was not willing to be a budding black Christ for his parents' Pope and Madonna act. Not the virgin, but the like-a-virgin one. Madonna, not the Pope. Though which of the two is more like a virgin is not for me to say.

Wriggling out of his mother's grasp he screamed at the top end of his little-boy voice, 'Leave me alone, white trash,' and ran down the bridge, Raj's 'How dare you speak to your Motherrr . . .' etcetera following closely behind him. He turned into the first narrow street that looked invitingly desolate, a bit like him, and kept running, hardly looking where he was going, blinded by tears of anger: anger at himself for having said that awful thing to Mumsy; and tears of shame: the shame of having said that awful thing to Mumsy; and the shame of tears. He knocked down a tourist and didn't even laugh.

He was soon to be more angry, more ashamed, more desolate. He was soon to get lost.

How in Christie's name (not Linford, not Agatha, but the auctioneers) was he going to kill himself at that stupid little bridge if he was not going to find that stupid little bridge for the rest of his living days.

V

Life seemed to be going down the plughole. He felt humiliated by Mumsy, humiliated by dadso, and worst of all, he had humiliated himself. Perhaps not. Not quite in that order of prioritized humiliation. I called the last – humiliating himself – the worst. However, that is a personal perspective: what I think. For Lahyayani Brendan Cenna, on that sunny spring day, being humiliated by his Mother was the *most* humiliating humiliation of all!

After turning yet another wild corner and getting into yet another samey street he thought he heard the thudding of heavy feet behind him. Imagining it to be dadso catching up on him, and wanting to avoid his unwelcome advance he dived into the alcove of an angular building that extruded to the left of him. He needn't have bothered. It wasn't dadso; but an equally unappetising sight. A tourist (who else). A tourist running. Running, with his camera (what else) bobbing up and down over his bare (how else), beer (what else) belly (where else), soft and pale with about five (perhaps six) straw-like hairs crinkling upwards in what seemed like a pathetic effort to escape into the heavens from their yukkily wobbling homescape. Lahya held on to his own stomach and retched mockingly.

Perhaps he should have been more sympathetic to tourists. After all, he, too, was a tourist. And in particular, like that tourist, a running tourist. But he did not have a camera jumping over a bulging belly. Besides, he was a captive tourist. Brought, not come. However, be that as it may, when the said tourist went past him without the least concern for his existence, much less whereabouts, he heaved a sigh of relief which ended in a sort of gasp as he was hit by the possibility that he might be lost.

He couldn't even remember the name of the hotel they had moved into after getting out of their shitholetel.

Who'd have believed a day would come when he will actually wish for dadso's presence. But, there he was, wishing if only that jelly-gutted tourist in flight, or pursuit, had been his undesirable and undesired pater!

He decided to retrace his steps. If he could get back to that stupid little bridge, and if either of those responsible for his existence was there . . . It would mean eating an overdone humble pie, but in the circumstances he was prepared to stomach it. Given the opportunity. Would he be given it? That was the big question. Would he be able to get back to that stupid little bridge? And if so, will either one of his parents be foolish enough to wait for him there?

He remembered seeing a shop with some near-death tables outside it. Piled upon the near-death tables were hands of post-death bananas, arms of emaciated yellowy cucumbers among heads of moronic lettuces besieged by assorted bodies of seriously sick or psychologically unsettled fruits and vegetables, all covered with a netting of sorts for the siesta break. He looked for the shop, found it with no trouble at all, and was about to take the street alongside it when he saw another shop with near-death tables piled high with deceased, disabled or psychotic plant droppings, all covered with a netting of sorts. If he took the street next to that shop he'd be going in a completely different direction. He had to think of something else. What else did he remember? Not much. He had been in too much of a mood to observe his surroundings with any degree of interest or enthusiasm. Not that he had any interest or enthusiasm for what surrounded him anyway. He had had about as much as he could take of gungy waters and cracky buildings and puky tourists.

Perhaps it would be better to stay where he was and hope that dadso would track him down. But it was too much to expect that *he* would succeed in anything *he* set out to do. Mother often remarked upon the fact, italics in her voice. No, he had to find his way back his own way, or come up with a different idea, not involving waiting for dadso.

VI

A few more attempts to get back to that stupid little bridge and he gave up. There was no end to the number of stupid little bridges stretched all over the place, like rigor-mortisised bodies, as in a Somalian village, or Ethiopian, or any one of those man-forsaken places.

As often happens, the harder you try, the more likely you are to mess up in a grand way. Such is the way of the world, alas alack, and there is nothing worse than the way of the world, unless it be the way of man, and as a man in the making, Lahya was in trouble of his own making, trying hard to get out, making it worse, as is the way of the world.

So there he was, stuck up a tower without a stairway, or a lift (elevator if you like) and not a passerby in sight, a multitude of tourists notwithstanding, in a manner of speaking, of course; though there are better ways of communicating than speaking, Doc Martens in particular, especially where tourists are concerned. And even if one did come along – passerby, not a Doc Marten – the one was going to be the one with a sense of humour designed for the occasion. The one who would have a good laugh and be on one's way home to tell in-laws and other enemies that one saw an idiot stuck up a tower without a stairway, or lift (elevator if you like) and not a passerby in sight, a multitude of tourists notwithstanding, save yours truly, who left him where he was so as not to spoil a good story with a happy ending.

The sun was hitting Lahya in the face and he was trying not to frown. He firmly believed that Mumsy's dictum of 'frowns on the forehead . . . etc.' was so relevant to modern life that it ought to be law, with at least a week's death penalty for all public frowners. If all the scowly wrinklies who went about with gashes gouged on their foreheads knew what Mumsy knew, the world would be a less frightening place to look at than it was.

However, whatever not frowning was going to do for his distant future, it was certainly not doing much for his present. He felt as lost with a stress-free forehead as he did when he went out of his way to crinkle it, just to spite himself, for being Lahyayani, the Little Black Courgette: LBC, or LBZ (Z as in zee, American-style, for zucchini) which it was to be later, and which he was to hate even more.

He even tried to follow the lost-child guidelines dadso had once given him and which he had promptly flushed down the crap-hole of his brain. Was there anything at all he could remember which might help locate their new fresh-smelling hotel with their very own fresh-smelling bathroom? Nothing! For once he wished that they were still in that stink-pot shitholetel of theirs. At least he could have stumbled his way to that. It was not too far from the station . . . brain-flash!

All he had to do was get back there, and ask. Before they checked out his mother had made sure to tell everyone where they were going – in case there was any mail, or telephone calls, or visitors, or in case they left anything behind, or just in case. Two incoming guests they met on their way out, informed of their new address, smiled at them, looked at them, looked again at them, looked away from them and smiled again. Friendly couple.

VII

Lahya looked around to see who he could ask for the way to the station having lost the urge to pursue his own initiative re navigational matters. Fate presented him with a promising candidate in the large shape of a policeman approaching from across a nearby gutter, or was it a canal. This imposing officer of the law was resting one hand, delicately, on hip while holding the other out in front, delicately, palm down and butt-swaying gently to some inaudible-to-the-naked-ear rhythm, possibly of the invisible-to-the-naked-eye genitals, praising the Lord for small mercies, or big, as the case may have been. This is not an insidious attempt to glorify the image of the carabiniere. He was a one-off: Lahya had never before seen another of his kind, nor saw one again, alas. He was the only type of policeman his mother would have warned him against, even though she was pro-police as opposed to dadso who was anti. Being in an anti-Mumsy mood, what better than to approach this balletic guardian of the law, thought Lahya.

He approached.

'Can you help me . . . please . . . sir,' Lahya spoke in his best Gravesendian.

'And how may I help you, young man?' asked the balletic guardian of the law in jolly Oxfordian. A lot became clearer.

Lahya explained that he was lost and wanted to get to the station.

'The railway station? That's easy,' – a seductive smile – 'Go straight,' began the balletic guardian of the law in jolly Oxfordian; a not very good beginning, for there was nothing straight in that ancient and renowned metropolis of that ancient and renowned country, at least that ancient and renowned northeastern region of it. Nothing straight that Lahya could see, beginning with the member extraordinaire, large, if limp, of the ancient and renowned polizia he had accosted.

Not only did he have a great way of walking and and talking, he wasn't bad at reading either, for he read the doubt in Lahya's eyes, and said, 'Come with me, I am walking that way.'

He started walking that way, while talking that way of his great love for Britain and all that it stood for. He had spent time studying there. He felt great affection for Lahya, hello hello hello, because he was from those precious Isles which had so fascinated him in his youth and which so repulsed the renowned and ancient conquerors of his renowned and ancient country.

VIII

Lahya entered their new, fresh-smelling room in their new, fresh-smelling hotel, all prepared for an excited and enthusiastic welcome from birther and spermer alike, an emotional reunion of the long-lost-one-at-last-found type. He was greeted with the warmth of a British summer by both.

The cause of this soggy chill soon emerged. The surprise factor which might have activated the pleasure glands was missing, snatched from Lahya's hands by the mouth of the desk clerk at their old shitholetel. He had telephoned the not-so-grieving couple to say that their long-loved short-lost offspring would soon be illuminating their abode again with his filial light, that he was being directed, guided and propelled in that direction by no less a personage than the oversized, if limp, what-have-you-got-in-your-holster-brigade member.

The disappointment of this mean reception was compounded by the fearful news that they would be having dinner at one of the establishments in San Marco. Lahya had vowed that if ever he heard 'My Way' played again, whichever way, or any of Frank Sinatra's or Ming's or Bing's ditties, whoever they were and whatever they did their way, he would begin producing from his nether cords his own music his own way with fragrant intensity and ceaseless continuity. Would he, when put to the test, be able to deliver? Probably not. An overwhelming sense of inadequacy and self-doubt gnawed at whatever remained of his already shattered self-esteem and he whined, 'Oh Mumsy, no Mumsy . . .' But Mumsy was in no humour for his 'Oh Mumsys and no Mumsys . . .' that day. It had not been a Mumsy kind of day at all, that day.

'Oh Mumsy.' He whined his most appealing whine yet again, but no response, yet again. Or rather, the most devastating response of all, silence. Mumsy liked dining out, especially at places where it was good for one's social image to be seen to dine. For the second time that day, she was on dadso's side! She did that when it suited her, and it drove Lahya absolutistly mad. He would never betray her by seeing dadso's point of view, ever, no matter how right he was; and yet, she, when it suited her . . . Suicide, patricide, or matricide: the choices facing him were increasing, as was his choiceless pique at the wimpishness of his being which would inhibit the carrying out of any of those choices, and which (wimpishness, just to remind the forgetful) added nothing to the lure of either black males or white females, regardless of colour or gender or age or size.

It was while eating a disgustingly large mouthful of some poor victim of cowcide that dadso let fall his pre-prepared bombshell. They would be leaving for Gravesend (he used the word home) the day after the next.

Mother well nigh spat out a mouthful of pre-dung in his face. Even Lahya choked. Gravesend! Suddenly Venice was a paradise of delight. Any day the revolting tourists of that drowning city than the revolting natives of that flotsammy town! At least not while he was so enjoying being miserable on a holiday which he was all set to hate for another week.

He could feel his soul being strangled by a million turbans as hairy faces peered at him with squinty eyes, dancing around him the *danse macabre* of the racially unhinged.

'But we are supposed to be here for another week!' screamed Marilyn in her voice of controlled hysteria.

That, dadso explained, was based on the price of the 'the other' hotel. Calculating the expenses of their new hotel, the 'allocated' monies would suffice for just another day.

Matricide was out of the equation now. Mumsy was once again the same old dadso-despising Mumsy Lahya loved to love. Patricide was out too. dadso was not worth the rigours of a remand home. Not to mention the demands of police questioning; or, the most fearsome possibility of all, custody by social workers. It was back to suicide.

Mother declared that his firm of blood-squeezing tax accountants could drain seven days' money out of some hapless client in seven minutes, but no matter, she would stay on regardless, spending her own money. No mention was made as to who would have the pleasure of Lahya. He pretended not to care. The soothing comforts of sweet death would take away the necessity of caring. It was *they* who will be sorry, *not* him. He would be well out of it. And quite right too.

Opportunity presented itself when they took a long boat-ride round the island to see the city at night with all the lights and the usual tourist garbage: dadso's attempt at appeasing progeny and mater. The moon was three-quarters on its way to fullness and decline; the waters were calm and cool; the ferrymen ugly, fellow sightseers uglier still. Nothing at all to live for.

He perched on the edge of the boat, determined to toss himself into the waters when no one was looking. Or perhaps, when everyone was looking. He couldn't make up his mind which would be better. Slipping away unnoticed was decidedly the more romantic, while plunging downwards with a swirl and a splash in front of all eyes was clearly more dramatic. As he pondered over the relative merits and demerits of either, a fat woman rose from her seat, lurched forward for no apparent reason, held on to her stomach, and manifested the reason for so doing. As her dinner dispersed into the atmosphere like tainted stars, another fat woman jumped up to assist, tripped over Lahya's foot, landed on his head sending him ass-first into the waters with the force and speed of a radically disturbed rabbit.

Immediate alarm brought immediate results. One man jumped into the waters, a rope was thrown, and amid shouts and screams of excitement Lahya was hauled up, but not before his shorts got caught in a hook somewhere along the side of the boat and parted company from the rest of him, along with his underpants.

Mumsy was amused beyond all sense of the occasion. Relinquishing the dolorous silence which she frequently adopted after an exchange of views with dadso, she giggled with over-abundant zest and wanted to know what it was they called him at school, Little Black Something or the Other . . . heeeeheheehehee . . .

Lahya head-butted dadso, just to get even.

Living is never easy. Neither was dying. Killing's worse, as he was to discover in good time.

IX

They did stay on for another week in Venice. dadso footed the bill *and* pussy-footed round Mumsy, buying her the most stupid gifts and souvenirs you can imagine this side of gagaland, and some other not-so-stupid things that she absolutely adored.

Oh the triumphant power of being white, gorgeous, and female. I should know, being gorgeous, female, and occasionally white.

He did a lot of muttering though, Raj, including the famous lines from the dear departed-in-haste Kennedy of Jacqueline fame: 'Ask not what your country can do for you, ask what you can do for your country.' He mumbled so you could barely hear the unaccented syllable of 'country'.

Ah, the vituperative helplessness of being black, ugly, and male.

PART II

New York

(three months later)

I

Raj's father was stabbed to death in New York. Seventy-eight times. One for each year of his life, the deepest cuts in and around the Big G-spot between the thighs. Not all murders in that great city are acts of random violence perpetrated by heartless strangers. Some are affectionately executed by loved ones. Or at least by those mindful of one's age and outstanding proclivities.

They had to leave Mother England, or, according to Lahya, 'Mumsy England' – for it was 'Mumsy's England, really' – and be in New York for the scattering of ashes. This in East River, behind the United Nations Headquarters, close to the 42nd Street visitors' entrance, six avenues away from the scattering of sex shops which Granddad ran with despotic munificence. The money for the very first establishment came from the ageing bride of Uncle Dileep, imported from India in the late 1970s. She, or rather her parents, had further provided for two extra taxis to supplement the two Uncle Dileep already operated. There was also the small contribution for a sixty-five-inch television, a double futon, a Sony VCR and a restaurant.

Mumsy was thrilled to be in New York because she hated New York. Any opportunity to tear it to bits from within was clitolatingly exciting. And the cake beneath the icing was returning home and telling one and all how awful it was, how crude and crass Americans were, in general, New Yorkers in particular.

There were three other reasons for the thrilled state of her psyche.

First, dadso's moaning and groaning *a* at the death of his father; *b* at having to find time to come to New York so soon after the holiday to Venice; *c* at having to fork out money for the trip) provided her with fulfilling opportunities to both mock and sympathise with him, alternately or simultaneously, both of which she enjoyed immensely.

Second, Granddad's sad demise and the manner of his exit from this blue planet with his New York state of mind. Mumsy hated Granddad. She hated the way he walked, the way he talked, what he did for a living. She hated the way he looked, especially at her. Things got really tense some six years ago when he accidentally cupped her left breast in his right hand while accidentally grasping her right buttock in his left hand in an accidental lurch while going up the lift – or should I say elevator – of Woolworth Tower. There were other accidents too. Apparently Granddad was quite accident prone when around Mumsy. It was not so much of a behavioural allergy towards her person alone. White women in general, white boys too, seemed to upset the natural harmony and balance of Granddad's character and deportment.

Third, unbeknown so far to Lahya, Marilyn was pregnant. Jamuna, the elderly bride of Uncle Dileep, was unable to have any more children after producing one perennially sick daughter about two years older than Lahya. It was, therefore, a sad delight for Mrs Raj Cenna to parade her pregnancy. Especially as she could not gestate what Jamuna had birthed: a chain of sex shops, two taxis and a restaurant, not to mention a sixty-five-inch television, a double futon and a Sony VCR.

II

Grandma Savitri, my favourite person in the entire Cenna clan, sat crosslegged on the double futon, clad in a white sari of mourning and looking happier than ever.

'I knew he'd come to a bad end,' she said in toothless aspirated Hindi. Her mother was fron Delhi, and she preferred to speak Hindi than Bengali. The rest of the family felt obliged to do the same in her presence. 'Told him so the very morning he got it!' She rotated her neck, thin yet ringed with layers of flesh that would have done the proudest of turkeys proud. She looked round at the circle of her devoted family for approval, smacking her gums and rolling the pan leaf in her mouth, the brownish red katha paste dribbling out the left corner of the twist in her lips.

Marilyn smiled knowingly. She had been subjected to Hindi on a fairly regular basis over the past twelve years or so by various members of the Cenna clan, but her knowledge of the language was curiously erratic. She understood selectively; and although resolutely refusing to speak or participate in a Hindi conversation, she could come up with an enlightening observation or a liberated remark at the most unexpected of occasions in colloquialisms that would have pleased the ear of a street urchin in Delhi.

Uncle Dileep and Aunt Jamuna had heard it all before and were duly unimpressed, but feigned interest. The sudden death of Granddad had left Grandma in charge of the sex shops, and much though she had harangued the old man for running a foul, impure and ungodly trade, she was now determined to hold on to them and 'make the best of a bad business'. This lent added muscle to the power she had over the family. Jamuna, devoted and dutiful to appearances, despised the crinkly old hen and felt sympathy, even affection, for the decrepit rooster, deceased. Dileep was fed up with everyone, especially Aunt Jamuna, who had borne him just one sickly daughter, Jayshree. Now, chasing fifty, there was no hope of her producing even a self-respecting cockroach good enough to compete with the ones provided gratis by the kitchen, much less a boy to carry his name forward into the big wild world to make it bigger and wilder. However, the restaurant was in Jamuna's name, for tax purposes, as were two of the now six taxis. There was also the probability of more good things to come when her father croaked his last in old Mother India. So Dileep had learnt to be civil, risking high blood pressure, a ruptured artery or a dysfunctional heart; the usual male opt-outs from the rigours of life.

'How can you talk like that! Mataji,' blurted Raj, 'I am sorry, but Bapoo . . .'

'Bapoo Bapoo . . . that is all I've heard all my breathing days. Now that he is finally off my belly, I do *not* want to hear his unholy name in *my* house ever ever . . .'

'Really, Mataji!' interrupted Raj with suicidal disregard for life, limb or inheritance, while Dileep mumbled in his brain: 'My house, she says; My house My house, says Jamuna; My house My house, says Jayshree; My house My house the old bugger used to say. It is everybody's house except *my* house whose house it is!'

As Dileep scowled to himself, frowns on his forehead, Lahya realised why his uncle looked so old and haggard, though he was nearly a year younger than his father. He touched his own forehead and was relieved to find it crease-free. He hated looking like his father. He'd hate it a million times more if he looked like his uncle. A zillion trillion times more – whichever was the greater.

'But I do agree with you in one thing,' continued Raj. 'Let us not take his name. Let him rest now. He is dead now. Let us *not* take his name. But with due respect, Mataji, it is *you* who . . .'

Savitri was livid at this second impertinence from her first son. She uncrossed her legs from the double futon and brought them down, henna-dotted feet hitting the red shagpile with a thud that shut Raj up in mid-sentence. Her right arm shot forward vigorously as her left hand angrily scratched the right armpit given airing by the first gesture. The fingers of her outstretched hand pointed at Raj's person with the ferocity of a thwarted life.

'I *know* he is dead. *You* don't have to tell me it. I know he is dead. And I *dance* that he is dead. Like *Kali*, the Mother Goddess. My Kali. It is *she* who killed him.' (*I feel flattered, but remain silent – pleading neither guilty, nor not guilty.*) 'And you want to know why she killed him? Because I asked her to. Went down on my knees and begged her to.' (*Here the woman speaks the truth!*) 'Kali has a thousand arms and a thousand knives, but she only used seventy-eight of them. Like I begged her to.' (*False. She did not; she is just making this up, for effect*) 'For the seventy-eight years he fouled our earth Mother with his filthy presence. Yes, he's dead now. DEAD. But he will not rest in peace. Not in this house, *my* house.'

'There she goes again . . .' mumbled Dileep in his brain.

'Not with his white sluts and his white boys, his black heart and his black face,' continued Grandma. She shut her katha-tainted lips tight, and scratched her right armpit again, this time more languorously, and with kittenish satisfaction.

For once Raj was refusing to play the mouse. He had spent most of his life away from home – boarding school in Calcutta, university at Allahabad, and then higher accountancy in London. He was jealous of his younger brother Dileep and five sisters who stayed home. Unlike them, he saw very little of his father, and had romantically idolised him by telling wonderful lies about him at school, at university, and then abroad, lies which he had almost come to believe. When Dileep left for America, his parents followed him to the USA rather than come to England to live with Raj, for which he was both grateful and resentful. The more he heard of his father's escapades, and the more bizarre they were, the more he envied him, never having the courage nor the sexual athleticism for amorous misdemeanours of his own. In defending him he seemed to be making a stand of his own against the world, against mankind, against womankind, against his mother, against Mumsy. Either that or he was unhinged by grief.

'But Kali is black. So was Krishna. And *he* had a gaggle of gopis, mostly white, yet he was a . . .' Raj's defence of the old man was brought to a dead stop.

'How dare you!' Savitri screamed, nearly choking on her pan leaf, the red katha escaping from both corners of her mouth. She wiped it away with her shirt sleeves before continuing, 'How dare you compare that old lecher to our Lord . . .' She managed to really choke, or make an excellent pretence of it; began to cough and splutter, beat her breast with both hands, moaning through rattling breath, 'I am dying,' choke choke cough, 'dying,' cough cough choke, 'killed by poison arrrrowws . . .' more coughing and breast-beating . . . 'arrows from my own . . .' heavy choking and violent breast-beating, 'own son. Save me . . . save me . . . Mother Kali from this . . .' hiccough hiccough hiccough, 'this mother-killer, this . . . this . . . ungrateful mother-killer. You are a Mother, the Mother . . .'

By then Dileep had rushed to her, put his arms round her and was thumping her back with what to a less than stupid observer could appear to be a touch greater force than might strictly have been necessary. He turned to his daughter, who was sitting all this while in the southwest corner of the room, left shoulder leaning towards the 2nd Avenue, back reclining against the 5th Street, earphones in ears, Sony Walkman in lap, quite oblivious to everything except the donging beat of Black Sabbath.

'Quick, Jayshree, get a glass of water for your grandmother! From the bottle, the non-fizzy one. Don't want any more gas . . .' This last as some of Grandma's windy emissions from her throat were dolorously accompanied by some windy emissions from her hind-quarters, equally noisy but less odorous.

'Some pineapple juice . . .' Savitri succeeded in articulating between upper and lower hiccoughs, tears of effort welling up in her eyes and trembling down her crumpled manila cheeks.

'Pineapple juice, putri,' echoed Dileep.

Jayshree did not pay the slightest attention to either.

'He was seventy-eight, for Christ's sake,' said Raj, in English, somewhat irrelevantly, raising his arms up in the air and letting them fall listlessly to his sides.

'I'll get the juice,' said Marilyn, rising with obvious embarrass-ment at her husband's insensitivity and glad to be doing something. On her way to the kitchen and nodding in response to Dileep's 'Thank you, bhabi' she gave Raj one of her looks. The day will not see light when he makes *her* cry like that! She'd walk out the door there and then. No. Throw *him* out. It was only Indian women who allow themselves to be treated like that by their men. She would

- 32 -

never have thought he had it in him, though. She gave him another look, this time differently.

'Seventy-eight, but he could still make a hole in a wall,' thought Jamuna, who had had the pleasure, even though she wasn't white, even though the result was just a sickly daughter. Still, that was more than what her husband had been able to manage. If only he was half the man his father was, she could have borne a son. Instead of blaming her, he should look into his own parcel.

Savitri was tired of coughing and was merely breathing heavily in Dileep's arms, eyes half open, nose twitching, armpits sweating; Marilyn was trying to pour some pineapple juice into her wintry lips, at once expectant yet reluctant.

'Look what you've gone and done now!' hissed Marilyn from between pursed lips as she looked askance at Raj, who was standing fidgeting to one side, trying to act more guilty than he felt.

Grandma gulped some juice, gurgled a little, choked some more, shut her eyes, opened her eyes, shut her eyes, and spoke, 'If anything happens to me, I want you to have the shops, even though you hate and humiliate me; me, who brought you into this world, after two-and-seventy hours of labour. My first born.' She raised one long and knotty finger, pointing it straight at Raj, even though her eyes were shut and Raj had shifted his position from where she had last seen him.

'The illegitimate daughter of a dog!' murmured Jamuna, almost audibly. 'Anything to create trouble, to set brother against brother against father against daughter against wife . . .' She longed for the days when widows were put on the pyre alongside their deceased and dreaded husbands and set alight. Her homely face lit up at the thought of the old woman's ashes flitting away in the Atlantic breeze. For one fleeting moment she was beautiful.

III

Lahya looked at Jayshree from an angle of seventy-five degrees approximately, and his brain shuddered. If that was a female . . . for the first time he had second thoughts about being a woman.

'What aaarrre you eye-balling me for?' Jayshree part-drawled, part-spat, as only she could.

'Just trying to figure out what planet you're from,' said Lahya, drawling, and trying to squint, as if in thought, without frowning; then suddenly, as if in the light of revealed truth, he smiled and snapped his fingers, 'Got it! Uranus,' making sure his 'a' was of the USA 'ass' rather than the British 'arse', and dragging it out.

'Better mine than yours,' Jayshree snapped her lips, then added, 'titface.'

Suicide, matricide, patricide, all were out. Cousincide was in.

Mumsy and dadso were some way ahead. Jayshree's scrawny legs had a sort of drag which made it difficult for her to walk so she lagged behind. Lahya had been instructed to stay alongside his 'sister'.

This was Marilyn's first adventure into the mysteries of the East Village. Jayshree was taking them to Tompkins Park, which she loved but where she was not allowed to go and where her parents refused to go.

Dileep was living in Queens when his parents first arrived with the dearly beloved bride. Later they moved to Brooklyn where they bought a deli and began to serve Indian food on the premises. They were there until two years ago when Raj and Marilyn last visited. Since then they had put in all their life savings and purchased a restaurant with an apartment above in the hopefully lucrative, definitely competitive prime situation at the corner of East 6th and

1st Avenue; refurbished it, restyled it and renamed it Jamuna – whose money it was that originally started the whole restaurant business in motion.

Lahya looked around for tourists, especially ones that might abduct and mutilate Jayshree. As long as they didn't rape her. She must die a virgin. Without ever ever having had it. Under no circumstances whatsoever, and from no one. But no one. Not even abducting tourists from New York.

Not that he was sure she hadn't already had it. There was such a knowing look about her. But then neither was he sure what all the fuss was about. All that fuss over sex. Something done with pissing parts, the shit-path bobbing up and down, and in some instances more actively involved; with lumps and cracks you were so ashamed of you kept them hidden from public view all your life. He felt an uncomfortably pleasant movement within his lower belly and a taste of bitter fruit drops in the mouth. A gasp of cold wind pushed itself into his lungs, eerily out of place in the heartless heat of mid-July New York: humid, heavy, and still. The skin on his back jumped twice; his buttocks tightened and a burning swelling began to stretch his Mumsy-bought Calvin Klein briefs. He wondered if it was sinful to wish he could shove a hand grenade, along with the hand, up the back of Marky Mark's Y-fronts.

The burnt sienna of his face got more and more burnt as his breathing became erratic. 'Oh fuck it,' his brain mumbled, 'I don't wanna be a man; I don't, I don't, I don't . . .' Memories of last night, and the night before, and the one before that invaded his veins. He tried not to count the number of times, and the shame and the guilt smothered his gullet.

He steered his mind to tourists again. Especially ones that would abduct and mutilate Jayshree. He couldn't see any. Any tourists, much less ones addicted to abducting and mutilating sad creatures like Jayshree. He was not surprised. Who would come to this cunt-piece of planet Earth! Who would like to abduct and mutilate Jayshree! Though most, if not all, of the natives seemed more than capable of abduction and mutilation in general, as a matter of principle, a point of honour, even if they might draw the line at abducting and mutilating Jayshree. In fact, Lahya would not at all have been surprised to learn that one hundred per cent of New

Yorkers were eager for abduction and mutilation, lived with the sole aim of abduction and mutilation, dreamed of abduction and mutilation, worked for it, visited museums and art galleries and theatres, rode the subway, smoked dope and snorted crack, went to restaurants, ate drank saw movies sang and danced and played with their assholes simply to enable them to abduct and mutilate in the most successful of ways, the American way. However, he was not sure of one thing. Whether the natives really were natives. It was hard to tell, with so many different colours and shapes and sizes and designs and styles of two-legged monstrosities dressed or undressed in so many different colours and shapes and sizes and designs and styles of what could slanderously be described as clothes. He was greatly surprised that with all the givens there wasn't large-scale abduction and mutilation going on all around him with maniacal avidity.

If there was one thing worse than the hairy legs of American tourists of various sexes, it was the hairy legs of American citizens of various sexes, if indeed citizens they were. Legs they certainly were. Mostly exposed in the degenerating heat, mostly hairy. His thoughts wandered into what lay between them, and once again his body began to respond in ways which led to guilt and shame and agony of what it meant to be growing up to be a man, amid less serious questions of aesthetics, ethics, and psychosis, not to mention sweat odours and emissions. Everyone knew men were rapists, and violent and evil and malicious and their parts were ugly or pathetic and funny, too large or too small, too demanding or not demanding enough, and that they had smelly feet and they snored and committed all sorts of heinous and unspeakable crimes, or were layabouts living on handouts and begging, or peddling dope and drugs and death. Getting drunk and beating up wives, their own or not; and masturbating. Especially black men. Oh, to be a gorgeous white woman. Or at least a woman.

'Shut up, you bitch,' he shouted at Jayshree.

The stony composure of Jayshree's stony features was rarely disturbed, but for once she was visibly shaken out of po-facedness by the sheer anger in Lahya's voice, by the unexpectedness of it. Her last sarcastic comment must have been at least three minutes ago. She responded to his challenge by widening her enormously wide eyes, contracting her enormously large pupils and sucking in her hollow sallow cheeks. Taking a shallow breath and jerking open her slit of a mouth which sat uncomfortably on top of a perfectly pointed chin, she exclaimed, 'Shut up yourself, donghead', secretly grateful that he had called her a bitch and not a dog, as most of her peers did in school.

'No, you shut up, dog.'

That was it. It was all-out war now. 'No. You shut up, you half-caste sleazebag.'

'Crippo monster.'

'Gorked-out geek, turd-eating nerd.'

'Lipless hole.'

By this time they had caught up with Marilyn and Raj, who were waiting by the Don't Walk sign at the corner of 7th Street and 1st Avenue. Seeing them, both members of the future generation of hope and regeneration dropped the insults but continued with, 'Shut up,' and, 'You shut up first,' and, 'You started it,' and, 'No, you started it.'

'What is going on, you two!' said dadso with a querulous note in his voice.

'Nothing,' said Lahya.

'He called me a bitch,' said Jayshree.

'No I did *not*, you bitch,' hissed Lahya. He jumped at the pole with the now Walk sign on it, and, wrapping both hands round it, began strangling it with all his strength as if it were Jayshree's neck.

'What on earth do you think you are doing, Lahyayani?' screamed dadso.

'Nothing. I am doing nothing. What do you think I am doing!' said Lahya as innocently as he could while still strangling the pole.

'Do you know what they call *him* at school?' cooed Mumsy, and before Lahya could even release Jayshree's neck, added, 'LBC. Little Black Courgette,' bursting into girlish giggles.

'Little Black what?' enquired Jayshree with scientific curiosity.

'Courgette,' repeated Mumsy.

'Zucchini,' said dadso.

Jayshree understood, and joined Mumsy in giggling. Only Jayshree's giggles were more like death rattles. 'LBZeee,' she hiccoughed between death rattles.

The gross humiliation of it all. And inflicted by Mumsy!!! He pushed dadso under a car. Not exactly under a car, though that is what he would have liked to do, but he pushed dadso, hard, and he fell into the arms of a near-naked black man who was roller-balling past at a hundred and ten kilometres an hour. Both dadso and the near-naked black man lay deposited beside the pavement, sidewalk if you like, while natives, if natives they were, of all colours, shapes, sizes, designs and styles sped past and over and around and above them with total unconcern.

'How could you . . .' started Mumsy, missing the opportunity to take political advantage of the situation.

'Hey beautiful, stay cool,' said the near-naked black man, Afro-American if you like, as he resurrected himself, helped dadso up, kissed him passionately on the lips and rolled away.

By this time Lahya had disappeared, running blindly forward through tears of rage and outrage.

dadso had a tingling sensation in his toes. He had never been kissed by a near-naked black man, not in New York, and seldom so passionately. It didn't feel half as bad as one would have feared.

IV

Lahya wondered if there was any chance of getting lost here in New York as in Venice. He surveyed the heat-drenched dismality of the scenic disaster which enmeshed him, searching for sad little bridges or sadder little lanes into which he could disappear, never to be found again. In vain. All he could see was gluey rivers of filth flowing out of string-tied dustbins, trash cans if you like, on to the even gluier rivers of filth bubbling along the pavements, sidewalks if you like; and, of course, the gluiest of all gluies, eye-damning butt-brained subhumans of multi-faceted varieties: animal, vegetable and miserable, beside the unclassifiable and unmentionable, drifting, streaming, waddling, peddling or piddling, here, there and everywhere in aimless purposefulness.

How right Mumsy was to despise this cacophony of a city, visually and odorously offensive, smearing the taste buds with a taste of testicular turds, and quite, quite uninviting to the touch, with its cuntinubilating dickulous inhabitants – heavy emphasis on the last syllable, ants. But then, Mumsy was always right. The city without flowers, she said. The city where the sun never shines, she said. Not even with blazing blue skies and the heat scorching your kidneys and drying up the juices of your heart – despite the three thousand and five per cent humidity. Though that part, about the sun never shining, was truer uptown where the buildings were so negroidly phallic. Here, in the East Village, the dope-dirty, piss-washed architectural crap-pots were lower both in class and height, allowing glimpses of the sun, at least along the avenues, even if the streets remained as dark and smelly as Pluto's subterranean alleys, or the anal passages of heterosexual males – homosexual anal passages getting more light, air and eau-de-toilette, naturally, or unnaturally, depending on where you stood, or which part of you did, at the thought of anal passages, hetero or homo.

Lahya found himself plunging through one of the above mentioned passages, tumoured and diseased, judging by the established fungusy establishments and all the to-ing and fro-ing going on within it. At one tediously inevitable crossroads the sign had no street number, just St Mark's Place. Hopes of getting lost were raised, but dashed immediately as he saw 2nd Avenue running in front of him, and signs proclaiming 7th Street and 9th Street to his left and right respectively. 'Home' would be two blocks left, down, and one block east, left again. How boring. Not even the dubious excitement of wondering whether you will ever find your way back, or be abducted and mutilated by Aliens, if no one else. Hope again. If ever there was a place in the world where Aliens abounded, it should be here. He scanned the surrounds once again for possible abductors and mutilators, this time for himself instead of for Jayshree.

Whether there were any about or not, Aliens and/or abductors and mutilators, no one took any notice of him, not even as a visiting Gravesendian from Mumsy England, much less as an objet d'abduxion (sic). Perhaps he should ask for it, as it were. That should make it easier, and serve him right too. He tried leaning sexily against a pole and half opened his mouth. No luck. A minute of that and his mouth was dry. Soon his lips would begin to flake, and that wouldn't be sexy at all. He remembered a moppet video his Granddad had once shown him in his sex shop when they were last here two years ago. Unfortunately when it came to the really interesting bits there was a knock on the door of the tiny office at the back of the shop and Granddad had to turn it off and him out of the shop altogether, not just the office.

He took off his shirt, wetted his lips with his tongue, and once again leaned against the pole, this time lifting one leg up, bending it at the knee and twirling his ankle. Still no interest. The next step, he recalled, was langorously putting the middle finger between the lips, and sucking it. That felt good, produced saliva and kept the mouth from drying, but no would-be abductors and mutilators. Now to be really daring. Bringing the index and middle fingers of his other hand to the nipple on the opposite side, and twisting it.

There he was, shirt off – well, that didn't count for much as there was hardly a shirt to be seen anywhere anyway – sucking the middle finger of his right hand with sensuously open lips while picking at his right nipple with the middle and index fingers of his left hand, yet no signs of any public arousal. What the heck. He straightened himself up, brought his hands down, and began pulling his jeans off. He pulled his jeans off. Now clad only in his sexily grey Calvin Klein briefs and white trainers without socks, he leaned against the pole again.

He could have been a part of the pole for all the excitement he failed to engender. By this time the moppet in the video had pulled many an eyeball out of its socket, not to mention the tongues she left lolling all over the place. But then, she was a *she*. And a white she at that. Blonde and Swedish and clever. What chance did he have, a stupid black boy.

Cursing heavily and loudly he stopped picking at his nipple, took his finger out of his mouth, pulled his jeans back on and thought of trying a more direct tactic. If he had to ask for it, why not ask? He had seen many a girl doing it *and* boys, especially at night, especially where his Granddad's sex shops were, and where his Granddad had taken him on one or two occasions. He had promised to take him more often and for longer periods but Jamuna put a stop to it. He had never forgiven his aunt for that.

Shirt carelessly flung across his left shoulder he approached a muscular young man wearing a number of rings, a money pouch, sandals, and nothing else. His eyes were hard, his hair short cropped and he looked mean. He had a dragon tattooed on his bulging right arm, and the head of a mile-long yard-thick snake seemed to disappear up the back of his left thigh. If anyone could abduct and mutilate, *he* could.

With New York-heat-desensitised head Lahya blocked the path of the strong mean man and said in his best voice, 'Would you care to abduct and mutilate me?' Then in true American brat fashion, added, 'Sir.'

All the hardness in the mean man's face melted away, his strong wrist flipped airily in the air, and with an oh-so-cute giggle he shook his massive neck and said, 'No! but you can me, any time,' pranced for a second, then before Lahya could recover from this rejection, added, 'Big boy,' and walked away with his previous macho gait.

Big boy indeed! Trust him to pick a visually impaired, intellectually challenged dungheap out of the three hundred million dungheaps within easy range.

Next he decided to turn his attention to an old man, bald and bent yet bright-eyed enough to be certified alive. Old men are always hankering for it and never getting it, his best mate in school always said. You can touch them for anything, he said.

'Would you like . . .' began Lahya, but the old man hurried past, as fast as his old legs could carry him, bending over further in an attempt to escape Lahya's enquiring gaze.

Perhaps he had tackled someone too old, too old to be interested in abduction and mutilation. He should try a younger older man. He was about to single one out when he saw two policemen and a policewoman strolling by. The woman was black and fat, her bust as huge as her huge bum, and she was chewing gum with the most determined chew he had ever seen in the most determined of Guernsey heifers. Her fat thighs rotated sideways as she moved forward, and her fat arms wobbled independently of the rest of her. The two policemen were equally short, fat and ugly, one white and old, the other young and Hispanic.

No way would he permit himself to be abducted and mutilated by any one of this terrible trio, and they would too, if they caught him soliciting their compatriots for abduction and mutilation.

He decided to go home for now and postpone abduction and mutilation to another less humid day. A little bit of breeze may work wonders for the libido of would-be abductors and mutilators, he thought. Well, I am not sure that he exactly thought that, his philosophy of life not yet encompassing the concept of the libido, or even if his philosophy did, his vocabulary did not; but he did think something like that, or so I choose to think.

Yes, he would go home. At least it will leave Mumsy and dadso worrying for a bit where he might be. And he'd be rid of that creepy cousin of his.

V

When Lahya was a few steps from the apartment he realised he didn't have the keys. Although it was a Saturday, Uncle Dileep would be out with his taxi, driving around as well as checking up on the drivers who worked for him. This was his routine nine days a week, thirty-six hours a day. Grandma resolutely refused to 'speak to the door' much less release it. He would have to go into the restaurant to get the keys off Aunt Jamuna, something he didn't relish doing. He'd still not forgiven her for not letting Granddad take him to his sex shops at night, two years and some ago.

He climbed the few steps down the road to restaurant level, walked past the long window where the sitar and tabla players sat in the evening for the live music sessions, and pulled open the door marked 'exit' on the inside. He was pleased at himself for remembering not to push it, as dadso did each time they came down, to Mumsy's 'He can't even open a door!' each time. Hesitating for a while above the 'welcome' doormat, he began treading the long red-carpeted aisle leading to the kitchen where Aunt Jamuna would be hard at work for Saturday evening's menu, while freshening up last night's leftovers for the 'lunch specials'. One of the waiters made as if to greet a customer with a smile but returned his face to customary gloom on seeing it was only that stupid boy visiting from England and whose father did not leave any tip the other day, even after a free meal.

It was nearly twelve thirty, and some of the 'lunch specials' were already inside the spacious dining hall which always managed to look more than half-empty when more than half-full. Dileep could never make up his mind whether they were lucky to have a much larger eating area than most other adjoining Indian restaurants, or if it was a problem, but could not come to any conclusion which lasted more than a day or two at a time. But then Dileep was never much good at coming to conclusions.

The walls of the hall were decorated with one picture each of the Taj Mahal and the fort at Fatehpur Sikri, two Air India posters inciting tourism; and large representations of three deities of Hinduism. Siva, who was Granddad's favourite, especially his Linga (unrevealed in the restaurant depiction). Ganesh, the elephant god, Jamuna's heart-throb, again with mammoth parts, again undisclosed in the restaurant portrait. And Kali, the eternal goddess, who burst forth from the brow of the goddess Durga to help combat and destroy the asuric, the demonic forces of evil, chiefly, if not always, male. Kali, the black, the ferocious, the vengeful and the just. Kali, who could destroy whom she chose, bewitch whom she fancied, bless and grant the deepest wishes of the heart whenever she was appeased and loved and honoured and worshipped with due respect and appropriate offerings. Kali who mated and sated Siva or whoever whenever her lust was awakened, killed and beheaded whoever whenever her anger was aroused. Kali, who could turn white and tender and beautiful if so her heart desired, or the occasion demanded. Kali, the great feminine principle without which the world would be at the cruel and insane power of the male drive. Kali, the ever-present, all-knowing, all-doing Kali. *Me. I.* Worshipped and revered by Savitri, as I should be by all who know what is best for them, and for this world of evil and conflict and torment.

VI

On his way to the kitchen Lahya surveyed the customers at the four occupied tables in the restaurant with an undisguised, unapologetic, damn-your-eyes nosiness.

On one, by the corner window with a view of both the street and the avenue sat a white man with short-cropped greying hair and a short-cropped greying moustache, wearing the shortest shorts Layha had ever seen, and the tightest. His companion, an overdressed, heavily made-up black woman, sat opposite him. Lahya remembered seeing them once before. They were two of the 'regulars', one of the friendlier waiters had said with a wink and a nudge, the reason for which Lahya didn't quite follow at the time.

On the other side of the aisle sat a lone young man: black denim shirt, black denim jeans, black sneakers, black-rimmed glasses. Another of the regulars.

A stout middle-aged man and a skinny older woman were devouring the menu on the table next to the young man. The stout middle-aged man had a skin so thin you could see the blood running through his veins, with cheeks the colour of peeled tomatoes. The skinny older woman's skin was leathery and of an indeterminate hue. Her face looked like it had suffered an earthquake of devastating proportions just before breakfast that morning.

A little further to the right a very young and very beautiful toothsome twosome sat gazing into each other's eyes with unmitigated lust. Lahya restrained the urge to go over to them and puke on their faces. He did not even pull their gold-blond hair out by the handful from the roots, thus sparing them total and instant baldness. He did, however, skilfully manage to pass a silently windy comment as he walked by their table, unnoticed, so absorbed were the doters in doting upon each other. On turning back to assess the results, if any, of his adroit performance, he discerned a clear change in their expressions and attitudes. Instead of looking into each other's eyes they were trying not to. Lahya smiled for the first time that day. Life had its little compensations, after all.

When he entered the kitchen Aunt Jamuna was bending over one of the lower ovens, her generous bum, swathed in a green and yellow sari of fine quality muslin, upended for the world to behold in all its overripe splendour. She looked up sideways as she heard the sound of someone entering, saw that it was Lahya, and grinned broadly, showing perfect white teeth set in a plump round face, fleshy, but unlined despite its forty-seven years, richly dark brown, and hot, as if it had just come out freshly baked from the very oven into which it was peering.

She shut the oven door and straightened herself up, 'Now what can I do for my moon,' she asked, drawing close to him and eyeing him tenderly. Lahya hated being referred to as 'moon', but gritted his teeth and refrained from asserting his terrestrial status. He needed the keys which were always tied in a knot round the loose end of Aunt Jamuna's sari and tucked inside its many folds round the waist, digging into the many folds of her flesh. She was generally loathe to part with them. The old woman wouldn't let her into the house if she didn't have her keys, and would then complain to Dileep that that thankless unworthy wife of his had neglected her the entire day. 'But it was you who chose her for me, not I for myself,' Dileep invariably felt like retorting, but never did. Whenever Jamuna did anything that pleased the old woman, which was when she displeased the now departed father-in-law, or any of the many friends and visitors despised by the old woman, Jamuna was 'her' sweet daughter-in-law. If not, which was the norm, she was 'his' wretched wife. But Dileep had learnt to live with it, as had Jamuna, though there were times she lost her patience, and then it was the clash of the titans. Dileep was only grateful he was hardly ever home.

'Can I have the keys to the house?' Lahya said 'house' as he would have back in England, not sure that living in a flat above a restaurant qualified as living in a house. 'I'll bring them straight back,' he added hurriedly without really thinking how he would manage that feat without needing the keys again; unless he wanted to stay out, in which case there was not much point in going in in the first place.

'Come here, my moon, I have a surprise for you. No one knows about this, not even your uncle.' She twitched her nose in a knowing manner and beckoned him into the pantry behind the kitchen.

She unlocked the door with one of the keys hanging from her sari, moved to one side to let Lahya enter first, then followed him and shut the door behind them, looked at Lahya again, twitched her nose again, walked up to the cupboard at the far end, opened it, reached high and picked up a lacquered terracotta jar from the top shelf, removed its lid and showed the contents to Lahya. It was full of flour, nothing to be so mysterious about anywhere, much less in a restaurant larder. Another twitch of the nose and her hand dived into the jar, and after a bit of rummaging around came up with a powdery set of keys. 'Here, take them. Keep them. For as long as you are here. But don't tell anyone you have them.'

'But they are bound to find out, if I . . .' began Lahya, joining in with the conspiratorial tone, wondering if he had misjudged Aunt Jamuna all these years.

'Just tell them you borrowed them from me. Or wait, you can tell them you got new ones cut. With your own money. Don't worry about me. I have two more sets hidden here. But when I don't want to go up to hear that old woman whinging and whining, I say I have lost mine somewhere, fell off my sari, or something. Then, when I am ready to face her sour face, I find them!' she giggled girlishly and slapped Lahya on the back. He had still not put his shirt back on and it was flung across his shoulder. 'My, you are hot and wet,' she said, as she felt his stickily perspiring skin, her hand lingering on Lahya's naked back. Lahya jerked away thinking he had been called a sweaty so-and-so, but the look in Aunt Jamuna's eyes was far from critical.

'Look what I have gone and done now,' Aunt Jamuna exclaimed, 'covered your back with flour!' As she hurriedly picked up a dishcloth to dust his back, she held his chest with the other hand, transferring some of the flour to his chest. 'Oh, sorry,' she giggled some more. 'Let me wash you up,' and despite Lahya's protests turned on the tap in the sink, washed her hands, and began to rub his chest with her clean wet hands, massaging the nipples ever so gently.

'I think I'd better run,' said Lahya and headed towards the door, 'Mumsy . . . Mum and dad will be looking for me,' he added, even though it didn't make sense if he was going up to the house, and it was them that he was he trying to escape.

His attempts to get out were thwarted as the pantry door was specially equipped with a self-locking lock on both sides of the door.

'You can never trust these bloody waiters – even the cook who comes to help me now and then,' explained Aunt Jamuna as she moved forward with her bunch of keys to open the door for Lahya.

'Bhagwan protect you, my son,' said Jamuna as if in parting, but then, before opening the door, continued, 'Back home in Calcutta I used to bath my little brother until he grew a beard. I will give you a good rub one of these days when you are tired. My brother loved it. Even after he was married he used to say he missed the baths I gave him.' She twitched her nose again and turned the key in the lock. Lahya was out of there feeling a bit numb, a bit confused.

VII

Back in the dining area Lahya's eye caught the many severed heads juggling round my holy neck, the many severed arms forming a skirt round my godly thighs, my many many hands with their many many swords waving about in merry vengefulness, and my blood-soaked tongue lolling out lustfully, craving for more blood. He stuck his tongue out at me and, grasping his crotch, jerked his hips in my direction, *à la* his most beloved person on earth besides Mumsy, a certain musical prodigy, the only black boy he knew who was gradually turning into a white woman, if not already turned. I liked the lad. Lahya, I mean, not the musical prodigy. Though I must confess to liking him too.

He was on his way out when one of the waiters stopped him. The one who had spoken to him the other day about the white man with the short-cropped greying moustache and the black woman. The waiter shook his hand and put his arm round his back. Lahya squirmed beneath the weight of it. His back was increasing in popular appeal by the minute, and his self-image was not high enough to handle it with any degree of equanimity, especially after the said image had taken a serious knock less than half an hour ago when not the slightest interest had been shown in his back, or the rest of him, while soliciting for abduction and mutilation.

'How're you doing, my friend?' said the waiter.

'Fine. I'm doing fine,' said Lahya, trying to get out from under the man's arm, but he held on to him with resolute firmness.

'Is your father still here? And your mother?' said the waiter, Bengali like the rest, but younger and taller than the others.

What a dumb question, thought Lahya. Of course they'd be here, if I am, thought Lahya, this man is a turnip; though later events were to prove that even Lahya could be wrong. For the moment he just nodded his head in assent to the man's question.

'You like it here?' continued the waiter.

Where was all this leading to? wondered Lahya, but murmured something like 'Yeah, it's OK,' this time making a successful lunge sideways and getting out from under the man's arm. He was about to leave when the man drew his face close to Lahya's and whispered, 'Want some free soda? Eh?'

Lahya was now on the verge of feeling a little afraid. Perhaps God had heard his roadside appeals and sent him an abductor and mutilator. Strangely, now that a possible abductor and mutilator seemed likely he decided he wasn't really too keen on abduction and mutilation after all. Not for just a soda.

The man sensed his apprehension and laughed. 'Do not worry my friend, I just want you to read a letter for me. You come from England. Your English will be good. It's from a friend. A girl. I met her here, she came for the lunch special. I talk fine, but don't read good, don't write well too. She thinks I'm going to be a doctor.' Lahya tried to picture the man in a surgeon's coat carrying surgical knives rather than in an apron carrying cutlery. 'She's gone to LA, to see her mother. I don't want people here to find out. Please. I am to marry my cousin and her brother works here. There, that ugly one with the fat stomach . . . giving me dirty looks. I think I go now. I will bring you a soda. On the house. On me,' continued the waiter and smiled what must have been his most appealing smile. 'But sit on that table, there.' The man pointed to the table next to the white man with the short-cropped greying moustache and the black woman, then winked.

'Why?' blurted Lahya, surprised into honesty, while imagining the reaction of Aunt Jamuna if she found him sitting 'on' one of her tables.

'You will like their talk. It is so crazy. If you are there, I will bring your soda and bring the letter, then I can listen too.'

Lahya's heart warmed to the man. Anyone that nosy had to be more than a turnip. By now he, too, was keen to hear what the couple had to say which so excited this lover-boy. 'OK,' he said, 'I will have a large Pepsi, no, Coke,' he remembered the musical prodigy, 'and a large portion of chips . . . fries.' The waiter's face fell marginally at this blackmail, but then perked up as he chirped, 'Sure I will.' He walked cheerily away, pointing with his elbow to the empty table adjoining the to-be-eavesdropped-upon couple.

Lahya put his shirt on.

VIII

Even before Lahya could get to his seat he heard the black woman's voice and the first thing he heard was that it was not a black woman's voice. It was a black man's voice.

'I haven't set eyes on the slut since she gave me the cat's litter box to clean out,' said the black woman's voice that was really a very made-up and dressed up black man's voice, angry, outraged and smug all at the same time, besides being very loud. 'I emptied the lot on her Slumber Beauty mattress where I saw her the other day, slutting on her back, legs open, mouth open, waiting for the white trash I thought to be *my* friend who just happened to be in the shower shaving his balls. You should have seen the look on her face! His face. If he thinks he can fool *anyone* with those shoulders, he must be as big a fool as his dick is small.'

The greying white man with the shortest shorts Lahya had ever seen, and the tightest, brought his hand to his mouth and went into a fit of squealy laughter. Between gusts of merry air he managed to whisper, 'Stay with cucumbers, girl, if you want a good stay, stay with cucumbers, that's what I say.'

'Oh no, I couldn't. I just couldn't. I am not made that way. Call me a freak, but I *like* them small. Why do you think I love that slut. Zucchini, that's the most I'll go for, a good, fresh, young zucchini.' This, just as Lahya pulled up the nearest chair and sat on it. The 'woman' heard the chair move and looked up. Their eyes met and she smiled. 'Zucchini,' she repeated to her companion who went into an even greater fit of squealy laughter. This time the woman joined him with her own brand of joyous noise which almost brought the traffic to a standstill outside.

That was it. Lahya had had enough of zucchinis for the day. With flushed face he rose abruptly from the seat he had only just occupied and marched out of the restaurant with a deepening scowl as the tall Bengali waiter hurried after him and tried unsuccessfully to restrain him with a Pepsi and an envelope.

'Your fries are getting ready . . .' he shouted in desperation to a disappearing-from-sight Lahya before turning back towards the counter. He could be fired if he left the premises without permission, and permission he was not likely to get.

IX

Lahya entered the little foyer of their apartment building and thought of ringing the bell of No 1 a few times, just to see whether Grandma would react in any way at all, to find out for himself if she really was determined not to let anyone in, or falsely accused of so doing, maliciously maligned. But good sense prevailed. If he did ring the bell, and nothing happened, and then he went up, she'd know it was he who tried to annoy her and hold it against him; cut Mumsy off her will or something mean like that which old people do.

He took out the bunch of keys given to him by Aunt Jamuna. There were a whole lot of keys in there; including, presumably, the keys to the restaurant pantry, and to the restaurant itself. Turning one in the outside door he opened it, greatly pleased with himself that he got the right one the first try. Up and in front of the apartment door itself he had problems. Just when he was about to give up in despair, thinking that Aunt Jamuna had played a dirty trick on him for one of the many unfathomable reasons women play tricks on men, bless them; just then one of the keys clicked the lock open. It was the one he had tried the very first time, and a hundred and three times besides. Thank God for that. A Chinese woman in the apartment opposite had twice opened her door to see what was going on, and had given Lahya a very suspicious look the second time round, the type of look that picks up the phone and dials the police. He had begun to regret his decision to return home – not that it was home.

Once inside, his regrets mounted. The red shagpile beneath his shoes felt greasy, and there was a musty unpleasant air about the whole place. The curtains were drawn, the windows shut, and the walls had a look of heavy despair about them. *You* can get out, they seemed to say to Lahya, what about us, where can *we* go! It was so hot and close that he had difficulty breathing.

He almost ran out when he heard Savitri's quaky and quaking voice coming from nowhere and everywhere, 'Is that you Jamuna, beti?'

Before he could stop himself he answered in as good a Hindi as he could manage, 'No. It's me, Dadiji.' Too late. If he hadn't spoken he could have slunk out pretending he was never there. No matter. He quite liked the old woman in a wary sort of a way. She had everybody running around in circles, and that couldn't be all bad.

'How did you get in, star of my eyes? Where did you get the keys?' She didn't miss anything, did she? 'And where is that ungrateful wretch of a father of yours, and your beautiful mother? I hope Jayshree has not turned them into crows with her accursed eyes.' Crackling laughter. 'One crow and a dove,' she amended, and crackled some more. Jayshree's hatred of her grandmother did not go unrequited. It was returned a hundredfold. Her anger at his father and praise of his mother were spot-on too. He was glad to have come home. Someone intelligent to talk to, someone on the same wavelength, even if it was a creepy old bat.

He still couldn't figure out where the old woman was, actually and physically. Then, as if she read his mind from wherever she was, 'I am up here, doing my pooja, in my little mandir, upstairs, the room in the corner.'

It was, for the East Village NY, a very large apartment with two storeys and a basement. Lahya had still not seen all of it as two rooms at the top and the basement were always kept locked while everybody crammed into the remainder. One of the always-locked rooms was in the corner upstairs. Lahya was quite excited about finally seeing what it was like. Halfway up he realised he was getting excited about going into a poky little locked room in a poky little New York 'house'. What *had* life reduced him to. Mumsy would *never* be excited about something like that!

Just as he reached the door of what Savitri had called her little temple and where she claimed to be worshipping, she called out, 'Come in, my darling boy,' as if aware of the exact moment his feet touched the threshold.

Lahya opened the door and was instantly hit with such a disturbing and disturbed combination of *déjà vu* and foreboding that he bodily reeled under the impact and almost backed out of the room. He would have too, if Savitri hadn't held him by the hand and pulled him in.

Too young to understand what could have happened, he knew better than an adult would have that something had happened. He could also tell that it was only the beginning. That there would be no escape from any of it any more. That it was too late.

But the feeling soon passed, and he was his usual clear-foreheadedly scowling idiotic self again.

X

The *déjà vu* was partly explained. The room was a shrine to Kali, and her various incarnations and representations adorned the walls, including the picture that Lahya had seen in the restaurant a short while ago. The one at which he had stuck out his tongue.

The centrepiece of the shrine was a larger-than-life statue of the deity at her most voracious and ferocious. At her feet lay burning candles and smoking incense and offerings of fruit and sweets, daubed with the red of sindoor to match the red of blood; and the dying body of a man made from a pale-ish white clay contrasted with the rich black of Kali herself.

'Now, if you want anything in life, star of my eyes, you ask Kali Mata,' said Savitri with a curious smile playing around her scarlet katha-stained mouth. 'It doesn't matter if you are not a woman. Actually, it pleases Kali even more if a man begs her for a favour. You look like her favourite child disciple anyway, the one who worships the very blood she sheds, see, there he is, by her ear. But if you do ask for something, you have to pay for it. With love, with adoration, with sanctified fruit and sweets, with money; and some-times, with blood. A tiger's or a buffalo's will do, though nothing pleases her more than human blood, male human blood. A male child would do, even a male infant. Offer her that, and you can have anything you ask. Anything!'

I smiled appreciatively at this elucidation of my powers and proclivities. For one eternal moment Lahya caught my smile, and the simple unadorned dread in his eyes was touchingly amusing. More and more I liked the stupid little boy.

XI

As Lahya and Savitri were coming down to the living room, the key in the apartment door turned for the second time in the last half hour and Jamuna entered carrying a vegetable thali in her right hand. She was about to bend over and bring her other hand down to the carpet, a token gesture of touching the floor as a mark of respect for her mother-in-law, when she stopped, and with a look of horror in her eyes said, 'You didn't take Lahya to that . . . that room . . . give him nightmares! He's from here, the Western world. He's not used to . . . he won't understand . . .' *Not many even from the Indian world will understand, evil witch that you are* . . . she mused as Savitri cut her short with a savagery which shook Lahya.

'Never you mind, I don't ask you where you take . . .'

It was Jamuna's turn to interrupt, which she did, swiftly, but in a sweet and sugary voice, 'I've brought you your lunch, Mataji. Hope you like it today,' meaning, *Hope you choke on it today*, then smiled broadly as she added an extra lie, 'Extra hot and sharp, made especially for you, Mataji. And something for you too, my moon. I thought you might be here,' this last addressed truthfully to Lahya.

Halfway through the meal Jamuna put her arms round Lahya and pinched his cheek. 'You have your school vacations now, Lahya, haven't you? You don't have to go back with your Mummy and Daddy. Why don't you stay on for a another month or so? Uncle Dileep will show you round Manhattan.'

'No I don't. I have another ten days to go to school before my vac . . . holidays. I took a week off especially to come for . . . for . . . Granddad's . . . because Granddad . . .'

'Really! That is strange. Our Jayshree has been off school for the past week.'

'Yes, my sweet boy, do stay,' said Savitri enthusiastically; and it wasn't always that she endorsed her daughter-in-law any which way, much less enthusiastically. 'This is your home too, you know. My home . . .' pause to emphasise that here the agreement was over, '*My* home is always your home, sweet boy.'

Lahya muttered something about asking his parents about it.

Lunch over, Jamuna gathered up the dirty dishes, put them back neatly on the tray and started to leave, but not before trying to persuade Lahya some more. 'Another ten days, Hannn! Well, by the time you leave, it will be five days only. Maybe less, if you count the weekend or something like that. Hann.' Jamuna resorted to the Indian nasal 'hann', or 'achcha' – both vaguely meaning 'OK ya' – when vocalising a longish train of thought. 'Why don't you stay on anyway? I will talk to your Mummy. And your Daddy, of course. By the way, they rang a short while ago, down in the restaurant. I told them you were here, so they don't worry. What happened? Why did you leave early? I bet you had an argument with our Jayshree. She can be difficult sometimes. Not like you. You are so sweet-tempered. If you come down to the restaurant, I'll give you a map of New York. Achcha. Show you where there are some interesting places you might like to see. Especially if you stay on. I'll ask your Mummy, if she rings again. I'll tell her you'd like to stay on and enjoy summer in New York. It is so damn cold and miserable in London. The last time I went it rained for more days than we were there. Terrible. Terrible, I said to your uncle. He agreed. Can you believe that? He agreed with me. So there. I will tell your Mummy you would like to stay. If they phone. Or when I see them. Yes. I think I better wait till I see them. But Raj bhaiyya said he might phone. In the restaurant.'

That was another thing Grandma could not tolerate. The phone ringing when she was alone at home. She could not tolerate the phone ringing any time, but she suffered it, reluctantly, if someone was there to answer it immediately. But not when on her own. It was a miracle she hadn't taken the damn instrument into the kitchen and boiled it in oil, as all perpetrators of evil ought to be.

Lahya began to wonder if he might really like to stay on in New York. It would be great to be away from school, and dadso, and ugly old Gravesend. But New York! Mega-puky, mega-smelly, mega-yukky New York. Mumsy's pet hate, New York . . . No. Thanks, but no thanks. That was it. He was going to be firm about it if Aunt Jamuna persisted with the crazy idea. No way would he spend another day more than necessary, much less a whole month, in mega-puky, mega-yukky, mega-slimy New York. Pissy, sissy, hissy New York.

At the door Jamuna turned once again and spoke once again, this time somewhat differently, in a far-away, misty sort of a voice which intrigued Lahya. 'It will be good for your Mummy, too. She'll need the extra rest. She had a bad time last time. The first months. Some women have bad last months, some bad first.' Her words intrigued him even more than the voice. What on earth could she mean? 'Last months'! A sudden dread got hold of his heart. Could Mumsy be ill? Could she be *dying* . . . His recently ingested food felt like surfacing upwards with a jolt.

'She's right, you know.' Grandma waited till Jamuna was out before admitting the woman was right about anything. 'She's right,' she continued, and just as Lahya was about to press for further details about Mumsy, she stood up, held his hand, and pulled him up with surprising strength. 'Come, come with me and help me throw my vile husband's things out of my room. I have put most of them in the trash can. I want the rest out too. On the streets. At first I thought of burning them, but that would purify them . . . And the river would cleanse them too. Out in the streets, dirty filthy streets, that's where his things belong. That's where he belonged. Even Calcutta was cleaner.'

'Is Mums . . . Mother all right? She is not . . .'

Savitri interrupted him with a boisterous chuckle. 'Of course she's all right. She's tough. We all are, we women. We have to be, to survive. Kali knows that. Don't you worry. You are a lucky boy to have a mother like your mother.' Lahya was reassured, but not quite. Some nagging lingering doubts and questions remained. What did she mean by 'she is tough'? Why did she have to be tough?

'Poor Jayshree,' Grandma prattled on, 'I can see why she is the pesty nasty creature that she is. With a mother like Jamuna. Come, we'll have a good shower after we have thrown his filthy stuff away.'

First a rub-down followed by the offer of a bath, now the

suggestion of a shower: did he have odour problems? He raised his free arm and did a quick nose-dive under his armpit. That's New York for you, he thought. You begin to stink along with everything else.

XII

It was their last day in New York. It was raining. Mumsy was delighted. dadso had wanted to go to Central Park but Mumsy said it was so full of weirdos on wheels that she 'just could not handle it'. First, there was the ever-present danger of mortal collision, so fortuitously and fortunately demonstrated only the other day when the black man, Afro-American if you like, ran into dadso, never mind that the latter had been unceremoniously pushed into the former's arms by his only offspring to date. Secondly, the sight of so many naked thighs, especially male, 'did something to her'. No one dared ask what.

So it was Mumsy rides again, and to the Museum of American Folk Art. The fact that it was so tantalisingly next door to Central Park added an extra bit of spice to Mumsy's victory, aided and abetted by Mumsy Nature herself shedding copious tears of joy from the heavens. However, it was Monday, and the museum was closed, which just goes to show that every dog has its day and dadso clucked with gleeful sorrow that poor Mumsy had been denied her heart's desire again. During their last visit too, unforeseen circumstances, such as dadso's toothache, had prevented Mumsy from doing her bit for the Red Indians, Native American Culture, if you like.

To add insult to injury, dadso booked a table for seven, for dinner at eight at the Jamuna Restaurant. Since the act was performed in front of the other invitees Mumsy was unable to explode vocally, so she imploded in silence. Jayshree and Savitri weren't keen on the idea either which made the situation even more exhilaratingly exciting. Mumsy said not a word for the rest of the morning and her demeanour threatened imminent self-combustion any time without notice. Their *last* night, and dinner at *Jamuna*. I mean, how mean can you get? Discount is one thing, disgrace quite another. And if the rest of the unsavoury Cenna clan had to be there, at least it could have been compensated by a more savoury cuisine; the unpleasant atmosphere of the family gathering offset by the pleasanter ambience of a less inelegant setting.

As the rain-drenched party returned home, the rain cleared. It was back to muggy heat and a soul-destroying sun whose reflected rays from glassy skyscrapers penetrated your psyche with psychotic fury and cut holes in your body where holes had no business. Then, upon Jayshree's insistence, another walk round Tompkins Park. Mumsy held on to Lahya for protection from the unending stream of over-tattooed leather-jacketed nail-studded ear-ringed nose-ringed drug-numbed drink-fucked dope-high flea-infested roach-ridden rat-bitten dirt-soaked unwashed uncouth unloved undesirables, unleashed in an equally unwashed uncouth undesirable locality on an equally unwashed uncouth undesirable community, determined that the next time someone jingled his or her paper cup at her nose and grinned for money and blessed her, she'd be sick in it. Not that Mumsy wanted to be uncharitable, unkind or ununderstanding, but she couldn't be untruthful either. So she declaimed her opinion of what she saw, prompting Jayshree to desire more time in the park, sit on a shit-coloured shit-smelling bench, admire the unadmirable and admit to the senses what was inadmissible to sense.

The most intelligent, most respectable-looking and the most conservative in attitude and perspective of those present were the dogs. Mumsy tried to befriend one in utter desperation, only to be verbally abused by the same in violent dog-slang. That was it; Mumsy retreated into silence again and Raj began to hum the tune of an Indian song which would have incited Mother Teresa to murder one of her recently-converted-to-Catholicism-and-recovering-from-disease-and-starvation protégés.

It was on the way back that things began to look up. Quaint little shops with the most utterly useless articles and objects in the entire history of mankind on generous display attracted the attention of Mumsy. The simple fact that dadso had no interest in them was enough to arouse Mumsy's interest and she started going into each and every hole and crevice business. Things ugly and pointless were scattered all around in such abundant excess in each of them to almost fill to capacity the throats and other apertures and passages of rugged all-American musclemen stars of gay pornos.

In one of these – shops, not throats or other apertures and passages of rugged all-American musclemen – Madam Something with a Ukranian name was advertising crystal reading, palm reading, tarot reading etcetera for a mere two dollars fifty. Nothing new in that. They were all over the place. Not all Ukranian, but almost. However, this particular one took Mumsy's fancy and she decided to have her palm read while holding a crystal in it, a feat which may have been impossible for some, but which Madam Something could perform with her eyes shut.

And it was with her eyes shut that she announced, 'Your first was a boy, dark like his father.' No prizes for guessing that, since Lahya stood there in all his glory; Jayshree and Raj had not-so-politely and politely opted to remain outside. 'Dark in colour and dark in mood,' the good Madam monotoned on. Then with a more cheery voice, '*This* one will be a girl, beautiful, with blonde hair and blue eyes, like you. She will bring joy and good luck . . .' Lahya didn't stay to listen any more. So that's what it was all about. The first months and the last and all that crap. To think that he had worried about his mother. And all the while she was planning to replace him with . . . with a blonde, white, blue-eyed little bitch . . . To think he had worried about her, and she a traitor, betraying him like that. Not even telling him about it, when all the world seemed to know. Aunt Jamuna, and Grandma, and no doubt dadso, who was the root cause of it, as he was of all trouble. 'I bet that cunt-lipped Jayshree knew,' he muttered to himself, face burning with anger, hands sweating and eyes hurting. Even that bloody Madam Fakelovotsky knew . . . He did his usual run and disappeared from view with Raj's 'What do you think you are doing, where do you think you are going . . .' following him to the end of the street.

He went into the restaurant again and read the friendly waiter's letter for him, 'borrowing' him with the excuse that he wanted *him* to read a letter in Bengali for him. The letter was so full of love that Lahya's sickness increased immensely upon reading it once. On second reading its funny side began to manifest itself, and by the time the waiter begged him to read it for the third time he could hardly keep a straight face. He had a feeling that he was not the first to have read the letter for the man, and wouldn't be the last. The way he kept prompting him, it seemed he had the damn thing memorised.

But as soon as it was finally over and Lahya managed to escape into relative freedom, ready to explode in hearty laughter, he couldn't. The pain of Mumsy's ultimate treachery and betrayal was back, magnified, and he rushed to strangle the nearest light-pole, kicking every piece of floating rubbish on the way with a strength which surprised and pleased him.

XIII

It was at the dinner table for seven at eight, placed strategically next to the white man with the greying moustache and the black woman who was a man, with a nudge and a wink to Lahya by the tall Bengali waiter, that Lahya announced his decision to stay on in New York for the summer holidays.

To his great dismay Mumsy did not seem greatly dismayed, although she did say all the right things: 'But I thought we had agreed you weren't staying! We discussed it all last night.'

'What about your school?' said dadso.

'What about my toothbrush!' said the black woman who was a man, Blossom. 'Did you know the slut removed her toothbrush from next to my toothbrush to a corner the very opposite end of the shelf, and that *before* I found the slut, legs up, ass forward, waiting for the white trash to finish shaving his balls in the bathroom, *my* bathroom. *My* bathroom from where the slut moved her toothbrush away from *my* toothbrush. Christ, how low can you get. I mean, what was my toothbrush doing to her toothbrush? Fucking it? And if so, darling, that was more than what I was doing to her. You know, I've never admitted this to anyone before in my life, but I never fucked the slut. Never laid a finger on her. Well, on her maybe, but in her, no; honey dear so help me God. I mean, the slut won't let me *come* anywhere near her.'

Burt, the white man with the greying moustache, jerked his chin at this confession as much as at the italics in Blossom's voice. Blossom continued without so much as a breath. 'All *she* ever wanted from me was housekeeping. And I thought it was love. Platonic she called it, because she did not *do* the other kind, too delicate and too sensitive. While all the while she was passing it round like cookies at a party. As long as they were white; know what I mean. Socratic I call it. Deviously clever and deserving death. Know what I mean.' Burt didn't. But he jerked his chin passionately.

'I think you are too young to be left on your own,' said Mumsy.

'Perhaps I am a bit old for her, you know,' said Blossom. 'Well, a year or two, or ten. Do you think I am too old, honey? Now don't spare my feelings. I have none left, anyway. Numb. That's what the bitch has left me feeling. Numb. Number than an Eskimo's dick on a night out fishing.'

'But he won't be on his own, Marilyn dear,' said Jamuna. 'How can you say that! We are family. Happens all the time. Perhaps not among white folk . . . sorry dear, I didn't mean like that. But we are family.'

'We know that,' said Raj, 'but still . . .'

'It's only a week more of school. Less than that. I'll get Ramesh to send me any work done while I am away. I'll have him sort the homework for me as well,' pleaded Lahya, for once addressing himself to dadso more than Mumsy. His father trusted Ramesh if he trusted anyone. Mumsy hated him.

'Can't you ask anyone else?' complained Mumsy, just as he had hoped. 'I can't stand that boy.'

'You know who I can't stand,' said the white man with a loud nasal whine and a greying moustache, 'I can't stand that dancer at the Gaiety, Moonballs, he calls himself, or something like that, the one with the premorse dick, truncated truncheon he calls it, or something like that. He acts like the world revolves round his sphincter.'

'So . . . mealy-mouthed, and creepy,' continued Mumsy.

'You mean polite and well-behaved,' said dadso.

'Butter wouldn't melt in his asshole,' said the white man with the greying moustache, Burt.

PART III

The Pact

I

'New York is a donkey's butthole,' said Lahya.

'And what is Gravesend like? *Your* butthole. Why don't you crawl back into it, fag,' said Jayshree.

'I'd rather be a fag than a faghag,' Lahya had heard the term only yesterday and was still not sure what it meant, but it sounded good.

'I'd rather be a donkey than a dweeb. At least I'll have a big one, not a little black zucchini,' retorted Jayshree.

Anything but that! Lahya brought out his worst insult, the one that *she* hated the most, 'Dog.'

'Bitch.'

'Come children, have some soup,' said Jamuna shouting from the kitchen of the apartment.

'Soup!!! Yuuuuhh,' Jayshree shouted back. 'I bet it is last week's leftover dal from downstairs.'

'Only for starting. I have a very nice surprise for you after. Something you really like,' tempted Jamuna, peeping out of the kitchen door.

'I thought papa was taking us out today. I knew it was too good to be true.'

'What is this papa papa business. Sounds like papadoms,' grumbled Savitri, coming downstairs after her elevenses pooja. 'Pitaji, that's what well-mannered Indian girls call their father.'

'Sounds like pitta bread,' said Jayshree and burst out into an hysterically shrill laughter. She hated laughing out loud like that, but she knew Savitri hated it even more, so it was worth it. 'And I am American, not Indian.'

'American, ha.' It was Savitri's turn. 'Have you had a look in the mirror? Black as coal.'

Jayshree was shockingly unperturbed at this humiliation from her grandmother. Lahya would have died, or killed.

'Black or white don't make Americans. It is the spirit. The spirit of freedom. Freedom to stand up to ugly old crones who get their husbands murdered for money.' Teacher rhetoric, pupil rumour, and Jayshree bravado.

Jamuna hurried back into the kitchen pretending she hadn't heard her daughter being so rude to her grandmother so she wouldn't have to reprimand her for telling the truth, and for putting the ugly old crone in her place. But Jayshree was an impertinent child of the devil, and should show more respect for her elders, even if they weren't betters. She'd let Dileep sort her out. Not that *he* could sort anyone out. If he could, Jayshree wouldn't be the brat she was. And in an Indian household! Even Americans had more manners than that. Her father would have killed a daughter like that with his bare hands. Still, she was a sickly thing, and not long for this world. So perhaps they had let her get away with more than they would have if she had been normal. Who would wed her, even if she were to live, which she wouldn't. Not for long anyway. She tried not to hope, and then felt guilty, and then begged forgiveness from Lord Ganesh.

'Bhagwan forgive this Hanuman's bastard,' muttered Savitri as she adjusted her sari round her thinning henna-dyed hair, unaware that she was speaking of her husband's bastard. 'Bhagwan forgive her. I never will.'

Just then Dileep came in, bringing one of his employee drivers along with him, a young black man recently converted to Islam, with large white teeth and a shaved head. Grandma hated all blacks, and all Muslims. She froze within herself, edging to the end of the double futon.

'I am afraid I don't have the time to take you for a drive today. But Daniel . . . Raschidde here will take you. You can go to South Street Seaport first. It is a lovely day for that,' said Dileep, trying not to look uncomfortable at having backed out, yet again, from taking the family for a day out.

Jayshree grinned with pleasure. Firstly she had won her bet with Lahya that papa would never take them out. Secondly, Savitri would refuse to go out with a black driver, even if he were a Hindu. Her wrinkled holes must be burning up inside that very minute at having him in the house, for however short a time. Thirdly, she enjoyed going to South Street Seaport. She loved the sea air.

'I'll go and bring some tea,' she said, getting up with as much agility as her awkward legs could manage, 'or would you like some orange juice, or coffee, Raschidde? Why don't you stay for an early lunch? Mama has made some delicious dal soup, and a surprise dish that will be absolutely scrumptious.' She tried to produce an erotic glint in her enormous black pupils as she flapped her eyelashes, miraculously succeeding in glancing askance at Savitri at the same time as she ogled Raschidde, Daniel until a month ago.

Savitri's reaction made even dying young worthwhile.

II

To Jayshree's incalculable horror Savitri came along and sat in the front seat *next* to Raschidde. Just because that was where Jayshree liked to sit, even with papa. With Raschidde, she would have loved it. The old crone had put one over her after all!

At least Jayshree managed to take the left window seat at the back, insisting Mama take the right so she could be next to Lahya, squashing him in the middle yet doing it because she wanted 'to sit close to and talk to her dear cousin'. Harassing Lahya would help ease her frustration.

Hardly had they moved than she whispered in his ear, 'You are history, you know that, don't you? Even you are not thick enough not to.'

'What are you on about?' said Lahya, genuinely surprised and forgetting to put on his sarcastic voice.

Jayshree looked at him in pretend shock. 'You really don't know, do you! You *are* that thick,' then cryptically shut up and started looking out the window at the dreary desolation of Houston Street going east.

'Come on, fishfa . . . Jay, open up that crack . . . ing mouth and . . .' He had to really lean over to Jayshree as affectionately as possible, so as not to be heard by Jamuna, nor betray himself with body language, following the suggestions of breakfast TV back home.

'You want to know. I'll tell you. Out of pity. Not that you deserve it.' She was dying to say it anyway, after having just thought of it. 'Your mother has dumped you. On us. My parents and yours made a deal.' Lahya jerked his head towards Jamuna, reflexively. 'Don't worry about Mama, she can't hear us. She's half-deaf anyway. Now listen. My Papa wants a son, which Mama can't have. Your dear Mumsy wants a daughter. It was all a joke. Mama asking you, your Mumsy complaining. All a put on. A set-up. Now that she is going to have a pretty little girl, your darling Mumsy is not going to keep you, is she! White ladies like daughters. She's had a scan or something to make sure. So, now you know. We get you, your Mumsy gets a daughter, your dadso gets the sex shops, and makes a bundle; everyone is happy. Except me. Stuck with you . . . One good thing, next to you I look great . . . and if you're as sick as your face, you might even die before me, with any luck.'

'What are you two whispering about?' said Jamuna trying and failing to catch what was being said, half-angry to be left out, half-pleased that Lahya was getting on well with Jayshree: the poor girl could do with a friend. She hardly had any. In fact, she did not have any.

Lahya had always wanted to be a gorgeous white woman. He had part of his wish granted. He turned white. If imperfectly, if temporarily. His blood left him. Where it went, he couldn't be sure; but it was certainly not flowing through his veins. His heart was not pumping it any more.

And to think that he thought *he* was punishing Mumsy by not going back home, that it was his choice, when all along it was she who was ditching him. How she would have smiled in her heart when he had dramatically announced that he would like to stay on in New York. *No wonder she hadn't looked greatly dismayed.*

This understandable error of perception should have been the least of his worries, presuming what Jayshree said was true, which it wasn't. Strangely enough, the re-lived humiliation and grief of that brief moment two days ago overshadowed both the terrible pain of the present and the joy he had been experiencing seconds earlier in anticipation of seeing the South Street Seaport. In imagining how he would mock it, no matter how nice it was, just because Jayshree loved it. It all seemed pointless now.

III

Lahya made up his mind to kill himself that night, for real. He would have too, had I not felt sorry for the stupid boy and gone to his rescue.

He had been given the second locked room in the apartment, opposite my shrine. A special favour indeed. Even Raj and Marilyn, along with Lahya, had been accommodated in Jayshree's room while the girl was moved into her parents' room for the duration, hence her extra good humour the past few days. The upper floor had a separate toilet and shower, as well as a little cubicle for a kitchen. The previous owners had rented it out to another Indian family. Jamuna refused to allow strangers into the house, and Savitri turned one room into her pooja room, like the one she had had in Calcutta, while the other was left for Jamuna's parents when they visited or should they decide to spend their last days with their eldest daughter in the wonderland aka the United States of America.

Lahya thought of various ways he could top himself. Eventually he decided to go to bed early, set his travelling alarm clock for two in the morning and execute his departure from this world at that romantic time of the night. The clock was a present from Mumsy, and it was appropriate to use it as an aid to self-annihilation. After all, it was her betrayal and abandonment which necessitated it.

He would leave the house, go down to 3rd Avenue, turn into 8th Street, walk east to Tompkins Park, noting along the way the street life of St Mark's Place by night for the first and last time. Jayshree had spoken of it with enthusiasm, and he couldn't die without allowing himself the pleasure of rubbishing it. Round Tompkins Park he would venture into the deathlands of Avenues B and C and on to the big road, whatever it was called, across it, over the bridge, through the park by the East River, then to the river itself, and jump.

Hopefully it would not come to that. Hopefully he would be set upon and boisterously slaughtered by some happy hood or a gang thereof, making it simpler, quicker, easier and more honourable. The last jump would require courage he may find difficult to invoke.

IV

Lahya did not have to make an excuse to go to bed early. He had been so down and distracted the whole afternoon, so broody and cloudy, so good to Jayshree, refusing to put peanut butter and jam on his cheese and mushroom pizza before not eating it, sighing more often than breathing and nearly bursting into tears when Savitri remarked he must be missing his dear sweet Mumsy, that Jamuna herself suggested he '. . . should go to his room and have a good night's sleep. That should settle his stomach'. Jamuna tended to blame all ills to which mankind is subject, from warts to wars and divorces, on a malfunctioning stomach. She even offered to come up and lie down with him for a while, tell him stories from India and massage his forehead and chest to soothe his body and calm his mind and bring on sweet dreams, like she used to with her little brother till he got married, but Lahya politely declined to be thus soothed and calmed and elected to sleep single. After all, it was to be his last night on Earth, what was the point in being calmed and soothed; and why sweet dreams when life was a nightmare. If he was to die alone, might as well sleep alone.

Up in his room he set the alarm for two in the morning and put the clock well away from reach, as Mumsy did, so that one couldn't just stretch out and turn it off, but had to get up for it.

He fell asleep with surprising suddenness. Were he awake he'd have been greatly relieved to be asleep for he had feared lying wide-eyed in bed for the entire night, or at least until a quarter to two, tossing and turning and sighing and crying.

The very next moment the alarm was hiccoughing away.

Everything was a black fuzz and an unnatural telephone. What was going on, and where? He turned to his left and flung his arm out to reach for the alarm, as he did back home in Gravesend in his own room in his own bed. His hand hit the wall with the great but normally unnoticed force inherent in any natural movement. He woke up with a yell.

One look around, and panic. He *had* been abducted after all. With quick but still sleep-jerky movements he checked his arms and legs to see if they were mutilated. Relief. Everything intact. Then why the pain in his knuckles? Perhaps they had dislocated his finger knots while pulling out his nails. And who were they? Aliens! The room looked like nothing on earth.

But even in the darkness of the night and mind, reality dawned – or illusion, if reality is illusion – as it always does, especially when you least desire it.

He had gone to bed fully dressed and he remembered why. He was to go out and kill himself, and he had not wanted to waste time undressing and dressing. A gust of sleep tried to sweep over him and he was about to lie back down and postpone dying to another time when the memory of abandonment and betrayal brushed sleep aside with a prickly broom whose bristles reached out to the very core of his soul.

First he had to go for a piss. Thank God there was a toilet next door or he would have wet himself. A minute ago nothing was farther from his mind than a piss, suddenly it was the most important factor in his life.

It was on the way to the little room that he caught sight of my room. At first it was no more than a slight jolt to his senses. He dismissed it, did his business, came out, and saw my room again, its door tantalisingly inviting, more so for being securely locked. My image reached out to him and he remembered what his Grandma had said. *Kali grants your wishes!* He wished he were dead. There and then. Save him the trouble of going down the stairs, out the apartment, down the stairs again, out, and then that long walk, just in the hope of being attacked and butchered; failing which, more walking, then a cold dive in the river, choking and drowning and gasping for breath and choking and drowning and gasping . . . He was too tired for all that. Too tired to live, too tired to die. If only Kali would grant him a quick and easy death . . . If only . . . If only

. . . If only . . . If only Kali turned him into a gorgeous white woman . . . If only!!!!!

Yes. That was it. If Kali could grant any wish, why wish for death? Why not wish for what he really wished for! If he were to become a gorgeous white female, *before* Mumsy produced her lily-white girl, then he would have the edge on the little brat. He would be the first, *and* he would not be crying all the time and being a nuisance and needing his nappies changed and all that shit. He would be already grown up. At the very least nearly twelve. Then Mumsy will be sorry she dumped him, then she will beg him, *her*, to come back to her and be her very own sweet Sigourney.

He went back into his room and picked up the keys Aunt Jamuna had given him. He had put them by his bedside. Not needing them any more, he would have left them there on his final way out, along with a brief note of thanks to his aunt for taking him in when his own mother did not want him. Armed with the keys he started towards my room to see if any of the many in there fitted the lock of my door. I made sure that the very first one did. He believed it to be a lucky omen, which it was.

V

As the door of my room opened, Lahya was enveloped in the holy glow of the huge candles that were always lit on either side of my clay replica that stood majestically at the far corner of the room on an elevated pedestal, surrounded by flowers and garlands and fruit and sweets and burning incense. I loomed above it all, black and beautiful, the tiny figure of Sadhaka, my beloved child devotee, hanging round my right ear, shimmering swords in all my hands, a chain of bleeding heads round my neck, blood-dripping tongue hanging out of my blood-dripping mouth; one foot balletically raised in the graceful manner of a temple dancer, the other firmly digging into the blood-soaked stomach of a dying man, young with long black hair, a white-skinned Indian of much-prized unmixed Aryan origin, his head half-severed, his dark eyes pleading for mercy, or death.

Lahya instantly knew that all I wanted was the dying body of a young white male and he would be a gorgeous white female, just like his mother.

PART IV

The Meeting

I

When Lahya came down for breakfast that morning Jayshree was hoping to see a despondent, half-dead boy who she would tease and humiliate for the duration of the meal, then take him aside and release him from his suffering. She'd tell him she was only joking. That his mother had not dumped him, and for some peculiar unununderstandable reason, still loved, or at least wanted him, as far as she knew. If he was going to be *that* miserable about the whole thing, he wouldn't be any fun to make fun of. Her vacation would be ruined.

What Jayshree saw was an eerily confident, self-assured boy with a sharp glint in his eyes and a determined set to his mouth. When she tried to provoke him by some comment about a non-existent news item in the day's papers regarding an undesired and undesirable boy child left outside a hospital chained to a lamp post like a dog, Lahya didn't even bother to respond. Well, if he was going to be like that, she wouldn't tell him!

Even Savitri commented on how well he looked, and Jamuna said triumphantly, 'I told you a good night's sleep will settle his stomach!'

Shortly afterwards, when Jamuna had gone down to get the restaurant ready for lunch and Savitri had retired upstairs for her pooja, Jayshree made several attempts to rile Lahya but failed. Worse than that, he declared simply that he was going to have a shower, change, and go out 'to see some friends'.

'What friends, I ask,' said Jayshree, hiding her increasing irritation and frustration, and in her best sarcastic voice, 'Who in his right mind . . .' But Lahya wasn't even listening. He was heading straight for the bathroom.

'I have the key to the basement.' She spoke suddenly but softly, playing her last card, in desperation yet not in the least appearing to be in desperation, putting on her most alluring voice, 'And your squinty little eyes will bulge out of your silly little head when you see what's in there!' If she could not rouse his anger, perhaps she could excite his curiosity.

She was right. He stopped where he was.

The cellar. That was it. That was the answer.

His main worry had been how he would get a dying body back up to Kali's altar. From the street into the hall, up the stairs past the prying eyes of the Chinese woman, then into the apartment, past the prying eyes of Savitri, if during the day; the entire household during the night; not to mention Jayshree at all times. Then up another set of stairs . . .

The cellar, basement if you like, would solve the problem. There was a trap door outside the entrance to the restaurant which led down to the basement. A few steps down from the street there, then a few steps down into the basement. He should be able to manage that. He did not have to go up to Grandma's shrine. After all, a goddess was everywhere. All she needs is devotion, and worship. In fact, if he were to set up his own little altar in the cellar, Kali would be even more pleased with him. Then, in the basement, at his own special shrine for Kali, he would make his offering. Then all his dreams would come true.

He had already figured out how he would get the body up to the apartment. His mother had left him a hundred dollars, to which dadso had added another hundred. Primarily it was a sort of a bribe for him to be good, for Aunt Jamuna had been instructed to confiscate the money, or any goods bought, if he 'misbehaved' in any way. The intended goods were a pair or two of Levi jeans, some CDs and a player, all of which were much cheaper here in the States than back in England. They would be his birthday present. Also, he might need money for some unspecified emergency . . . various little excuses which passed for reasons when parents wanted to do something that would satisfy their conscience and prove to the world, the child and themselves how caring and concerned they were as parents.

He had decided to buy a pair of cheap (stolen) skateboards, among the many items of all sorts on sale anywhere and everywhere, night and day on the village streets, from old telephones to used condoms. He'd rope the skateboards together, put the body in a black bin bag and tie it on top of the skateboards and then roll it along by pulling the rope, as he had seen a bum carrying his worldly belongings around town.

Surprising how active his mind had been since his encounter with the goddess in the early hours of the morning!

Not surprising what he was willing to do to retrieve Mumsy's lost love.

He still had a few difficulties with the thought of killing some poor innocent white man. A young and strong and good-looking one too, for that was what Kali would like. But then he thought of all the bad things that white people had done to black people and people all over the world. For centuries. How many white people had made fun of him, insulted him at school and other places. He recalled every racial incident that he could, of Bangladeshis killed in the East End of London, beaten up in Blackpool, houses burnt, police brutality, and so on and so on . . . Yes, it would be a justifiable act of retribution even if there was nothing in it for him; much less when his entire future depended on it.

Yes indeed he should do it. And yes indeed the cellar was the place. He might even lure a living sacrifice down there. Especially if there was something interesting enough in there to lure someone, as Jayshree had implied, and do him in on the spot. Fresh blood, at the altar itself. That would make the whole thing easier. And better. A great, great deal easier. And a great, great deal better. He was grateful to Jayshree for the train of ideas she had set in motion.

He was not too excited about the fact that she had the keys. Chances were that among the many in his bunch there was one to the cellar as well. But just to be on the safe side he would humour the repulsive creature. Also, she was a good ally to have, both in and out of the house. She was cunning and devious enough to be useful. Her creepiness was a pain in the neck, but it was also an asset. Everyone who knew her hated her; all who didn't know her pitied her. Both emotions came in handy, depending on one's objectives.

'Let me have a shower and change anyway; then we'll go down and see. OK, honey . . . darrrling,' he smiled, and winked.

Good God, wondered Jayshree, what's happened to this boy! He's changed since last I saw him. Did Shiva visit him in the night and sort his linga out for him? And if so, what am I letting myself in for? A tingle ran down her spine. Still, he can't be worse than Granddad. A shiver ran down her spine.

I must get copies of the keys cut as soon as possible, thought Lahya, before Aunt Jamuna asks for them back.

The one thing Lahya did not give much thought to was how he, a skinny little boy, would manage to kill or mortally wound a strong healthy young man, whatever his colour. But in the United States of America, anything was possible. Certainly in New York. Or so everybody said.

II

Lahya had his shower in the upstairs shower, after which he changed from one pair of black jeans and a black top into another pair of black jeans and a black top, put on his white sneakers, as he sneeringly called them now, and came down only to see Jayshree was nowhere in sight.

The ugly witch, she's tricked me, swore Lahya, and turned round to go back up again to get his keys before venturing out to scour the streets and avenues for possible candidates to grace Kali's altar with their blood. By now he had half-convinced himself that it would not only be justifiable to take the life of a white man, but an honour for the one chosen.

He had just reached the first step of the staircase when he heard a sort of groan. Following the sound, he nearly tripped over Jayshree lying doubled up behind the double futon. At first Lahya thought she was playing up, but soon he realised she was in pain. Her normally twisted face was twisted beyond recognition. Drops of cold sweat large as dew drops were pouring out of every visible part of her skin, and she was hugging herself with her arms around her knees in the most helplessly pathetic manner he had ever seen.

He knelt beside her, put one arm under her neck to raise her head up and asked if he could do something to help. 'My pills, in my room, get them, please,' Jayshree's voice was barely audible, and she was having difficulty articulating words. Lahya was about to ask where in her room when he had an idea, 'Don't worry, I'll get Grandma.' He was about to put her head gently back on the carpet but was stopped by the look of terror on Jayshree's face. She let go of her knees and brought a clawlike hand to grasp Lahya's arm,

'Don't, don't call Grandma. She'll hide my pills. Take me to my room. Please. I was only joking. Being silly. Vicious. Your Mummy has not . . .' She stopped as another wave of pain roared through her body. She bit her tongue to avoid screaming, and Lahya could actually feel the impact of her pain go through his own body.

Almost without thinking, and without fully taking in what Jayshree had said, either about her grandmother or about his mother, he put both his arms under her and made an effort to lift her up. He needn't have tried. She came up in his arms like a paper doll. She could have hardly weighed more than a child of three. The rather voluminous dresses that she wore were intended to conceal the fact that there was nothing to conceal.

Lahya carried her to her room and laid her down on her bed. She pointed to the top of her cupboard and told him to get a rolled up old blouse that was lying pushed right at the back. Lahya did as he was asked. Hidden within the blouse was a bottle of pills. Under her bed was a bottle of still water. With more than a little help from Lahya, she greedily swallowed two of the pills before falling back on the bed, almost lifeless. In fact, for a few seconds Lahya really thought the wretched girl had departed this proverbial vale of tears. He was about to get up and call Savitri when Jayshree once again extended a clawlike hand and held on to Lahya. As if reading his mind, she repeated what she had said earlier, 'Don't. Don't call Gran . . . that woman. She wants me to die. I have to hide my pills before she hides them. She is . . . evil. And I don't mean bad. I mean evil . . . she can kill . . . cast spells . . .'

Lahya looked at the poor girl. She was clearly delirious. But there was pleading in her eyes, and a soft gentle air hung around her frail little body like an aura of light. Lahya felt his heart move with a strange feeling which he did not recognise as love, but which brought with it a blissful sense of peace, and it felt good. He stretched out his hand and ran his fingers through the girl's tangled hair. She smiled weakly, and Lahya saw that she was beautiful.

The moment passed, but pity, even concern for the girl remained.

'I lied, I lied about . . . about your mother dump . . . leaving you. I was only being . . . nasty . . .'

Lahya should have been furious at Jayshree's lie, but he wasn't. He should have been elated at Mumsy's faithfulness, but he wasn't.

He was in one of his periodic numb states. The only thought in his mind was the absurdity of wanting to kill some poor white man. How could he have even considered the idea, much less tried to plan it in some detail?

III

Jayshree fell asleep. Lahya covered her body with a single white sheet and came out into the living room just as Savitri was coming down from her pooja session.

'Don't you look smart,' she said with a happy smile, coming over to Lahya and giving him a gentle hug. 'My sweet, sweet boy. Raj is a lucky man to have a beautiful son like you. And a beautiful, beautiful wife. Tell you a secret. I am normally not liking white people, especially white women, but I do like your Mumsy.'

Lahya's heart warmed to the woman. Jayshree must be really crazy to have said the things she said about her. It must be the pain.

'A wonderful, wonderful woman. Your Mumsy,' continued Grandma, 'I pray that no evil fall on her pretty golden head.'

For no particular reason Lahya felt a steel blade go through his heart. A white-hot steel blade.

'I was just talking to Kali Mata,' Savitri said, sitting in her favourite pose, feet up and legs crossed beneath her on the double futon. 'I was praying for a healthy and beautiful baby girl for your mother, with golden hair and blue eyes, for I know that is what she wants. Kali has promised me that so it will be. Of course, I will have to keep my end of the bargain. For if Kali makes a promise to you, and you promise something back, as you have to, and is only fair, then you'd better keep your promise. *She* always does, no matter what. But if you don't keep yours, she *makes* you. Makes you pay for it anyway. *Her* way. And her way is not an easy way.

'She takes what bites. Bites your heart. Bites the heart of your children, or parents, or loved ones. In my case, something might happen to your father, for I love him even though he is so wicked to me, as you know, my sweet moon. In your case, if she promised you

~ 92 ~

something and you didn't keep your promise, something might happen . . . to your mother. For it is she you love the most.

'But of course nothing will happen. Not to your father, for I always keep my promises to Kali. Not to your mother, for you haven't promised anything to Kali. So, there is nothing to worry about. There. And everything to be happy for. Especially for a beautiful golden-haired blue-eyed baby girl to be your little sister. I am sure you will learn to love her as dearly as your mother will love her. Oh how she will love her beautiful blue-eyed daughter with long golden curls and a diamond-white skin.

'Did you like your grandfather?' she quietly turned to him and asked, changing the subject unexpectedly and pointlessly, then without waiting for an answer relaxed back into the futon and shut her eyes, the red trickle of katha negotiating its slow way down the corners of her mouth.

Lahya's mouth dried up and parched and heated as his eyes turned moist and greasy and cold. He had better go and scour the streets and avenues of Manhattan for a suitable candidate to kill.

IV

Out in the pre-noon heat of a blindingly sunny day Lahya began to realise more clearly the difficulties of his mission impossible. There was no shortage of healthy-looking young men, black or white, many good looking, some even walked normally. The trouble was, how to get one.

It would have to be during the night. A sneak attack. Some of the drop-outs in and around Tompkins Park would be the easiest targets. They looked dangerous but were more vulnerable than those who claimed to be threatened by them. Even Lahya could tell that. Though dirty and smelly, most were young, most were males and, more surprisingly, most were white. Many had good bodies and attractive features, if full of holes and metal. He could not get away with it during the day. Even with rejects and disposables. Not just because of his size and strength, or the lack of it, but because he needed the body afterwards. It was not as if he could shoot or stab someone and then escape into the crowd, or get lost in one of the many little shops scattered all over, open most of the time and where his size would be an advantage. He needed the body. That was the prime purpose of it all. Yes, it would have to be the night. Not that that would be easy, what with the pale creepy lights that deluged the night scene, and the police that haunted the area like disease-defying pesticide-resistant death-proof infestations.

Best would be if he could entice a prospective into the cellar; but for that he'd have to know more about the cellar, see it for himself, check it out.

For the time being he'd better get the keys cut, and walk around getting the lay of the land.

As often happens in Manhattan, you want something, you look

up, and there it is; from instant enlightenment to penetrative sex or Greek food. Facing him, 1st Avenue and 7th Street, was a hardware store. And not just there. Until recently Lahya didn't know what a hardware store was. Now there was no escaping a hardware store. Everywhere he turned there was a hardware store, next to a laundromat. KEYS CUT, signs indicated. He went into the first store, as joyfully as he was capable of being joyful at the moment. Once within, his joy became fuller.

The owner of the store was an Indian, but the person to whom he shouted out, the key artist, artisan if you like, was a young white man, built like a truck, muscles bulging everywhere, skimpy little shirt with sleeves torn out, invisible shorts, offensive thighs, big bare feet, wavy brown hair, glasses. Probably spent his entire life working out, but the greyish brown eyes behind thick glasses looked shrewd and not entirely brainless. Kali would like him. Knock off his glasses and you could render him helpless, at least momentarily, and that moment might just be enough.

'Excuse me?' the young man said for the second time as Lahya, lost in the possibility of dragging the said young man's heavy cadaver around town, mumbled something about keys in a voice even he could not make out, much less a full-blooded American not used to Gravesendian English. However, when Lahya had the sense to pull out the bunch of keys and dangle it under the nose of the prospective, he understood. 'What, AAALLL of them!' he exclaimed with dumb stupefaction, proving that intelligent eyes were not all they appeared to be. 'You'll have to wait,' he said and moved away somewhere behind the shelves and disappeared. Time was one thing Lahya had no trouble with.

It took longer than he had thought. While waiting, Lahya christened the big guy 'Dirk', deciding he ought to give a name to this prospective, and to others as they came along. That would make it easier, in his mind, to index and prioritise them, than if he had to think of them in terms of their descriptions all the time.

By the time Dirk returned with the bundle of keys Lahya almost asked him if he would like to come to his cellar, basement, after he had been to it himself, of course; but he settled for just handing the money for services rendered, saying, 'Ta, Dirk.' Dirk said, 'Excuse me?' in his questioning voice, with a startlingly bored expression on his bespectacled face, returned the money and pointed him towards the Indian man. Lahya concluded – perhaps erroneously, for one can never be sure in such matters, least of all in New York – that Dirk would not be interested in seeing his basement, not without just cause. If it had to be Dirk, he would have to wait for him outside the shop till he packed up work, or find out where he lived. And then with something definite to offer as a temptation down in the cellar.

Lahya also bought a new key chain from the store, one which ejected a surprisingly long and lethal knife at the push of a button. By the time he had completed the tedious task of forcing the new keys into the new ring secured to the end of the concealed knife, he was so fed up with life he decided to go back home instead of searching for more prospectives or examining the lay of the land. There were too many keys jangling in his pocket, and they were heavy. Might as well get rid of the old set, return it to Aunt Jamuna or put it away in a drawer or whatever. Also, he was a bit worried about Jayshree. Best go and see how she was: better, or garotted in her sleep by the grimalkin.

On his way back he heard a familiar voice and looked behind him. It was Blossom, talking to Burt. They were both heading his way, presumably to the Jamuna. Burt saw Lahya look at him, recognised him and smiled, 'Hi there, kid. You walking down to the restaurant?' They didn't need to be wizardly clever to have gathered that he was something to do with the place.

'That way,' said Lahya, suspiciously, still annoyed at their bringing up 'zucchini' during their conversation the first time they had 'met', in a manner of speaking. 'I'm going up to the house, the apartment.'

They were in step with him by now.

'My toothbrush. I told you about my toothbrush? Or did I? Did I tell you about the mailbox, honey? She pulled our names right off the mailbox. And it had taken me a full hour, well I lie, a full half hour to write them out, in my best handwriting. You know what my writing is like. I only did it because the Super told me to. "You are new, honey," he said to me; nice man, always calls me honey. "You are new, honey," he said. That's when we just moved in, see. "You are new, honey," he said. "Better stick your names on the mailbox. The mailman won't know you, and may leave your letters on the stairs or something, for the world to look at. People are always moving in and out. In and out," he said, "in and out. Letters get lost." So what do I do, write out our names, in my best handwriting, and stick them on to the mailbox, one above the other. When I get home that night, guess what. And no gifts for guessing . . .

'And that was *before* she changed the message on the answering machine. All I'd recorded was, "No one's home, dear caller. If you have a message for Petal or Blossom, leave it after the tone." That's *all*. Cross my rocks and hope to live. She changes it. Just the phone number, and please leave a message. No mention of names. Like she was ashamed to have my name next to her. On the mailbox, or on the machine. Even her fucking toothbrush was too good for my fucking toothbrush, know what I mean. Can you imagine what I felt! Can you even begin to imagine! So, when I saw her, lying flat on her back, legs open and mouth apart, for that bit of white trash, shaving his balls in *my* bathroom . . . I lost control. Can you . . .'

'Did he . . . she have a separate bathroom of her . . .?'

'Now you're being stupid, Burt. Of course not. But that is not the *pooiiint*. You can be so insensitive sometimes. Anyway, as I was saying, can you blame me? Perhaps *you* might, but no one else will. and I *Have* asked a few. Now don't interrupt when I am trying to say something. I know exactly what you're going to say, and apology accepted . . . No one can say I hold a grudge, no matter how insensitive anybody is towards me.

'Now, as I was saying, befoooore I was interrupted, I have asked a few, believe me, I have asked. They all agree with me. Some say they would have done worse than what I did, which was nothing really, except to tell the slut what I thought of her and that bit of white trash of hers. Now if she had come out into the open, told me about him, been *honest*, not that *she'd* know the meaning of the word, then I would have said OK, if it's a bit of white trash you want, then it's a bit of white trash you want. But no. She denied flat out that there was anything between them. I said I can well believe *that*. Nothing between you two, when it comes to it, not even a condom. *And* I don't like my phone number left on the machine. Know what I mean? Can't tell which gimpy geek will get hold of it, and then, before you can say sniff that crack, you are up to your clit in turd talk. Now, I am all for people doing their own thing, I am, but I draw the line at them doing it over my phone. Now is that fair or is that fair? Am I asking too much if I don't want my earholes screwed by the likes of that . . . that . . . what film was it, you know, the one with the . . .'

Lahya excused himself at first sight of the restaurant. On another day he would have liked to linger on. Today there were darker things on his mind.

He entered the apartment almost on tiptoe and was relieved to see that Savitri was not in the living room. Unlike Jayshree, he had still not quite decided against her, but he was wary. Wary, until convinced one way or another. He continued his silently silently approach, partly so as not to disturb Jayshree if she was asleep, and partly not to attract the attention of Savitri, whether she was upstairs or in her bedroom.

He climbed up the stairs and entered his room with remarkably noiseless ease, considering he was clumsiness-prone. He put the old set of keys in one of the drawers and was wondering whether to go down and have a look to see how Jayshree was feeling when he remembered that new sets of keys were not always perfect. Some didn't work. So he took out the old set again, and began the task of transferring the old keys to the new chain, the one with the knife. It was a long and frustrating task. Life certainly was not worth it. Not his life, anyway. But Mumsy's was. So he had to soldier on. He had just managed to push the last key in when he thought he heard someone talking. He tried to listen – but nothing. He must have been imagining. He put the new set of keys away, this time on the old key ring, and was about to relax back for a while before deciding on his next move when he heard the talking again, unmistakably, and followed by the sound of rather loud, familiar laughter. He came out of the room just in time to see Jayshree and Savitri emerging from the room opposite, my room. Jayshree was clinging on to Savitri's arm in a most affectionate manner, while Savitri was engrossed in telling her something which both found distinctly amusing. He couldn't tell what she was saying as she was talking in Bengali, and although Lahya understood, and even spoke Hindi, and therefore Urdu of sorts, he had never learnt Bengali.

All their eyes met at the same time. The surprise in Lahya's ridiculous face was ridiculously apparent. Jayshree registered no expression. Neither did Savitri. But they both stopped talking, and they both stopped laughing.

V

Lahya returned to his room and shut the door.

Half an hour or so later there was a knock, and before Lahya could ask who it was or say come in or whatever, Jayshree was in.

'I came to thank you for helping me this morning, but don't let it go to your head,' she said, trying to be friendly, yet keeping a distance.

'So!' was Lahya's articulate reply.

'So, let's go down to the basement. The old . . . I have to get her smell out of my nose. Thank God she's gone for her after-lunch nap before her lunch. So, we have time to ourselves without either her or Mama snooping around. Soon, we can go.'

As Lahya looked unsure, she understood his reasons. 'I have to humour her now and then. And her Kali. Pretend I am a devotee. Otherwise she'd have my liver for breakfast.'

Lahya didn't know what to believe, or whom. But the cellar was important to him. 'OK,' he said. He still couldn't bring himself to say anything insulting. It would take time for that spirit of camaraderie to re-establish itself, if ever.

The door to the basement stairs was a step up from the main bathroom door. Jayshree teasingly inserted her hand in her blouse and brought out a pair of keys. Before she turned one in the lock, she said with the usual twisted smirk back on her face, 'Hope you are not easily shocked, dear cousin of mine!'

There was another locked door at the bottom of the stairs. Jayshree used the second key. Once inside, it was huge, the size of the entire restaurant above it. There were two other doors, one leading to the trap door on the sidewalk, the other opening into the restaurant. One of the keys fitted into one, the other into the other, said Jayshree, implying she had all-round access to the place with her special keys. Lahya was dying to have a good look at them to see if they matched any he had, but he resisted the temptation. He couldn't have been sure anyway, so there was no point in arousing her suspicion.

Lahya was not easily shocked, but he was shocked.

Back in his room he locked the door, thankful he had a lockable door.

If sex was like being ticklish, he thought, it couldn't be a DIY job. But it wasn't. Whether this was good or bad, he couldn't make up his mind.

The best thing about the basement was that it would be so easy to make a little shrine for Kali down there. It already had two shrines in it anyway. The whole place reeked with incense and candles and other paraphernalia of holiness.

And it was carpeted and heated and decorated, furnished with comfortable chairs and divans and tables, with a television and video along with the widest selection of porno videos this side of Heaven, magazines you would kill for back in prudish old England, a camcorder, radio and stereo CD player, sex aids of all sorts, drinks, everything, even a little kitchen, and the best bathroom ever he had seen in New York. It would be great to entertain a prospective in there, provided he didn't live to tell the tale.

The two shrines had altars for yoni and linga. Jayshree didn't have to explain much for Lahya to understand. The cellar was Grandpa's study.

VI

Mumsy telephoned that evening and Lahya was happy. However, he was brief and brusque with her, otherwise he would have cried. Which made Mumsy angry and she was brief and brusque with him, handing the phone over to dadso. Lahya put the phone down, just to get even. By the end of it all he was more miserable than ever. And he still wasn't sure if Jayshree was telling the truth when she claimed Mumsy had dumped him, or telling the truth when admitting to lying. Neither scenario excluded the 'fact' that Mumsy was going to have a beautiful new baby, a girl, and that the very thought of it hurt him, and made him want to hurt back.

What *was* life all about, and why do we spend all our time hurting most the people we love the most? Lahya had no answers to these questions because he did not have these questions. If he had, he might have come up with an explanation astounding the world, illumining the souls of wo/mankind, turning all and sundry to Buddhas and Christs.

Of course I could have explained to Lahya, had he asked, but he didn't.

Savitri does me a grave injustice by portraying me in the simplistic terms of reward and punishment, painting me with a dark brush tainted with blood, and telling the boy that if promises made to me are not kept, I avenge. That would mean I had expectations. I do not. I do not have expectations. I do not avenge. If terrible things happen to those or theirs who break their vows to me, it is their own fear and guilt that has brought them about, or their greed. Not me. My true passion is love, not vengeance, which is anything but.

However, the stupid boy was not to know that. Both his greed to be a gorgeous white female, and his need to prevent any harm coming to his very own gorgeous white female, Mumsy, demanded blood. The blood of a beautiful white man, young and supple and desirable, clever and kind, loving and lovable, for nothing less was worthy of me. So *he* believed.

He had to quit being sorry for himself and get on with it.

The first thing he had to make sure was that he had the keys to the basement. If not, he would have to befriend Jayshree. His relationship with her was at a curious stage. From fear and loathing it had transcended to an absolute moment of love, then degenerated to suspicion and mistrust; and then, in the cellar, something else happened. Surrounded by that sexual aura, he had a vague and uneasy feeling, even a painful feeling, that something was expected of him. He had to make some sort of a move so that Jayshree could have either the pleasure of accepting, or the pleasure of rejecting. Pleasure always belonged to the woman, to man only the risk. Not that risk did not have its pleasures, but Lahya had neither the age, nor the experience, nor indeed the intelligence to understand much, if any of it. But he did know that something was expected, and that he had failed.

Jayshree looked quietly angry on their way back up to the house; and when he said he was tired and would like to go to his room and rest for a while, she had sneered, 'I'm sure that's all you *can* do!' Lahya had again understood and not understood. But then there was that call from Mumsy and the world was a bright and cheerful place again. For about fifty seconds.

He couldn't go on like that. Not as long as he was a man, however unripe and pitiful a specimen. He had to get up and do something. Only when he was a woman. Especially a white woman. More especially a gorgeous white woman, would he be able to lie back and enjoy life. Until then it was work work work. And pain. And shame. The pain of never doing enough. The shame of never being enough. The pain of being a man, however unripe and pitiful a specimen.

And if, to relieve himself of that pain and shame, to achieve pride in himself and joy in life, he had to take a life, then amen. He had his rationalisations and justifications pat by now.

In the middle of the night he crept downstairs to try his keys on the cellar door. He began with the two most likely for the type of lock. The first one didn't fit. The second did, and worked. The first worked on the second door below.

Satisfied, he went back up to bed. Before he could make any plans for getting hold of Dirk the next day, or whoever, he was fast asleep. It had been a strangely exhausting day.

VII

It was at just before twelve midnight that Lahya saw Ariel Van Damm.

Just as one day was in the final throes of death, the other not yet born. One fragment of linear illusion melting into another, maya and samsara colluding to delude.

The day had been as painful as an unlubricated anal enlargement. Uncle Dileep had a bad stomach, vindicating Jamuna's stance on ill-health and inefficiency. So he stayed home for the morning, an event so rare that he decided to celebrate it by playing cards, especially to amuse and entertain Lahya. Lahya would have considered chicken plucking while blindfolded and naked with one hand tied behind his back more amusing. But he dared not voice the idea for fear that Aunt Jamuna might take him at his word and invite him down to the restaurant kitchen for a bit of chicken plucking while blindfolded and naked . . .

In the afternoon he managed to get away and hovered around the hardware store. Dirk was there, in jeans and shoes. Perhaps the Indian woman at the cash counter that day was less partial to naked flesh than her male counterpart the day before. After about half an hour's hovering, a long time for a restless boy, he gave up; mainly because, try as he might, he could not come up with a good reason, or the courage, to ask Dirk over to his basement at about eleven that night. Surely, for a New Yorker such an invitation would not have been overtly unusual, nor aroused undue curiosity on the part of the invitee. But Lahya was still British at heart, much though he would have challenged that assertion, and a Gravesendian at that, however he may have wished otherwise. He did not have the casual facility to tender such a proposal to the man who had only yesterday cut his keys for him; and even though the keys were many, and it took a long time to do them, it still did not form the basis of that open and carefree relationship where you feel easy to ask someone over to your cellar at twenty-three hours, not for a British person, especially not an under-twelve British person, no matter how reluctantly and accidentally British, and no matter how close to being fully twelve.

He spent the evening sulking, tried hard not to miss Gravesend, even harder not to miss Mumsy, and had another early night, refusing to watch *Northern Exposure*, even though he liked it, or the *New Generation Star Trek*, even though he hated it. It was always more fun to watch what you hated so you could have the pleasure of complaining all through it, ruining everybody else's enjoyment, not to mention having something to moan about the next day.

He thought of setting the alarm for half-past eleven to go out and hunt for a prospective around midnight, but couldn't be bothered. Tomorrow, he said to himself, stripped down to his shorts, opened the window of his room to let some air in and hoped that humidity and heat regardless he would sleep till late the next day.

However, when he woke up at precisely eleven-thirty, after having just dreamt of me, he decided it was ordained that he should go out and hunt for a prospective. An 'or else' seemed to hang about the air.

Fighting ordinary fears – fear of the unknown, fear of the East Village by night, fear of night itself, fear of picking up young men with intent to kill – by the extraordinary fear of divine retribution, and egged on by divine compulsion, he put on some clothes and shoes and peered down the stairs to see if anyone was about.

He had planned to go through the cellar. Partly because he needed the practice, but also because opening the front door was likely to attract attention even if no one was in the living room watching TV or whatever. The cellar staircase was near the bathroom, so, if challenged, there was an easy answer. The upstairs bathroom was minimal, without a bath, or indeed a mirror or a cabinet, and it would be understandable if he preferred the one below.

Luckily, everybody seemed to have had an early night, or was out. He had no difficulty in quietly letting himself down to the basement. Resisting every temptation to explore it further, or to examine some of the magazines with a more academic eye, he made his way to the door leading out to the pavement. The restaurant was still open but no one saw him emerge from down below; no one could, unless specially looking out.

He walked up to Tompkins Park, heart thudding with a mixture of terror and excitement, marvelling at the life and goods on offer at that time of the night all along the sidewalks. Once again he resisted the temptation to linger, even though it was all so fascinating, so different from anything he knew back home. But some powerful inner drive was leading him on. Round the park, diving into shadows at the sight of police persons, and into territory where the brave feared to tread, once the burial ground of mercilessly butchered Native Americans, now the habitation of the equally despised and deprived.

Behind the park, past Avenue B, and all was silence and emptiness, except for the odd car screeching along.

Where was he going, and why?

The answer was approaching straight in front of him. Tallish, graceful, dark eyes, long black hair, flawless white skin, twenty-something, and beautiful. Lahya darted behind a tree to see without being seen. The young man came to the crossing, the sign said DON'T WALK, and a few cars were going across. The young man stopped.

Inspiration hit Lahya like a waterfall, even before he could give a name to the young man. When the next car came hurtling by, he would run out of his hiding place, into the young man, and knock him straight under the wheels of the vehicle. From what he had heard about New York drivers, he was sure none would stop to help. True, he didn't have his skateboards to transport the body, but at this time of the night and in this area he could hide it and come back for it later. But what if the driver stopped . . . he'd see to it if it came to it. His heart was beating so fast his brain couldn't hear itself for the pounding.

He saw a car coming. He ran full force, aiming at the back of the young man. The young man moved to one side for no apparent reason. Lahya went straight into the car and was flung aside as it sped past, faster than before. At least he had been right about New York drivers.

VIII

Lahya lay on the road doubled up sideways, unable to move or speak, more out of shock than anything else, having miraculously escaped real injury, when he saw out of the corner of his eyes another car heading his way at what seemed like twice the speed of the one that had just knocked him over. In less than a second I am omelette, he thought. Instead of his whole life flashing before him it was Jayshree's face that came to his mind. EEYYUK, he retched in disgust. Just then, instead of black car tyres, he saw a pair of male legs with excessively developed calf muscles virtually jump into the air and be by his side. Their owner carried him away in his arms, missing the oncoming car by an eyelash, nearly losing his own life saving his. An angel, thought Lahya. No wonder he had no fear for his life. Angels cannot die.

The angel laid him carefully down on a cleanish patch on the sidewalk and sat beside him.

'How are you? Are you all right?' Lahya heard the softest, gentlest voice he had ever heard, with more concern in it than had been shown to him by anyone he could remember offhand. Not even Mumsy. He couldn't quite place the angel's accent, he was not very good with accents, but it was clearly not an American accent, which was understandable. An angel would know better.

Lahya looked up into a pair of deep black eyes, almost unnaturally so, above a cute button nose and full pink lips. A mass of deep black hair, almost unnaturally so, hung loosely all around the angel's face, down to the middle of his arms.

'What were you doing here, running like crazy, in the middle of the night? How *old* are you? I think I'd better call the police, or the ambulance. How old *are* you? Will you be all right? If I leave you here for a while? Where are your parents? Have you any bones broken? There is no blood. Are you in pain? Do you live around here? Can I take you to your home? *How* old are you?'

Lahya was getting a bit cheesed off with the angel's incessant questions, and his obsession with his age. He didn't think it was any of his business. Anyway, if he was an angel, he ought to know. 'I am sixteen,' he said. And with his voice, his memory returned.

The angel was no angel. He was a prospective. The one he had just tried to kill. And he had ended up saving his life. Lahya felt ashamed of himself. Not for the first time in his life.

'Sixteen! You look like six to me.'

'I *am* sixteen,' said Lahya, determined to stick it out. After all, he would be twelve in less than a month. 'It's just my voice. I've always had a squeaky voice.' Ariel looked at him with unconcealed disbelief, thinking, well, he can't be that hurt if he can lie like that. Lahya continued, 'dadso . . . my dad is short. And thin. Always has been.' It was good to blame dadso for everything. And right too. After all, he wouldn't have been an ugly black git if his dad had not been an ugly black git.

By now Lahya could sit up, which he did, but his head reeled and his body trembled. Ariel was squatting next to him on the very edge of his toes, outlandish calf muscles looking more outlandish than ever. He steadied Lahya by putting his arm around him.

'Are you sure you're all right? I think I should call an ambulance, or police, paramedics . . .'

'No. Please no. I can't stand the blues. Or doctors. They make me sick. I'm all right.'

'So you are from England,' said Ariel, thinking Eastender Paki in trouble in New York. On drugs??? He was running around like crazy in the heart of the night in the stomach of drugland. Even he was afraid, and would never have been there that night had there been an alternative. He tried to remember a somewhat similar experience he had had while on LSD. He thought about a couple of Eastender Paki friends, sort of, when he was in England not too long ago.

Lahya was annoyed that the not-angel had so quickly guessed his accent, while he could not guess the angel's. 'Where are you from?' It was his turn to ask a question.

'I am Dutch. My name is Ariel. Ariel Van Damm. I am from Amsterdam. But I lived in England for ten years. Do you know that New York was once called New Amsterdam?' And then, without waiting for an answer and standing up, 'Come, I'll take you home. Do you think you can walk, or should I carry you? You are a very lucky kid, you know. You could have been dead by now. Or paralysed. Why on earth were you running like that? In the middle of the night? Where are your parents? And where do you live?'

'My name is Lahya,' was all Lahya said. He tried to stand up, but his legs had difficulty holding him up. Ariel held him close to his body for a second, then made him sit down again, once again squatting next to him.

Lahya liked Ariel. He liked the way he looked. He liked the way he looked at him. He liked the way his body felt for the brief moment he pressed himself against it. And in the passionate grip of the night, he liked the smell of his sweat. So much so it made him uncomfortable, and he couldn't understand why it made him uncomfortable which made him more uncomfortable. But he did not like all the questions. He never liked questions. Under any circumstances. In the present circumstances, particularly not. He'd have to come up with some good lies, quickly. He could not allow himself 'to be taken home' at that time of the night. Left outside, perhaps? But the way his legs felt, he doubted if he'd have the strength to weave his way down and up through the basement, and up again.

He pressed the L button on his mental computer, and waited for a list of lies to create itself, from memory, from experience, from imagination.

IX

Halfway to the Hare Krishna House Lahya fell asleep in the taxi.

However, when the taxi stopped and Ariel got out to pay the driver, Lahya stirred a little, opened his eyes and looked around him in a daze, trying to figure out where he was and what was going on. Ariel was relieved. He was not entirely ecstatic about agreeing to let Lahya stay in his room for the night; he certainly did not want to be seen carrying the sleeping boy in his arms into the House and then up to his room. Him tagging along behind was bad enough.

True that in the true spirit of Manhattan, House rules were liberal and the residents more so. Nonetheless, dragging a previously unseen, half-asleep skinny little boy of colour by a male of no colour to one's room about one o'clock in the morning could have raised an eyebrow or half. Especially when that particular uncoloured male was an object of mystery and curiosity anyway, spending most of his time in his room, or out, rarely mixing with the others, and almost never eating in with the rest; known to some as Garbo, or the antenna, and to a couple of British and one Australian inmate as the one who washes out the whitest. Fortunately, Ariel did not meet with any looks on the way, for he met with no eyes. Most people were either in their rooms doing whatever took their fancy – which could, in extreme circumstances, even involve sleeping – or out, or in the TV room or the dining room or whatever, and Ariel managed to take Lahya, still unseen, to his room on the second floor, third by American tradition.

The Hare Krishna House, situated on 16th Street between Union Square and 5th Avenue, where East meets West, was originally founded for Hare Krishna devotees. Over time, the place acquired the dubious status of a profit-making charity, with most residents recommended to it by word of mouth, not necessarily based on religious enlightenment or inclination. Now, of about the forty-five occupants of single or double rooms of various sizes and character, only three were Hare Krishna people. Even the management was chosen for its commercial expertise rather than cultic alignment. With two exceptions, all the residents were white; with three exceptions, all were young, the majority male. Mostly students; or looking for work or resting actors and dancers; or looking for fame, publication or exhibition, artists and writers. And an absolutely incredible sixty-five per cent were not gay men. That is if you included the recently dead, and those who were not men, at least not principally so.

Lahya entered a pleasantly large room, the most spacious and the most expensive in the House, next to a large luxurious bathroom, a window looking out on to the garden, two cupboards, one walk-in, its own sink, a full-length mirror, an antique writing desk, a dressing table with capacious drawers, and a coffee table with two straight-backed and one sofa chair.

X

'How can that washing powder afford it?' said hairy Harry, so-called
for he had thick matted hair of all different colours where he should have
had skin, except on his head where there was plenty of skin but no hair.

'You know as well as I do, light of my alimentary,' said one of the
two Adrians, the one with more rings than fingers, but who could
unfortunately not wear his favourite ring around in public, and could
only do so on special occasions, when not sitting on it. 'Horizontal work
is hard, for men, honey, and I mean hard, but it pays well.'

'O my Gawwd. Isn't that amazing!' said Mabelene, wide-eyed with
excitement.

'I think you are being hard on him,' said one of the three Christophers,
the tall one who didn't look any taller than the two shorter ones because
he walked with a stoop.

'He wishes,' ejaculated Daniel. Then mixing his metaphors with his
orange juice, he added, 'Have you seen the line of men that streams up
and down to his room?'

'Only on some days. And those are actors and dancers. He designs
costumes for them.' Christopher continued his defence of Ariel. 'They
visit him professionally.'

'I rest my case,' Daniel ejaculated again.

'Amazing!' Mabelene was so thrilled.

'Designers make good cash. And his family has money.' Christopher
was not to give up easily, 'His father's a film producer in Holland.'

'A film producer in Holland! That's like a cricket captain in America,'
snarled hairy Harry.

'No, dear,' said Adrian, 'that's like a film producer in England.'

'Ha bloody ha,' said hairy Harry.

'Oh my Gawwwd,' said Mabelene, getting a little bored by it all.

'Maybe the sprite has magical powers,' mused Jon, who had more manuscripts returned than sent out.

'With that nose and those teeth, not to mention the creamy muscularity, I bet he has,' agreed Joe, an older man with tears in his voice. It was not just envy or the tragedy of lost youth; Joe always had tears in his voice, even when at his happiest.

'You are all jealous bitches,' said Mary Jo from Boston, Massachusetts; and Lee Ann from China, San Francisco agreed. She agreed with everyone. The secret of her popularity. More queues of men streamed up to her room than travelled the subway by night.

'I think his real name is Klaas,' said Ms Rosenberg, adjusting her teeth.

'Amazing.' Mabelene's excitement was back.

'Oh no. It really is Ariel. I've seen his passport,' Joe cried into his coffee.

'Ooooh . . . And what else have you seen of him?' Adrian began to twist and turn the ring round his middle finger.

'He should be so lucky,' hissed hairy Harry.

'He's Dutch, not German,' said Adrian two.

'I said Klaas, not Klaus!' Ms Rosenberg adjusted her teeth again.

'A bit too classy for Adrian,' said Adrian two.

'Amazing,' said Mabelene.

'I once knew a man who had passports in seventeen different names,' thought Jon aloud.

'Oh my Gawwwwwd,' said Mabelene.

'You would, wouldn't you!' said Lee Ann from China, San Francisco. Jon, though not gay, had never shown any interest in Lee Ann. Usually even the gays doted on her.

'I'm sure the films his sugar daddy makes in Holland won't be requiring the costume designing talents of his beloved son, since they won't be requiring any costumes.' Daniel took a few hasty puffs at his king-size and blew the smoke towards Ms Rosenberg. They were not allowed to smoke in the TV room, and Ms Rosenberg was always the one to convey rule-breaking to the management. But the manager's husband was a friend of Daniel's and he always got away with it.

'However, hauuwever, they might be requiring the – shall we say – bodily talents of his son . . . I mean dance is big in Amsterdam.' The second Adrian looked around for general consensus and approval. Among the many rumours floating around about Ariel, one proclaimed that he was an ex-ballet dancer who quit professionally at the height of his career due either to a back injury or to a jealous boyfriend removing his rocks, thus rendering him unattractive in ballet tights. He was also said to be a French spy working for the EC to discover American attitudes to Europe in general and France in particular; some could have sworn he was a famous somebody researching a book, in disguise and incognito, substantiated by the fact that he often wore wigs and changed eye colour; for others that was a sure sign of a pure and simple hustler who was neither pure nor simple.

'And jock straps are big in dance,' said hairy Harry.

'You can all stop being so jealous of the poor boy,' said Mary Jo from Boston, Massachusetts, fully intending to make them more jealous. 'He needs space for his designing, so he's getting an apartment of his own and moving out of here.'

'Aren't we all, honey,' sighed Daniel. Although the Hare Krishna House was a clean and comfortable place with many facilities, and ideally situated, getting out and having one's very own apartment in NY was everyone's dream, seldom realised. Many had been in the House for years, some went back to parents or home towns, some had to take refuge wherever when rent money ran out.

'He really is,' said Jon. 'In about a month. I know the girl whose apartment he has taken. We used to be in NYU together. As soon as she moves out, in a few weeks, Ariel is moving in. Beautiful apartment. Balcony with a garden.' Those who did not like Ariel before, abhorred him now.

'Lucky Garbo,' said Joe, cheerily as ever.

'Good to see your antenna rattled,' said hairy Harry, turning to Daniel for no particular reason, and saying rattled in a passably good imitation of an American accent.

'Your speech is going the way of British cricket,' retorted Daniel.

'Isn't that just amazing!' said Mabelene looking truly amazed.

'Ha bloody ha,' said hairy Harry.

XI

Ariel sat Lahya down in the comfortable sofa chair and said, 'Are you hungry? Have you eaten? I can get you something from the kitchen. A cup of tea, orange juice, some cookies. There must be some food left over, or I can make toast or something. An egg?' As he spoke, in his very soft, very gentle voice, he looked straight into Lahya's eyes, his own intense and penetrating.

Lahya could have done with something to eat, and orange juice. He liked American orange juice, so much richer and tastier than the one he was used to in England. But he shook his head.

Ariel again looked deep into the boy's eyes. By then he had had a bucketful of lies from him. However, there must be some truth in it somewhere for him to be running around like crazy in the middle of the night, and east of Tompkins Park at that.

Abused by his father, clear sexual implications, but not directly stated. Beaten by his uncle; his aunt making him do the family laundry instead of his homework resulting in punishment at school; friends calling him names and a neighbour's son forcing him to shoplift odd pairs of shoes from the ones on display outside. Now this last was so odd that Ariel thought it must be true. Abuse by father must have some foundation. The uncle beating him up was the reason he gave for running out of the house in the middle of the night. If he went back that night, he would be crucified. He'd wait till tomorrow to let uncle cool down. With any luck, he would have forgotten the whole incident. He was dead drunk; when his head cleared in the morning he wouldn't even remember. This last Lahya had emphasised on the off-chance that Ariel might escort him home the next day and meet the uncle. No, they won't worry if he didn't get back home. He often stayed out nights, and this Ariel could well believe. In fact they'd be only too happy if he got lost or was killed. His life was insured for three hundred and seventy-five thousand dollars, which could go up to half a million in case of murder. Actually, it was pounds and not dollars, making it even more.

The boy was trouble, and dark trouble. Something within Ariel kept warning him, and if he had listened to that inner voice, he'd have let him be where he found him and run in the opposite direction, faster than the crazy boy himself. But he liked children – *sixteen! he must think I'm blind or something* – and since he was not sure if he'd have any of his own . . . Besides, he could not have just left him like that, whatever tricks he was up to . . . But only until the morning. He was having nothing more to do with him after that. Of that he was definite.

'Well, if you're sure you don't want anything,' he said out loud, 'but I am going down for some juice and cookies for myself. I'll bring some up anyway, and if you change your mind . . . First, I'll make your bed for you; it'll only take a minute. You must be tired. You are a very lucky boy, you know. You could be dead, or without a leg or two. You must learn to look where you're going.'

Lahya looked at the bed in the room. It was large enough to fit three. He would have quite liked to cuddle up to Ariel, but the thought began to make him feel uncomfortable again, and he looked away from the bed, up at the wall.

Ariel went inside the walk-in cupboard and came out with a folding camp bed, which he opened out, and with meticulous care began to spread a clean sheet over it. That done, he brought out a pillow, and carefully rolled it into a clean pillow case.

He patted the mattress, and winked at Lahya. 'All yours. I'll get some cookies . . . Wait a minute, before I go.' He walked up to the sink, and looking into the mirror above it began poking his eyes, or so it seemed to Lahya. Then he brought both hands to his head and pulled off his long black hair. He turned round and faced Lahya. He now had bright emerald-green eyes, and golden blond hair.

Lahya gasped, blinking his eyes.

'Surprised?' said Ariel. 'Well, I am full of surprises.'

'You look like my mother,' exclaimed Lahya, 'except she has light-blue eyes . . . You look just like my mother,' he repeated incredulously.

Ariel's sense of humour failed him. *Will this boy ever stop lying? I mean, I can take a lot of shit, but his mother a blue-eyed blonde!!!! That takes the Jaffa.*

Ariel himself was not exactly addicted to truth and regarded so-called truthfulness as a highly overrated, dubious and perverse virtue, more a tool for moral blackmail by friends, lovers, what-have-yous and the merely nosey, than possessing any inherent value. Honesty was quite another thing. It was always good to be honest. And one could be perfectly honest while being quite untruthful, for example in telling those one loved that one loved them, while lying through one's teeth about where one had been the night before last. Honesty about one's emotions did not mean setting one's right to privacy on fire. All of us were entitled to reveal as much or as little about ourselves as we liked, while being totally honest about how we treated another human being and how we felt about him or her. Honesty, even fantasy and self-preservation were more important by far than the truth – unless one was speaking with a capital T and in absolute terms – for the sake of others too, not mere selfishness.

Also, one had to make a distinction between revealing the truth as truth is – if one is ever enlightened enough to discover it; articulating the truth as people saw it, which could differ from group to group and person to person; not releasing verifiable facts in general; withholding verifiable facts about oneself; telling hurt-preventing lies; telling interesting lies; telling hurtful lies; telling stupid lies; and *being stupid*. This boy had begun low, and, moving lower down the scale, had hit the last.

XII

In the early hours of the morning Lahya had a strange dream. He dreamt he was in the big bed lying next to Ariel. Ariel turned over to his side and put one arm across Lahya's back. Lahya felt a gust of hot sweaty pleasure run through his veins, but when he tried to look up and smile at Ariel, he saw it wasn't Ariel at all, but Aunt Jamuna. And then, before he could reconcile to that, it was not Aunt Jamuna, but a strange creature with the legs of Jayshree, the face of Savitri, and the arms of Kali. And those arms were wrapped round his body at various points, making it unable for him to move, to breathe, to scream . . .

He woke up, his body shivering, his heart stomping, and his head jumping up and down as if pulled by a string.

A sheet of moonlight had rolled itself in through the window and was spread over Ariel's body, naked except for a pair of grey Y-fronts and a pillow squashed between the thighs.

It was either due to the after-effect of the accident, or the fear and desire of the nightmare, that he was overwhelmed with a strong urge to cry. Strong and irresistible. His whole being shook, hiccoughs of pain jerked through his parched throat, tears began oozing out of his eyes like blood from damaged skin, and he began to sob in a pathetic, robotic sort of manner.

The noise of his sobbing was so loud and unpleasant that it woke up Ariel. He had been in a deep sleep. Deep, but not a peaceful sleep. Disturbed and disturbing images of his recently dead grandmother, and his ballet teacher who had died some time ago were dancing round his body in a sacrificial dance, a dance inviting him to join them, wherever they were. Inviting, urging, coaxing, threatening.

He was only too relieved to be out of it all. But it took him a minute or two to realise what had woken him up. The poor little bastard in the camp bed was doubled up, sobbing his life out. He may have lied about the reasons for his trouble, but in trouble he surely was.

He got out of his bed, went over to Lahya's, put his arms around him, held him close, and said, 'There there. It will be all right. Whatever it is. It will be all right in the morning.' His voice was like the murmuring of a mountain stream or the touch of morning breeze.

Lahya felt showered by a roaring torrent of grace.

He clung on to Ariel with all his little strength, and smiled, 'I love you. I love you so much. Don't go. Don't go away and leave me alone, Mumsy.'

For the first time it was Ariel's turn to feel uncomfortable. A warm tear from Lahya's eyes made its way down to Ariel's stomach, tickling a nipple along the way.

Rather abruptly he disentangled his body from Lahya's and moved back to his bed. 'Try and go to sleep now, kid.' He smiled his smile and bared his teeth, 'See you in the morning.' He couldn't handle being anybody's *Mumsy*, much less this sad little boy's.

Fortunately for Lahya, he was already half-asleep. He sort of smiled back in response to Ariel's voice rather than words, and slid downwards into a lying position on his bed, the blurred boundaries between Ariel and Mumsy, life and nightmare merging into a blank and black emptiness.

XIII

Later that morning, almost eleven o'clock, Lahya sneaked into the restaurant to make some plausible excuses for being away to Aunt Jamuna. He figured she was likely to be the most understanding and forgiving, not to say gullible. He was quite disappointed to discover he had not even been missed.

Jamuna just smiled at him and hoped that he had a good night's sleep.

When he had not come down for breakfast, she had wanted to go up and wake him, but Savitri had said, 'Let the poor boy sleep. He's not been feeling too good lately, what with missing his mother and his home.' And that was that.

Once the initial disappointment was over, however, Lahya was quite pleased. It meant he could be out more often looking for prospectives without being found out and cross-examined.

Life did have its little compensations. And big ones. He was so happy to have made a new friend. He was determined to see him again, and again. Just to make sure, he had 'forgotten' his wallet with a five-dollar bill and some telephone numbers in Ariel's room as an excuse to call back. He had also stolen Ariel's keys. One for the House, one for his room. Who knows when he might want to take refuge from whatever. On a scrap bit of paper he had Ariel's telephone number, written in Ariel's handwriting. He held on to it in his palm like a very precious stone.

He thoroughly enjoyed his lunch that day, and looked so happy and cheerful that both Jamuna and Savitri remarked he had finally come to enjoy New York and stopped pining for Mumsy. Jayshree didn't look too pleased about it, but she didn't look too displeased either.

Lahya spent the afternoon hovering about the hardware store. Dirk's massive white body was back to being his favourite for the chop.

XIV

Later that evening Lahya walked over to the hardware store again, waiting to see when Dirk would come out, and then either follow him and see if he lived close by; or try and strike up a friendship by asking for a light, or a sniff or a touch of snow in the heat. He had to haul ass and get his shit together if he was to make any progress in his white shark mission.

However, while hanging about, he saw two young men involved in deep conversation, using eyes, hands and hips as much as words, and got involved with another of his recently acquired leisure time activities: listening in to New Yorkers talking. It was more entertaining than TV, more educational and with a marginally higher intellectual content. Certainly a deeper dramatic impact. Actually he was quite lucky in that he could do both, keep Dirk under surveillance, *and* hear the voices of Guppy and Puppy, as he chose to call his audio-dicks. His face turned slightly sideways presented him with a clear view of the hardware store, beautifully positioning his ears in just the right direction to catch the words from his left, opposite the metallically fortified Tunnel Bar.

Guppy and Puppy were waiting for a companion to turn up.

'I can't stand the Tunnel. It's like a . . . tunnel. Wonder Bar is so much nicer, cosy, you know . . . with a little bit going on, on the side, you know, but not *oppressive*,' said Guppy. 'You can take your pick, or not . . . no pressure . . . you know.'

'And their screen is big,' said Puppy.

'I know. A *regular* screen. Not that I go for all that porn. I prefer the real thing, you know. Something you can get a hand on.'

'Or in,' said Puppy.

'Or in, if you like. Anyway, I'm not going in here till Rich comes.

I will when he does, for his sake; he likes it, God only knows why. I bet even *He* is puzzled, in all his omni-whatever. In the meantime I'd rather sweat in the heat here, and the Tunnel can stuff its air-conditioning up its tunnel as far as I'm . . .'

'Is that him?' interrupted Puppy, all excited, pointing his nose at a big black guy in shredded shorts and a shredded shirt, much like Guppy's, coming from the opposite direction, the shape and size of his recumbent black dick outlined through the exposed crotch of white panties. It had a generous, friendly look to it, and was kosher.

'Oh no! I wouldn't mind though, if he was. Not that I go for black guys personally. Highly overrated, if you ask me. Give me any night, or day, a white shaft with a purple head, and a blond butt with a pink slit for an a.h., just below the tomatoes, or above, depending on your angle. I don't like rings, especially the wedding kind – you know what I mean, too tight and there for life. This reminds me of Julia, my secretary. You know what she's done, gone and fallen in love with John who works in computers! Wants to marry him in September. Can you believe that? She's so pretty, and so young. Can't be a day older than you, if that. And he must have hit his fortieth a few years ago, at *leeeast*. And skinnier than a pencil dick.'

'You mean the one with glasses and a bent nose?'

'Exactly. Can you imagine *annnyone* falling in love with that!'

'Women have no taste, do they? They fall in love with all sorts, especially if they're a soft touch or a clever mouth.'

'Exactly. Breeders are *so* insensitive. *Crude*. Their aesth . . . sensi*bili*ties, aren't fine-tuned like ours. No wonder the best Arteeests, and the most creative people in the world, and I mean *really* creative, are gay, always have been. I mean I could never love a forty-plus-plus-plus skinny man with a bent nose, no matter what. Women do it *all* the time. With *worse*, as you said. Now if there was big money . . .'

'Or big talent. You have to admit. A great actor, or a designer . . .'

'Perr . . . haps. I'd be tempted, I must admit, but wary. *Too* full of themselves, actors and designers. But *taste*. Great taste is import-ant. Sartorially, tonsorially, colour matching, people who *can* tell the difference in blue and azure; and furniture . . .'

'Furniture, now that *is* important. I can tell a man by the chair he sits on . . .'

'I can tell a man by something else he sits on. But I am wicked. Getting back to what we were saying. Furniture. The bed. The bed. That is crucial. Absolutely . . .'

'And underwear. The ultimate test. You want to find what a man is really like, take his pants off . . . I always say.'

'So that's the big talent you look for in a man . . .'

'OOOh. Barbed tonight, are we! What am I doing hanging around with you then? Honest!'

'Hee, hee and who's barbed now, poison-tips . . . You know what, Harvey has decided to come out.'

'What, again! I'll believe it when it happens.'

'Sounds like he means it this time. Says he's taking the yoke and brats to Florida next week, just to . . . Well he didn't say yoke and brats, but I do, and I don't care who knows. Have you seen her, and them! I mean sometimes I wish I had kids, but when I look at his, my balls ride up my ass, honest to God, they do!'

'You know I could never live a lie like that. I came out before I was born . . .'

'Which wasn't that long ago, and am I grateful for it or am I grateful for it! Came out before you *came out*, I'll remember that. But you are right. These closet fags make my cum freeze. No thought for the rest of us who are *suffering* for our honesty, and *dying* for our dignity. Now if I had my way . . .'

Lahya never got to find out what Guppy would have done had he had his way. He did find his neck in a vice lock and his body lifted high up in the air by a forklift truck.

He had been lost in the Guppy–Puppy interchange, despite the fact that he didn't understand most of it – or because of it. Not only was it grown-up talk, and sex talk, but pervo talk, something beyond his wettest dreams in the streets of Gravesend, and something which both excited and disturbed him, firing a nerve somewhere in the belly of his being in a manner both frightening and fascinating. So much so that he had let his eye escape the hardware store.

XV

'I don't know what your game is, bozo. But I catch you hanging around here again I'll make a pizza topping of you and eat you raw.' It was Dirk.

'Nothing. My game is . . . nothing,' blurted Lahya, in mortal danger of being murdered by his murderee. The sheer panic in his voice calmed Dirk, and he dropped Lahya.

'You better be right, bozo. We've been broken into twice recently. And if you're keeping a lookout for someone, or sizing up the place . . .'

'No, no. I swear. I swear on my dead dad. No. I was just waiting to see you,' he decided that for once truth was the best way to diffuse the situation. As long as it wasn't the whole truth, and a lot else beside.

Dirk's curiosity was aroused. 'See me! Why???'

Lahya hadn't had the time to think this one through. Once again he decided to stick as close to the truth as possible. 'I wanted to ask you if you'd like to buy some videos.' Then, catching the blank look on the other's face, added, 'You know, dirty videos.'

Dirk was speechless for a second, encouraging Lahya to greater expansion, 'Homo, hetero, Indonesian, Hispanic . . .' Lahya hadn't seen any, but he'd seen the boxes labelled in the basement, and he rattled them out as he remembered them.

'You mean you're peddling sick videos! I've seen younger than you selling dope, but . . .'

'It's my Granddad, see. He is sick, I mean not well.'

'What's your Granddad being sick got to do . . .'

'My father's in jail. We need the . . .'

'I thought your father was dead.'

'No. Yes. That was my first dad. This is my third. We need the money. For Granddad's medicines. Doctor's bills.'

Dirk was once again reduced to momentary silence and thought. Lahya once again pushed his advantage, 'My mother has left us, with the . . .' He was about to say 'milkman' but remembered, just in time, that they didn't have milkmen here in the US of A. 'With the post . . . the man who brings in letters.' Unable to decide between postman and mailman.

'Let me get this straight. Your first dad is dead. Your third dad is in jail, your mother has run off with someone, your grandpa is sick, and you are pushing porn to pay the bills!'

'I knew you'd understand.'

'Why should I buy from you? I can buy them anywhere. It's not like crack or anything.'

'Two for the price of one? Four even . . . I am . . . we are . . . desperate, for money. The bills are mounting . . .'

'Bills do. What's it got to do with me? You think I'm some kind of airhead nerd . . .' His eyes behind the glasses took on a hard, mean look.

'All right, all right. Don't get mad. I was only asking. It's a free country.'

'It may be a free country, but it ain't your country, from what I can tell.'

'How can you say that? This is a nation of immigrants. It belongs to me as much as it . . .'

'OK. Can it. I can do without a lecture from a knee-high twerp. So where *are* these fancy videos of yours, if that's what you're here for, selling them. I want proof. We've been broken into twice, and the one reason they hired a big guy like me, with a record . . . and I don't want to be tricked by a fast-talking kid while his three dads are planning . . .'

'I've got them, here, the videos, just a block away. In the basement. Come with me and I'll show them to you!' Fear was turning to confidence, to hope.

Dirk hesitated. 'I can't . . . Not tonight. I'm seeing a friend. But tomorrow. Meet me here, same time. And if anything happens to the store before that, I'll personally hunt you down and set you on fire. Is that clear?'

'Clear, Dirk.'

'What? What did you call me? Did you call me a jerk?' Dirk was obviously not Dirk. He took a menacing step closer to Lahya.

'No. Of course not. I said . . . Turk. Yes Turk. That man over there. He's a Turk I know because my cousin's married to one. A Turk. She's visually disabled. Partly. See you tomorrow. Here. Same time. Sleep well. Sweet dreams.' Lahya began retreating pace by pace into the night.

Guppy and Puppy stopped talking as they witnessed the little scene played out by Dirk and Lahya. They couldn't hear much, for Dirk was shouting in a hoarse whisper, and Lahya's squeaky voice was squeakier than ever, but precisely because they couldn't hear, it appeared like a drama of violence by a big man on a small child. They saw Dirk pull Lahya bodily up in anger, and could also see the expression of rage on his face and in his demeanour, the fear in Lahya's eyes.

'Wasn't that disgusting,' said Puppy.

'Telling me, all that meat. I mean, I like a bit of muscle same as the next man, but that was gross,' said Guppy.

'Since when was gross too gross for you? I bet you'd melt like sugar in the oven if he lifted you up in the air like he did that kid. I *meant* the *shirt*. All those flowers, and all those colours. I can't *bear* to see anyone in Hawaiian shirts. They went out with the fifties.'

'Lean cuisine. That's what I like. Not skinny, not thin, lean. Muscled, but . . . tight.'

'All that body, it's wasted on heteros. They don't know what to do with it. Or what to put on it. A Hawaiian shirt, for Christ's sake. And the top *threeee* buttons undone.'

'Exactly. You noticed that! Did you? I did too. I mean, you either button right up to the top, or unbutton right down. Three open is neither here nor there.'

'So passé.'

'Exactly!'

XVI

The next morning Lahya was in a mad rush to build some sort of an altar for Kali in the basement before her offering arrived.

He went into one of the many esoterica-selling shops to enquire about statuettes of Kali. A skinny white boy with rings in ears, nose and left nipple, green and orange hair on one side, shaved on the other, was in deep meaningful conversation with his boyfriend of greased-back dark hair and blue eye-shadow with matching lip colour. At Lahya's approach the blue lips moved aside, with just the right balance of sulkiness and seductiveness, as the ringed nipple turned his attention to Lahya. He smiled a pleasant smile, showing uneven teeth of a light beige hue, complementing the waify pallor of his skin. Lahya explained what he wanted.

The nipple was extremely understanding but extremely sorry that they did not stock that item. However, he was extremely helpful and gave the locations of at least three shops that would. One on 3rd Street, or 4th and 2nd, but it only opened three days a week, the other on the West Side in Greenwich Village, and yet another on St Marks. Lahya bought some incense from the many coloured incense jars, going for ones promoting love and the granting of wishes. He also bought five huge candles, red for blood, green for peace, yellow for happiness, white for fulfilment, violet for luck. He also bought similar coloured glasses to house the candles. Finally, almost on his way out, he came back for a set of tarot cards with pictures based on Indian mythology. Then he headed for the nearest shop to look for Kali.

He found her. He bought the best one that he could afford, almost a foot high. There were also a few postcards depicting Kali in her various moods and in varying situations, from squatting on the white linga of a white Siva, to riding a many-fanged tiger while in her white-skinned epiphany. Lahya bought a collection.

Once back home, Lahya was tempted to ask for Jayshree's help in setting up the temple. He had never done anything like that before. But then he decided against it. He could never trust Jayshree. For a start, she'd ask too many questions. He'd just do the best he could, and if Kali was the great goddess she claimed to be, she would understand, and forgive all acts of omission or wrongful commission on his part. He prayed to Lord Jesus for help.

XVII

The altar was set. In a corner, on a corner table draped in white lace taken from Savitri's wardrobe, my statuette in its centre, my picture cards on walls on either side. Candles. Incense. Fruit and sweets. Red sindoor dotted around, and streaked on the food.

Lahya placed the most comfortable chair in front of the TV and made sure that the video was working. He would make Dirk sit and preview something he might like to buy, or, even if not willing to buy, just 'for a laugh'. Then he would come from behind and hit him on the head with the standard lamp, strategically placed just behind the chair. Once he was knocked unconscious, then would come the kitchen knife.

He found a rug in the back of one of the cupboards which he spread beneath the chair, and stuffed old newspapers underneath the rug to soak up the blood. He took out a bottle of wine with a couple of glasses from the drinks cabinet and checked to see that the cooker was in order for tea and coffee if required.

He was doing all that he considered necessary, as if guided by a higher intelligence, and fired by something greater than his own need to be a gorgeous white woman; which was there, nonetheless, and of which he was acutely aware; as great as his need to protect Mumsy from any harm; which was also there, and of which also he was acutely aware.

Not thinking, either of the consequences, or of the act itself. Just preparing for it, in the most rational and sensible manner. Not thinking of the life that he was going to take, but preparing for the sacrifice he was going to offer. Not thinking. Just doing. Very like him in some ways, very unlike in others.

XVIII

The time came. He went to wait for Dirk outside the hardware store.

He was cold and shivery in the choking heat of late-July New York. Never in his life had he felt like he felt that night. Not even when he tried to push Ariel under a car. That was a spur-of-the-moment act, quite spontaneous, almost natural, almost playful. This was different, planned, reptilian . . . *demonic*. The word came to meet him physically, rising out of the half-light, half-dark midsummer night like a genie just released from the bottled-up depths of some passionless heart.

I didn't mind. I didn't want to control what he thought or felt or did. It didn't really matter. Or if it did, it was too late. I was only trying to help him realise his dream, even though he was only a stupid little boy. *And* I liked him. I particularly liked the way he tried to hold his tears back by contracting his throat muscles and concentrating on the back of his head while making sure he did not crease his forehead. It was quite, quite funny.

XIX

He waited, but no Dirk.

He waited some more. Still no Dirk. He couldn't be sure of how long he waited. His sense of time was all warped. He had periods when he felt like he had waited for years, and then moments which passed as if they never were. He couldn't even see Dirk anywhere in the store.

The store began to shut, not being one of those all-night businesses. Lahya had to make a decision, and quick. With the sort of courage which comes from dedication, devotion or brainlessness, Lahya went into the store and said, with a near-normal voice, 'Is Dirk around? He's my friend. I just wanted to . . .'

'Who?' asked the Indian woman behind the counter. An Indian man came and stood next to her. They looked wary. Perhaps they, too, had seen him loitering about the shop, like Dirk, and were suspicious, like Dirk.

'What's the matter?' asked the man, with T's harder than dadso's.

'He wants to know about some man called Dirk,' said the woman, sounding more puzzled than suspicious.

It was then that Lahya's mistake dawned on him. 'Dirk' was *his* name for the man, not the man's name. His claims of friendship would seem less solid now.

Fortunately the man with the hard T's helped him out. 'He must have said Patrick. You misunderstand. All the time. All the time you misunderstand. Do you want Patrick?'

Patrick sounded nothing like Dirk to him, but he latched on to it. 'Of course. That's what I said in the first place. Patrick. He's my friend. Well, actually, my brother's friend. He's sent me with a message. They were to meet today but . . .'

The woman looked sad. 'Very sorry, but Patrick won't be meeting anyone today. Not tomorrow, too. He had . . .'

'He fell and broke his leg, in three places.' The man wanted to talk about the exciting event himself, his voice bubbling over cheerily. 'He was just putting boxes up on the shelf when his foot slipped. Such strong muscles, such weak bones. A little fall, and three . . . what do you call them, fruc . . . fractures. No, fractures. Just there. Over there. No no, behind you, on the top shelf.'

'I don't know how you can be so happy about it,' said the woman, frowns in her words, frowns on her forehead. 'Think of the insurance problem. Now if you had employed that Australian, like I wanted, he had no Green Card, so no insurance problem. With Patrick, God only knows what . . .'

'He was a criminal. What d'you call it, ex-con. We did him a favour. I don't think he will make any claims. I will speak to Lakhani tomorrow. He'll sort it out. OK. You worry for nothing, all the time. All the time.'

Perhaps Kali did not want Dirk. No point in wasting a life that wasn't wanted. Lahya was relieved, immensely so; it was as if Dirk's enormous weight had been sitting on his chest and was now lifted.

Lucky man, that Dirk. Three broken bones were better than one broken neck.

PART V

Renunciation

I

'Every time I look at you, you look paler and girlier than last I looked at you. Are you turning white? A white tart or something? Our very own Michael Jackson of the Indian community? Pity you can't sing like he does. Or do anything like anybody does.' Jayshree was trying to be at her best and her most entertaining for 'our little guest', as her mother dotedly referred to the boy she never had. Jayshree well knew that Marilyn had not abandoned her little black son for a pretty white girl; but *her* mother would cast her aside quicker than a snake its skin if she could have a boy of her own, regardless of colour, looks or brains.

Lahya didn't quite know how to respond to this somewhat unexpected line of attack. A part of him was almost pleased, another felt threatened. Did the witch know something? Had Kali told his grandmother about their pact, as he suspected, and passed on the information to Jayshree? Did those two hate each other, as they publicly proclaimed, or were they in it together, whatever 'it' was, as they seemed to be in private?

He chose not to respond as a response. At least for the time being.

'Did anyone ring for me?' he asked casually, bending over to tie his shoelaces, pretending as if it were no more than a mature attempt to change the childish subject. In reality it was a question he had been dying to ask and couldn't not for any longer. He was desperately praying for a call from Ariel telling him he had left some money behind and suggesting a meeting. Lahya had left both telephone numbers with Ariel, the one for the restaurant, and the home number. He was hoping he would call him anyway, money or no money, just to ask after him, and maybe want to see him, money or no money; but at least . . .

'At least you can talk. I thought New York had got your tongue.' Then after a long enough pause to keep him guessing, 'Who'd call you?'

Jayshree would have been more than willing to make friends with Lahya, especially after he helped her, but Lahya had been so withdrawn lately, either physically absent, or mentally, that she had seen it as a personal snub and gone back to being her usual charming self again. The *nobody is going to like me, so what's the point in making the effort* approach to life and the living.

Lahya tried to look nonchalant and cool about the 'Who'd call you!' taunt, for he didn't want to give Jayshree the pleasure of seeing how disappointed he was. He would have to call Ariel himself. He had been thinking about it since they last parted but could not build up enough courage to act on it. Could it be that he *did* call, and Jayshree was not telling him? He looked at her, directly, for the first time in a long while. He couldn't see any signs of hidden glee which she would have had, had that been the case. His face fell right in front of her eyes, and he tried to repair the damage by grinning foolishly and remarking that he was not turning into a white tart, but she sure was burning up like a right fart.

Jayshree was about to say something, but stopped. She put her hand of cards down – she was in the middle of a game of solitaire, her favourite pastime when not listening to hard rock or heavy metal – and looked at Lahya again, this time with a different look in her eyes.

'You haven't fallen in love or something *sick* like that, have you?' she almost whispered, then suddenly and surprisingly began laughing her hysterical laugh and clapping her hands as if derisively awestruck at the prospect of Lahya in love. With the uncanny insight of the debilitated and the destined to die young, she was able to see what Lahya himself could not have understood, much less acknowledged.

Lahya's reaction, a mixture of anger and guilt and denial sent Jayshree into further fits of hysterics, most of it masking her disappointment. She would have given anything to be the object of Lahya's desire, even though he was just a kid, and an ugly kid at that. Better to be wanted by anybody than nobody.

On his part Lahya felt equally inadequate. He was *not* in love with

Ariel. He was no *queer*. But even if he was to fall in love with him, Ariel could never love him, an ugly little black boy. *But*, if he was a gorgeous white woman, then, then perhaps, perhaps, he himself might *choose* to fall in love with Ariel; and then, perhaps, perhaps, even *he* might, just might . . . He kicked Jayshree's chair and swept aside the carefully spread cards on the table. 'You stupid bitch!' he screamed and walked to the front door and out.

'Lahya is in love, Lahya is in love,' sang Jayshree's bitter voice as it followed him into the corridor. If only she had known who with, her self-pity might have turned to pity for him.

Neither cousin knew the meaning of love, not having experienced it, but, without realising what was happening to him, Lahya was in the process of falling helplessly and comically in love. Or, to phrase it differently, falling in helplessly comical love. Of course he would have denied it to the death, and quite truthfully, so far as he was aware of the truth. But then, not many, older and wiser than Lahya understand the lies of truth.

II

Once outside, Lahya was taken hostage by one of the many festivals held in the Village. This was one on 1st Avenue. Very different from New Road, Gravesend.

It was early in the day and some stalls were being set up while others were in full swing of business. Colourful and strange objects of desire, from voodoo dolls to botty comforters and dick warmers sat or stood comfortably alongside articles of daily use such as socks and jeans, all displayed with the simple vulgarity of the truly innocent or the hopelessly corrupt – the shifting hallmark of everything American. Food and drinks of all nationalities and tastes were being stuffed into mouths of all nationalities and tastes with a tastelessness that cut across all nationalities and tastes.

Police loitered at intersections, permitting traffic on the criss-crossing streets while keeping the avenue clear of all vehicles except those carrying equipment and merchandise connected with the festival. Music from radios and cassettes invigorating the tropo-sphere was gradually losing out to the live bands roaring further along, but not without strong decibellic resistance. But the biggest spectacle of all was the spectators. Some had chosen to cover parts of their bodies in honour of the occasion, others had decided otherwise. But in every case was a case, and in every step a stepping out.

Lahya felt like dancing. And why not? New York was the only place he so far knew – and had he known more he might still have come to the same conclusion – where you could dance or sing or kill or cohabit in the middle of the road and in clear daylight, or a stormy night, and yet be ignored at best, at worst admired.

He began to dance. A few others joined him, a young black man with smooth and dry armpits, an old white woman with hairy and sweaty armpits, and a young mixed couple holding on to each other's buttocks as if they had been transplanted by mistake and they were trying to retrieve their own. Lahya imagined the white boy with the black girl's ass, and the black girl with the white boy's butt. It made him dance more energetically. If only his father saw him now, he'd be horrified. This made Lahya dance all the more energetically. The young black man with the smooth armpits eventually moved away, as did the couple; but the old woman carried on, cheered along by some new revellers getting in step.

Almost unconsciously Lahya heard this most beautiful and gentle of voices, followed by a laugh which cut through the pains of life, a laugh which gods reserve for the blessed few even to hear, much less possess.

He turned his head, and there, slightly ahead, on the other side of the road, was Ariel. He was so happy to see him and his first instinct was to run forward and surprise him. Then he noticed the young man with Ariel. Medium height, black hair pushed backwards, nothing remarkable about him. Lahya wouldn't have thought anything of him, but it was the manner in which the two walked together that made him hesitate. There was an air of intimacy about the way Ariel's whole body swayed towards the other from time to time, touching his arms or back with the swing of his own arms. At one point they stopped to look at a stall, and Ariel held on to the other's shoulders and brought his neck close to the back of the other's head, his golden-blond hair brushing against his jet-black crown.

Surely they couldn't, *he* couldn't, he *couldn't* be one of *them*. No, that could not be so. He stopped dancing, stopped thinking, and would have stopped breathing if he could have. As he stood, foolishly and uselessly in the middle of the road, both the men turned, for whatever reason, and Ariel caught sight of Lahya. His bright face brightened a little more. 'Hey, Lahya. I've been thinking of you.' He waved his arms in the air to be noticed, and to call Lahya towards them.

Lahya flushed with joy. *He remembered my name. And he's been thinking about me!* Just then the other young man put his arm round Ariel's waist, they both looked at each other, nodded their heads almost in unison, and began to laugh. Lahya turned and began to run as fast as he could in the opposite direction.

'Hey. Lahya. It's me. Ariel,' shouted Ariel as he took a quick step towards him, but as Lahya's squirty little frame began to disappear in the crowd, he shrugged his shoulders and was about to turn away when there was a screech of tyres, followed by some loud and not very pleasant verbiage.

Ariel rolled his eyes and clicked his tongue. There he goes again. He was sure it was Lahya, and he was right. As he made his way through the train of people, he saw Lahya, held by the back of his neck and jerked about by a fat Hispanic man. 'You want to fucking kill yourself, you go stuff your head up your mother's ass, not under my . . .'

'Don't you talk about Mumsy . . . my mother, you wet-back, cunt-head, douchebag, draft-dodging traitor to the USA . . .' Lahya was trying to think of every insult, especially with an American resonance to it, while simultaneously trying not to burst into tears.

The fat man, silenced and stilled for a moment by this unexpected tirade, released Lahya, simply so he could have his dominant hand free to give the little creep a fiver in the mouth he'd remember for the rest of his life, if he was left with any. This split-second relief was enough for Lahya to outplay his opponent's strength with his agility. He head butted the fat Hispanic in the groin, while at the same time jumping on his bare toes that stuck out of open sandals. The fat Hispanic yelled and made a lunge towards Lahya, but misjudged his direction as tears of pain blurred his vision.

Lahya, already on the other side of him, made another of his runs, this time in the reverse direction, and straight into Ariel's stomach. Ariel gasped, but managed to quickly push Lahya behind him, between himself and his friend, manoeuvring sideways synchronistically. Like a beast with six legs, the three edged towards a popular Hungarian food stall allowing themselves to be overwhelmed by customers. The fat Hispanic rushed past them, and then back again, when he saw a red-bearded man disappearing with his car radio, his jacket, and his back seat. Cursing and shouting, he turned towards one of the loitering policemen. As he was gesticulating and shouting and not very coherently trying to explain to the even fatter Hispanic policeman what had happened, the tyres of his car screeched for the second time in the last five minutes as it was driven away by a very respectable-looking man carrying golf clubs and a briefcase. The fat Hispanic clearly remembered seeing and admiring him during his altercation with Lahya.

'Why am I doing this?' said Ariel to himself. 'This boy is trouble, dark trouble.' An uneasy foreboding swept across his normally cheerful face. He turned to his companion and said, 'I'm hungry, are you?'

III

'You know me, I'm always hungry,' said Ariel's friend with a smile and a wink.

'That's what you say about me,' laughed Ariel, white teeth glistening in the sun, a slightly uneven lower set giving them an extra edge of excitement than prosaically perfect ones. Lahya felt the aroma of Ariel's breath generated by the laugh diffuse into the atmosphere. He breathed it into himself, and it was like wine. Stolen wine that he sometimes took a sip or two of back home whenever he felt like doing something daring and when no one was looking. He thought he was going to suffocate by the sheer intoxication of it. A feeling of imbalance unsettled his limbs. He steadied himself by leaning against a parked van.

'Poor kid, you are still in shock. I think you must be living in a constant state of shock because of something or the other,' said Ariel as he stretched out a hand and held on to Lahya's shoulder to support him.

'Let's go eat then,' said Ariel's friend.

'All right, so I will go now,' said Lahya as casually as he could, wondering whether to ask about his wallet. Apparently Ariel had not even noticed it or he would have mentioned it. Better leave it for now as an excuse for future contact.

'Aren't you coming with us?' said Ariel, genuine invitation in his voice.

'Well, if you really want me to. I mean you don't have to . . .'

'I know I don't have to, but I want to, unless you don't want to. By the way, this is my friend Yoast, with a J and two Os. Condon. Joost Condon. Some people call him Used Condom,' at which they both laughed and looked at each other. Lahya felt like he was being made fun of, though even he could tell that the name did sound quite funny, if that *was* his name. However, he could tell Ariel really did want him to come along, and that was what mattered.

So it was settled. They'd go and eat. Lahya was so happy he wanted to think about something miserable, just to make sure it wouldn't go away, as happiness does when you are at your happiest.

He would have quite enjoyed something from one of the stalls, but they opted for a place in St Mark's Place. Fortunately it was on 1st Avenue, and, sitting out in the indented balcony, he could savour the festival spirit while relaxing in a comfortable and interesting café.

As Ariel and Joost were ordering, Lahya said he would just have some Coke, as in Cola. He wasn't sure what to order, and he wasn't sure who was paying, so he thought it best to play it safe and simple.

'Have something to eat, go on,' said Ariel, making his voice softly persuasive and quietly appealing, his disturbingly green eyes looking into Lahya's eyes with such intensity that Lahya felt he was going to feel dizzy again.

But Lahya had made up his mind. He was not going to be a greedy pig, otherwise the offer may never be repeated. 'Thank you, but I promised to eat with my cousin. She's a cripple see, and she'll be very disappointed . . .'

'Now now now, *don't* let's go down that street again,' said Ariel, half-mocking, half-serious, voice a bit richer and deeper and sharper than before.

'Ariel!' Joost almost shouted. 'That's not nice, if his cousin is . . .'

'You don't know him like I do. He has quite an imagination. He insists that he is sixteen, at least he did till I got twelve out of him, and I doubt even that. Also, his mother looks like me, except that she has blue . . .'

Lahya jumped up, face turning as red as a muddy-brown face can. 'Just wait here for me. Please. I'll only be two minutes. Less than that.' And before they could stop him, he was off and running again.

Ariel rolled his eyes once more and waited for another crash. But none came.

Lahya was not back in two minutes, but he was in five. He lived only a couple of blocks away, and knew exactly what to get, and where it was.

'Here.' He thrust one of Jayshree's photographs under Ariel's nose. 'That's my cousin.' It was one from a pack of family photographs recently taken by his parents in New York. The picture was unmistakably of a girl not of sound body, and if looks were a criterion, not of sound mind either.

Ariel and Joost were only just recovering from the awe-instilling apparition of Jayshree, when, with a flourish that a magician of world fame would have envied from the bottom of his pile of tricks, Lahya presented the gentlemen with a picture of his mother. It was a professional portrait taken some years before, and among the many Lahya always carried everywhere with him to give himself some pride in his origin and background which appearances denied him. Marilyn's golden-blonde hair and sharp blue eyes were at their most alluring. She did, almost uncannily, look like Ariel.

Ariel was clearly thrown, but before he could say anything, Lahya spoke, 'I know what you are thinking. This can be anybody's picture. Well this is one with Mumsy and me, taken two weeks ago, only a few yards from here. And no. I am not adopted.' Here Lahya played his trump card by bringing out a picture of his Mumsy holding him up shortly after birth, followed by a few more of the early stages of his growth in his blue-eyed, blonde Mumsy's loving arms. There was no picture of his father.

'Just because I am an ugly black kid does not mean I can't have a beautiful white Mumsy. You think there is something so special about you just because I am ugly and black . . .'

'Hey hold on, hold on,' Ariel got up and put his arms around Lahya, whose whole body was convulsing by now, and he was sobbing without actually crying.

'You can laugh at me and call him Condom, or me, or what you like, just because . . .' stuttered Lahya.

'Just take it easy, take it easy. Calm yourself. Nobody's making fun of you. And you are *not* ugly. You are just . . . different. Beautiful in your own way. I would love to have your skin colour. Honest I would. Dutch people love dark skins.' He almost added, 'That's why we have so many Indonesian prostitutes of both sexes,' but didn't. 'Everybody is different, that is what makes life interesting.'

'I know I am different from you and my mother. Like a cockroach is different from a butterfly. You don't have to tell me.'

'There you go, putting yourself on the floor again. You are not ugly. And I am sorry. Really sorry for not believing in you. But you must admit, you do tell them sometimes, don't you? I should know, because I do too. Takes one to know one. So there. We are even now. All right. I really am sorry. I will make it up to you. Listen. *Jurassic Park* is on. Would you like to see it? We can go see it together. And I will buy you something to eat then, if you have to eat with your cousin today. There, is that a good idea?' Ariel was thinking of ways to alleviate the boy's misery in some way. If all this is true, he thought, about his mother and his cousin, then perhaps the rest is true as well. His father screwing him, his uncle knocking him about. Poor kid, and he was rather sweet. It would be nice to cheer him up. He liked children anyway. He wasn't sure if he'd ever have any. There was that one time . . . but he didn't want to think about it.

'And you are right. Condon is not his name. It is Harmensz Berlage. Joost Harmensz Berlage. It is such a mouthful that we make a joke of it, and invent names. I sometimes do it for myself. If I quickly say my name is Ariel Van Damm people look at me as if they haven't heard. So I make something up. Only with strangers. Joost does it more often. It's an old joke. Nothing to do with you. We weren't making fun of you, were we, Joost?'

Ariel transferred his gaze to Joost, and a quiet shift came in the focus of his eyes, more than the mere obvious, as if he was seeing through a misty magical veil of changing colours; the voice at the last three words seemed to fragment itself into a masterly composition of musical notes.

Lahya could have killed Joost.

That was a thought. He looked up and studied Joost more carefully. Very ordinary, but then Ariel seemed very fond of him, so perhaps he was not quite as common as he appeared to Lahya. Anyway, he was young, white, and there was nothing wrong with his skin; though it wasn't quite as white as he would have liked. Yes, he would do nicely.

But then he looked at Ariel again, saw the love in his eyes, or what he thought was love, and although it broke his heart, he knew he couldn't break Ariel's heart. What if someone did something to Mumsy, or Ariel? He'd die, die of pain. He couldn't do it. Not to Ariel, and therefore not to Joost. He'd have to start looking around.

'What's the matter now?' said Ariel.

'Nothing. Nothing's the matter. Why do you ask if anything is the matter?'

'Just that you looked . . . so . . . so . . . never mind. Here comes your Coke, and if you change your mind about anything else . . .'

Lahya looked at Joost again. There were ugly black hairs on his knuckles, thick and twisty, and they were brushing against the mayonnaise smoothness of Ariel's shoulder. Ariel smiled for no reason at all, raised his arms, spread out his elbows, interlocked his fingers and cradled his neck in his hands. Then he leaned backwards in his chair, stretched out his naked legs to their full length, slipped his strong dancer's feet out of open sandals, and smiled again, dreams dancing in his eyes, making them change colour with the light and shade of their character, full pink mouth fuller and pinker, the tip of his nose glowing with happiness. Joost also lifted his arms and clasped his hands behind his head. The fluffy blond of Ariel's armpit hair glistened with a wet golden glow in the sun. The fuzzy black of Joost's armpit hair was matted with sweat, coarse and wiry and smelly. Perhaps Joost deserved to be killed. If only for Ariel's sake. Surely he could do better. Surely he should do better.

No reference was made to Lahya's wallet, a Christmas present from Ramesh, but halfway through the meal, as one of those obscene American ice creams was ordered for the boy, Ariel checked to see if he had his keys. 'Keep losing them all the time,' he explained, 'two sets in the last month alone.'

IV

As Ariel and Joost were checking out the cheque, working out how much each would have to contribute, including the all-important tip, a black man came to the railing of the café's balcony and jingled his paper cup at them.

'I can't handle these people,' said Ariel, 'I'd rather pay more taxes.'

'I don't think you'd like doing that either,' commented Joost as he retrieved some coins from the money spread out on the table for the bill, and leaned over to deposit them in the rattling cup.

'I swear I would, it's this . . . this . . . confrontation I can't take,' said Ariel.

'Thank you, God bless you,' said the black man, and held on to Joost's hand as a gesture of gratitude.

Despite the intense heat, the black beggar was wearing a heavy shirt and a jacket, both coated with greasy dirt and soaked in sweat; trousers of a black gabardine-type material; long, thick, woollen socks which showed through the tears in the decomposing gabardine; big black boots, leather cracking in criss-cross streaks all over their surface; and a grey felt hat. He couldn't have come in contact with water for a considerable period of time. There were signs of a pinkish skin disease on his hands and around his lips and cheeks which stood out in odd contrast to the dirty blackness of the rest of his visible flesh. The smell off his person could have been grasped in your fist and carried for days without dispersing. Mumsy would have been sick for a millennium if presented with such a one at her dinner table.

Joost brought his other hand and placed it above the man's hand and held it between both of his own for a brief moment before withdrawing and going back to settling the bill.

Lahya's vision was fragmented. Unlike the day when he suddenly saw Jayshree as radiantly beautiful for one illusive moment before a return to seeing her as she *really* was, he could now see the beauty and the ugliness side by side, and a lot more besides. The black man was neither black nor white nor man nor horse, he just was, and yet he was black and white and man and horse and butterfly, dadso and Mumsy. Joost was as beautiful as Ariel and Ariel was Lahya himself, and no one was no one yet everyone, and all were there, side by side, merging, separating into their individual entities, then receding and converging until nothing was static and nothing moved. Only one thing was certain. Everyone and everything was so bright. Lahya's eyes hurt, and tears began to roll out of them in big red drops. His whole body shook and convulsed and he felt cold, so cold, and yet so happy. He had never been so happy in his entire life.

'What's the matter? Are you all right?' Ariel's gentle voice was bathing him like the waters of a mountain spring would a tired rat. Joost was trying to massage his forehead and Lahya could smell the black man in his hands.

The young and pretty waitress looked quite concerned. 'It must be the heat. We had an old lady faint here only last night,' she said. 'I'll get him another soda, on the house.' How kind and wonderful and beautiful everyone was. Lahya smiled. All was well. All was definitely well.

When he got home, he wasn't so sure. Jayshree had fallen off the stairs and had had to be taken to the hospital. There had been a small fire in the kitchen which set Aunt Jamuna's sari alight. It was a miracle that she did not get burnt herself, thanks to the quickness of one of the waiters who turned the fire extinguisher on her, leaving her feeling ill, but uncooked. Mumsy had telephoned and he was out.

By the time he went to bed, everything was back to being as shitty as ever. But a sort of doubt remained. A sort of positive doubt. But there was the other kind too. If, if Ariel liked plain-looking *men* with dark hair, would he like him if he turned into a gorgeous blond *woman*?

Perhaps looks weren't everything, as Mumsy often told him when she gave him a hug. Perhaps love asked for more than beauty, or less; more than sex, or less.

But then gender was beyond beauty, beyond sex, beyond love. It was power. Power as in the power of electricity, energy. Power as in pleasure and in flinging one's red shoes up in the air and wearing silk and diamonds, or nothing, if you dared, and having mere humans melt into semen at your feet with desire, or as dew with adoration.

Just as colour – or rather, not being of colour, was power. And freedom. The power to pass through immigration and not be taken into a 'special' room for questioning while Mumsy fidgeted outside elegantly, like a heavenly being condescendingly awaiting emergence of the shit brigade from a septic tank; freedom from being examined like dirt in a pure world, dirt that should have been swept away by an enlightened being with a hard brush and a dustpan, if not by an energetic vacuum-cleaner salesman demonstrating what a hygienically spotless universe should be like. The compensation of having a desirable dark dick or a mysterious all-devouring black hole for the excitement of some opening or a stretch of white flesh was not enough, whatever the Dutch might say.

Lahya didn't exactly think in these words, but he felt in these words. I think. I can certainly feel it.

Life was becoming more and more complicated.

V

That night Aunt Jamuna came into Lahya's room. She woke him up with a glass of cold chocolate, freshly made and with extra cream topping. She also brought him some delicious rasgullas and gulab jamuns in a rich syrupy base, wonderfully cool for a hot summer's night. Lahya had been feeling thirsty and hot in his dreams, and his throat was sandy. He couldn't have hoped for a better treat.

Aunt Jamuna was wearing a light-blue robe of Indian silk which she removed after a while, saying that since her sari caught fire that morning she was frightened of having any clothes around her body. Uncle Dileep was doing another of his late-night shifts, and Jayshree was in hospital. Aunt Jamuna was lonely and sad and wanted to talk to Lahya, who must also be lonely and sad, away from his friends and town and dear Mumsy, and would understand what it was like. She did not want to turn the light on as Grandma might come in to turn it off, thinking that Lahya had forgotten to do so before dropping off to sleep. She was old and didn't sleep well, sometimes wandering about the house at night, or going for some Kali worship or quiet contemplation or a piss.

Actually Jamuna herself had just been for one, and it made her a little itchy, down there, because of the heat and the acidity, and if Lahya could scratch her, just so, down there, she'd cook him a special something the next day. Sometimes she went for a little massage by a local woman and paid her twenty dollars; she could let Lahya have some of that money if he could rub a little 'bitter' oil on her body. She produced a small bottle of sharply peppered olive oil from the folds of her flesh and poured some of it on to Lahya's hands.

Easing herself more comfortably on the bed, she opened her legs and her lower lips. Taking Lahya's oiled hand in her other hand, she led it to that little bit of flesh that felt specially itchy. It was like a wet nipple and felt squishy and squashy and made Lahya laugh even though he was trembling for some reason and not really feeling like a laugh at all; but then he thought of Ariel and was sure *he* would laugh and that made him feel very excited.

Of course it was only fair that if Lahya was going to give her a little rub-down with the tasty, tangy oil, she should do the same for him. After all, she was so much bigger and stronger than him, and it would be no problem for her at all. She used to do that for her little brother although he was twice the size of Lahya, even at his age, and a real giant by the time he was married, still longing for a rub-down by big sister. It didn't matter if she got some oil on Lahya's shorts and top as she pulled them off. She'd wash them for him personally, first thing in the morning.

In the clandestine light of the night their bodies appeared paler and softer than in the candid brightness of the day, and Lahya remembered with a sharp ache the moon-bathing of Ariel's skin. It all became quite confusing. Abruptly he was sucked in by the larger, softer mass of his sweet aunt and he couldn't tell where she ended and he started and how Ariel fitted into all of it. Sometimes his face was no more than a third breast between her two breasts, and sometimes it was like being reborn, his head emerging from between her thighs and seeing the world for the very first time, in an entirely new light, in the moonlight, a much pleasanter and gentler and softer light. Like Ariel's skin.

Of course, he had seen some of the magazines, but that was nothing like the real thing. Nothing like it at all. He understood why Jayshree had been so disappointed that day and felt guiltier than ever for not making her feel good as he was now making his aunt feel good, and she him. Yes, it was altogether a good, good feeling, and he soon forgot about the guilt of his past lapse in the pleasure of the good he was doing then, and the good done to him.

Eventually, Jamuna felt tired in a happy, relaxed sort of a way, a bit giddy and light-headed, and her itch went away. Then she suggested they go down for a bath and a rub-down. Couldn't possibly sleep with all that oil on their bodies. Lahya thought so too, though he couldn't help feeling it was a bit naughty and self-indulgent to be having a bath at that time of the night. Mumsy would surely have thought so. But he was not going to tell Mumsy about it anyway. Not just because he had promised Aunt Jamuna that he won't, but because it is good to have some secrets of one's own. Mumsy must have thousands. She didn't even tell him about the new baby until the Ukranian gypsy woman or whatever revealed it for the world and him to know. And no doubt Ariel had a few secrets tucked behind the many voices of his eyes and the many colours of his voice.

She got the water just right. Cool, without being cold. She had a knack of getting things just right. From behind a cupboard she brought out a big bristly loofah which she ran all over Lahya's body. It tickled him, making him laugh. She laughed, too, when he rubbed the same over her body, pushing it in between her breasts and thighs. But then she decided he'd gone too far and needed to be punished. So she spanked him a bit, and pinched his fleshy parts and poked him here, pulled him there and even left a few teeth marks on one or two places of interest.

However, all good things come to an end, and it was time for Lahya to go back to bed. Aunt Jamuna was feeling a lot less lonely and a lot less sad than when she had come up, and it made him feel happy to have made her happy. No need to be too proud of himself though, for she had done the same for him, too. Life was on the up again. And Ariel was his friend.

VI

The up-beat feel continued into the next day.

Three letters arrived for Lahya. One from Ramesh, one from Mumsy, and one from dadso. Lahya was quite drunk with happiness. His first real letters. He even enjoyed receiving, if not reading, the one from dadso.

He couldn't make up his mind whether it was dadso who tried to show his special concern for him by posting his letter separately, or whether it was Mumsy who wouldn't allow dadso to save a few pennies by sharing the envelope; but in the end it didn't matter. It was good to get letters from anyone, but especially from Ramesh, and of course, sweet Mumsy.

Mumsy did not mention anything about how the beautiful white thing within her belly was progressing. In one way he was glad that she did not, but it also annoyed him that Mumsy wasn't 'sharing' the creature with him. Once she was actually out, he would be out, completely. But he did not want to dwell on such dark thoughts, not today, when he was enjoying the first real letters of his life; just after enjoying the first real sex of his life.

And if all that wasn't enough, he got a call from Ariel saying that *Jurassic Park* would have to wait, but he'd be happy to take him to Central Park, if he wished. He was going to Lincoln Center to see a dancer friend of his. He could meet Lahya at Union Square and they'd take the subway from there. Would he like to? Would he, indeed! Lahya was so excited he could hardly decide which of his two jeans to wear.

VII

Lahya got to Union Square at five to eleven, twenty minutes before time. He looked around nervously, trying to run his eyes all over the little garden with its very own statue of Mahatma Gandhi tucked away in a corner. He didn't dare concentrate on any one spot in case he missed Ariel in another. He hoped he had got the directions right and was near the correct entrance to the Subway from among the many that branched out in all directions all over the place. To make matters worse, it was a market day and the place was full of all sorts of two-legged curiosities littering the place like hyperactive kangaroo turds.

Lahya looked at his watch every five seconds, only to find the second hand had moved just one tick forward during that period. Quarter past eleven came, the appointed time, and still no sign of Ariel. A couple of hours later it was half past eleven. No Ariel. It was almost quarter to twelve and Lahya was about to go back home, on the verge of tears – tears of despair at not seeing Ariel, tears of shame at having been made a fool of – when he heard the most beautiful laughter in the world. Ariel was walking his cat walk, his cat eyes glowing like green diamonds in the stark light of the stark midday sun. With him was another friend of his, both carrying bags slung across their shoulders.

Lahya was so pleased to see Ariel, more pleased than he had ever been to see anyone, more so than seeing Mumsy; and he had only met him, what, twice! He felt guilty, disloyal to Mumsy. But more than that, he felt frightened, frightened in a sense he could not describe, much less understand. Frightened, not just emotionally, as in the fear of losing someone you loved; but spiritually frightened, though he would not have been quite sure what that meant.

Something like being frightened of God, or Jesus, or Kali; frightened of someone you were supposed to love, but who you knew had the power to punish you, arbitrarily, wilfully, and severely.

He thought of Aunt Jamuna and last night. It had sort of gone out of his mind over the many hours that he had been waiting for Ariel. Seeing him brought it all back, and the possibility that there could be a link between what happened last night and meeting Ariel made him all the more frightened. It was like being suddenly confronted by a rain forest while ambling along Gravesend High Street.

He was disappointed, too. Disappointed that Ariel was not alone. He had been prepared for the fact that Ariel would be seeing a friend of his at the Lincoln Center, whatever that was, but he had hoped to have his company all to himself before that, on the Subway, and for at least some time after. Anyway, he was here, and they were going to Central Park: that was happiness enough. Mustn't be greedy for anything, especially for happiness, his favourite teacher at his first comprehensive always said. Make the most of it when it comes your way, for it has a way of turning nasty if you don't.

'This is my friend Andy. Andy Zuckermann. He is a photographer. He has to photograph this dancer friend of mine I am going to see. I am trying to get a contract for designing costumes for a new ballet he is in. While my friends are doing some pictures, you and I can have a wander round the Park.'

That was great news. So Lahya *would* be alone with Ariel in the Park. In a way because of this friend who was with him. And to think that he had been annoyed to see him.

Ariel did know how to pick them, though. Short. Squinty little close-set eyes, a drawbridge for a nose. Rough-looking dark hair. Voice like a donkey in distress. Compared to this one, Joost was a beauty.

Still, he was friendly enough. Either naturally so, or Ariel had told him of the boy's abused status and he was trying to be nice out of worthiness. Possibly both. Said he also photographed some rap and soul singers and groups – with unspoken but heavy emphasis on black – and if there were some he'd like to meet, he'd take him along. But only for a little chat and an autograph. After that they'd be all too busy. He'd phone Lahya if he was doing anyone he thought he might be interested in. But in case he forgot, he gave Lahya his phone number to call him sometime and find out for himself.

VIII

Down in the Subway, underground if you like, and in the tube, train if you like, Lahya felt exhilarated and full of joy. Strange, for he hated the New York Subway. Mumsy wouldn't travel by it even if it meant missing her hair appointment. The filthy state of the stations, the filthy state of the trains and the filthy state of the people who used them was all too much for her sensitive nature.

Nothing was different, yet all was different.

The stations along the way were yellowy and brown with dirt and decay. There were aromatic and designer patches of last night's urine and this morning's blood along the platforms and in the carriages. Beggars with bodies that stank and clothes that stuck to the onlooker's eyes as they stuck to the wearer's skin with the stagnant sweat of poverty and decay.

The people in the train were mostly Hispanics or blacks, fat old women and youthful tarts, the odd office type rubbing butts with the endless hoodlum variety; bush forests of armpit hair, coppices of leg hair and impenetrable jungles of head hair, baldies excluding.

The whites were often women desperately trying to cling on to middle age and failing. Years of dieting had taken away the natural voluptuousness of maturity as evidenced by Aunt Jamuna, and replaced it with a sickly half-dead skeletal body, wrinkles deeper than trenches, and a pallor of skin which overdoses of make-up only served to intensify with a glaring lack of subtlety.

Some non-gay young men could be seen reading a book while trying desperately to look gay. Some gay men sat around with studied nonchalance, legs open and shorts torn, prepared for any intrusion into their lives or parts.

Children outdoing each other in crassness, fatness and ugliness underscored the American way of life: eat eat eat till you are twelve then diet diet diet till you die. Their jelly bodies wobbled about with the undulations of the train, their belly faces smiling when they had little reason to, and looking happy when they had less, considering what undoubtedly awaited them in this land of opportunities.

Yes, nothing was different, but all was different. A week ago this spectacle would have filled him with loathing second only to his self-loathing. Today he found it moving and touching. Picturesque. Quaint. And sad. In a nice way. A way that made you want to do something good and wonderful and kind, something to make the world a better place, something to make you a better person.

Ariel laughed his laugh a musician would have given his life to compose, his voice split into colours of the rainbow and he whispered into Andy's ear, 'Some black people are so black!' Lahya jerked his head and looked up at him. There was no look of derision in Ariel's face. Instead, almost an awe, an envy, a lust. His lips were brushing against Andy's left ear. Lahya thought he saw his tongue dart out for a moment and lick the lobe. His face went red, his brow furrowed and he forgot to unfurrow it, all was back to normal again: ugly and smelly and Third World – just as Mumsy said. But then Ariel put his arm round Lahya's waist, looked down at him, and said, 'How do you like it so far, Kiddo?'

'My name is Lahya, not Kiddo,' said Lahya in a sulky voice. But the skies had cleared. He could feel the soft firmness of Ariel's fingers digging into his angular little hip, and a charge of pleasure ran through the largest organ of his body down to a smaller one through the body of his bones. Ariel's breath, as he spoke, smelt of honey and Obsession and mangoes and Poison and papayas.

IX

Out in the sun and Lahya recognised the place. This was where the tragedy of Mumsy and the Museum of American Folk Art was enacted.

Andy was continuing a strain of conversation started a little while ago in the train when most of it had emptied itself out at 42nd Street.

'I was about to take a picture of the dancers, bobbing their dicks about when this man . . .' Andy was stopped mid-sentence by Ariel who elbowed him with a grin and pointed towards Lahya.

'No worries. Kids these days! They know more than we do, let me tell you. Besides, we've all got dicks, haven't we . . .' He turned round to address Lahya directly when Ariel stopped him again, this time by pinching his stomach and whispering, tongue almost darting in and out of the other's earhole. 'I *know* we've all got . . . you certainly have, more than your share, despite your chop job.' Here he laughed his angelic laugh with a devilish joy, '*But* I'm sure the boy will find out what he wants to find out, in his own good time. Without your help. He probably gets more than he needs from his own . . . forget it.' Serious now, almost sombre. 'Don't you think you had better go? Tone will be waiting. I'll see you here in about two hours' time.'

'Make it four.'

'So it's going to be like that then! Only don't have a nervous breakdown in the middle of it.'

'Better than having one two-and-a-half years after the event.'

Ariel laughed, 'You are so mean to me. I should never have told you about it. Anyway, be gentle, if not quick. Four hours can do a lot of damage to a body, especially a dancer's body.'

'You are the expert. Anyway, it's nothing like that. You know taking pictures takes time. You've had yours taken.'

'I *know*. That's why I know!'

'OK. I'll go before you get any more silly ideas. See you in four hours. Take care.'

He kissed Ariel on both cheeks and was about to go but Ariel held on to him, gave him a strong hug, a quick kiss on the lips, and a slap on the neck before releasing him.

Lahya tried not to look but couldn't help it. He wished he was back home, in Gravesend, where he knew what was what, what was done and what was not and what it meant. Here, all was confusion. Rules of life and conduct as he knew them did not apply in New York, and you could reach a false conclusion based on the obvious, or miss out the right one simply because it was obvious.

'And give my love to Tone.' Ariel's mellow green eyes merged with Andy's brown ones so completely they both assumed a liquid hazel appearance.

'As if I won't; so calm your fluttering heart,' assured Andy as he started off in the opposite direction.

'He's cute, isn't he?' said Ariel, looking at Andy's retreating back.

Lahya, almost in tears without quite knowing why, also looked at the retreating back of Andy. A few steps and he turned round to smile and wave at them. Lahya tried truly hard to discern any hint of cuteness, but failed. Perhaps cuteness meant something different in Manhattan. It certainly meant something different to Ariel than it did to Lahya.

He looked down to prevent Ariel reading his response to Andy's cuteness in his eyes. The feet of a man walked past him. Their toenails were unclipped and yellowy with ragged edges. They were cuter than the whole of Andy. But then, perhaps, he was . . . jealous. This was the first time that the J word had walked into his mind and he felt deeply ashamed of himself. Ashamed, and unsure. Unsure even if he wanted to be a beautiful blonde woman any more. Ariel seemed to like ugly men with dark hair. Perhaps there was hope for him yet, as he was.

X

The next four hours were the happiest of Lahya's short life. By the time he got back home he hardly remembered any of it, except the happiness. Overwhelming, overpowering happiness.

The happiest part of the happiness was when Ariel held his hands, looked into his eyes, and said, 'You know, Kiddo – OK, Lahya.' He released Lahya's hands and raised his own as if in mock surrender, 'Lahya, right. You know Lahya, I like children. And you know what, I would have had one of my own, like you. Well, not like you, not as old as you, not sixteen.' Here he laughed his laughter which changed the character of the world, the nature of the beast and turned all suffering to joy. 'Not sixteen but five.' He fell silent and looked up at the blue sky with his green eyes and his green eyes turned blue as they reflected the sky while the blue sky turned green as it reflected his eyes. 'I was so happy. But my wife, she didn't want a child. So . . . so . . . we didn't have it.'

Lahya felt like crying. He was so sad. Sad for Ariel's sake. And so happy. Happy for Ariel's sake. If he became a gorgeous white woman, when he became a gorgeous white woman, he would make Ariel happy; perhaps even . . . it was all so foolish and so silly and so . . . so . . . wonderful. Ariel did not really like ugly men with dark hair. At least not just them. It would be worth his while becoming a gorgeous white woman after all. If only for Ariel's sake. Everything was going to be all right. Yes, it would. It would. It had to. Kali had said so, or as good as. How faithless of him to have ever doubted.

'Was your wife . . .' Lahya began. He wanted to say, 'Blonde,' but hesitated. 'Was your wife,' he began again. 'Was your wife Dutch?'

'British. Come, I'll show you where the skating rink is.' And he lifted Lahya off the ground, like he would a ballerina, and threw him up in the air and pirouetted and caught him in his arms again and danced another step or two, carrying Lahya with the palms of his hands before gently and gracefully depositing him on the ground. He bowed, then started to run, 'Let's see who gets there first.'

British! Chances were she was blonde. Surely white, and of course, a woman . . . after all, she was pregnant, unless he was much mistaken. Lahya *had* to get a white male body to get a white female's body. He just had to. Now more than ever.

He ran as fast as his thin legs could manage, trying to catch up with Ariel. But he didn't have to, for Ariel turned round with a shout and rushed back and caught up with him.

They had ice cream, and cappuccino, and ate pizzas and Russian salad and ran around the lake and scared ducks and swayed from tree branches until even in New York one or two people eyed them strangely to see what they were up to.

XI

Andy came back with not one, but two dancers, both of them black, which more than surprised Lahya; he couldn't say why, after all the man *was* into heavvvy rap and soul photography.

One of them, Benjamin, was *really* black, as Ariel might have put it. The other was Tone, and he was a sort of milk-chocolate colour. Both had dancer's bodies and long necks, but looked quite different otherwise. Benjamin had almond-shaped black eyes without the whites being too prominent, as with some really black persons. His lips were full without being too full, and he had a nice friendly smile. Tone's mouth was tight and compressed, slightly lifted at one corner along with an eyebrow, as if in a state of permanent cynical appraisal of whatever it observed. He had transparent, snake-like eyes, colourless, passionless. He spoke like a snake, hissing his syllables softly; and he walked like a snake, gliding unexpectedly ahead of you, or twistingly behind you. He suddenly said something from one side of you when you were sure he was on the other, and appeared to appear and disappear at will. He scared Lahya, who tried to walk so he could keep an eye on where Tone was, but one blink, and he was somewhere else.

On the way back they took a taxi. Ariel loved taxis, so he said. Andy sat in the front; Lahya had to squash in the back with Ariel one side of him, which was like sleeping in the same bed with Mumsy. Ben was on the far side with Tone pressing against him on the left. Lahya felt his naked snake-like arm devouring him, and when he turned round to smile at him, it was as if he would spit out his tongue and bite-inject some painful poison into his system that would see the end of him before he saw the end of the day. But on the other side his sweat was mingling with Ariel's sweat, promising life eternal.

Ariel dropped Lahya in front of the restaurant. He came out of the taxi to wish him goodbye, which he did by giving him a great big hug and a gentle kiss on the lips.

'Will I see you again?' asked Lahya, half afraid to ask, more afraid not to.

'Of course you will. I'll give you a call.'

With this promise he went back to the taxi, smiled at Lahya, parted his rich lips, bared his kinky teeth, and, raising his arm, exposed his golden underarm crop.

For that unrepeatable moment Lahya couldn't have cared whether he was boy, girl or goat. It was perfect the way it was.

XII

Jayshree was back from hospital, either because she was better or it would have cost too much to stay on, he wasn't sure which. Still, he was happy to know that she was home, and surprised that he was happy. Perhaps he was happy just because he was happy.

However, the happiness was soon to wear off. Three days on, and he could hardly remember it.

Ariel didn't call.

Jayshree wouldn't come out of her bedroom.

Grandma Savitri burst into crackling laughter in the middle of his breakfast and asked him if he had enjoyed his midnight bath. He could have died there and then.

No help from Aunt Jamuna either. In fact, her behaviour had gone quite strange, making him feel quite uncomfortable. He had expected her to be more than her usual effusive self since their friendly encounter the other night. She seemed to have gone cold, or mysterious, irritable or embarrassed, he couldn't make out. She barely spoke to him, except once, to ask for her keys back. He was glad he had had the duplicates made. He brought down the bunch, telling her about the copies of the apartment keys, but remaining silent about the others. She just nodded vaguely without showing much interest. Nonetheless, Lahya got the feeling that she was not best pleased about him having the apartment keys either. However, she said nothing, and he didn't probe any further. At first he put her behaviour down to Jayshree's illness, but then the seed of a thought took hold in his mind and shot forth into a blooming monster of a something or the other in no time. *He hadn't been good enough.* Aunt Jamuna had been disappointed in him. He wasn't surprised. He always knew he was no good, not for anything, and certainly not as a proper man. His father wasn't, as Mumsy well knew, and made clear at any given opportunity. Everything was the fault of that scrawny little black man, but what could he do. Except become like Mumsy.

It was high time he made a serious search for someone to help him keep his end of the bargain with Kali. Nothing less would alter the course of his life for the better.

That afternoon he went into Jayshree's room to ask how she was feeling. She looked so pale and wan that his heart went out to her. He sat by her bedside, held her hand and tried to cheer her up. 'You'll be all right before you know it. Chipping away at me in your best . . .' It was dadso's metaphor and he said it without thinking.

'What sort of a fool do you take me for, you Little Black Zucchini. Of course I'm not going to be well, and well you know it. I am for the kerosene and the matchbox, and the sooner I get used to the idea the easier for all.'

There was such fire in what she said and how she said it, Lahya wasn't even offended at being called LBZ.

Perhaps he could make her happy in a different way, like he did Aunt Jamuna. Well, he hadn't really – made her happy that is – otherwise she wouldn't be acting the way she was. But she was a big healthy woman, with the appetite of a big healthy woman. Jayshree was weak, sick, young. And inexperienced. At the very least, less experienced. He remembered how disappointed she had looked the day she had taken him to the basement and he hadn't tried on anything that was in the magazines they flicked through together.

He didn't really fancy her at all. At least Aunt Jamuna had a bit of flesh on her at the right places, even if there was a lot of it at not the right places. And her face was, well, a proper face, if nothing else. Not twisted and contorted like . . . he tried not to think about it. If you had to do a good deed, you had to do a good deed, and with the best of attitude and as cheerfully as possible.

He bent over the prostrate Jayshree, put one arm round her shoulder, the other upon her dry little breast, and leaned forward to kiss her lips, thinking cod liver oil is good for you.

Jayshree let out a yell, brought her left fist up and caught him on the chin while elbowing him in the stomach. 'You sicko pervert. Get out before I pulverise you senseless and chop your little zucchini for the dogs.'

Lahya was so stunned with pain, fear and shame, the last thing he could do was get out. He could not even move. Jayshree saw the helpless rigidity of his petrified features and took pity.

'What on earth do you think you were doing? Just 'cause I am ill and weak don't mean you can . . .'

Lahya found his voice. Trembling and in tears he tried to explain, 'I was only . . . I thought you might . . .'

'Thought what? Thought I might . . . *like it*? You mean you, *you* thought *I* might . . . You mean you were doing it out of . . . pity! Not even . . . not even horny. Just feeling sorry for me . . . Oh Bhagwan. That is the limit. Shitface. Go lick a dog's ass and never, never come near me again, or I'll, I'll, I don't know what I will, but I'll think of something. Be sure, pencil dick, I *will* think of something . . .'

Lahya could just about stumble out of the room.

He had to talk to somebody. He had to talk to Ariel.

He went to the phone. Fortunately, due to Savitri's abhorrence of the damn thing it was kept out of the way in an alcove by the rarely used dining area.

He dialled.

After a few rings, on came Ariel's beautiful voice, on an answering machine.

He tried later. Answering machine again.

And later. Still the answering machine.

The fourth time he decided to go for it.

After the tone, 'Hi Ariel. It's me. Lahya. I just . . . wanted to talk to you. Thank you. I really enjoyed myself . . . the other day. Will you see me again? Er . . . give me a call.' And then, unable to stop himself, 'I love being with you. I wish I could be with you all the time. I . . . I . . . love you. So much . . .' All the fear and guilt and sense of inadequacy concerning Aunt Jamuna and Jayshree suddenly came to the forefront and he started to cry before he could put the phone down.

XIII

Lahya waited for a return call from Ariel for the entire evening, but none came.

His only relief was that Jayshree did not mention his evil behaviour to Jamuna, or anyone else. He would have to kill himself if she did. He still might, the way things were going. If it wasn't for Ariel . . . Life was certainly worth holding on to, as long as he had the friendship of Ariel. He did realise that his message yesterday had been a mistake, but he hoped Ariel would understand, and forgive. If not, he'd explain. He'd say how sorry he was. It was just that he was worried. His mother was ill. His father was dying. His uncle had threatened him with a sawn-off shot gun. Anything. Anything to explain his foolish message, and even more foolish crying. He did not want Ariel to think he was a crybaby likely to stick to him like glue. That would put him off him completely. For ever and ever and longer.

The next day he decided to phone Ariel early, when he was likely to be home, but not too early when he might be asleep. How to get the right balance. Nine might be too early. Ten too late.

At about a quarter to ten he dialled, but put the phone down after two rings. At ten he dialled once more. After about the fourth ring he was about to break the call again when he heard Ariel's voice. It was like being bathed in cool waters after a day in the Sahara. All it said was, 'Hello.'

'Hi,' said Lahya, 'it's me, Lah . . .'

'Hi. Listen, I am on the other line. I will call you back later.'

Lahya waited by the phone. Five minutes were one hour. Half an hour everlasting. Lahya gathered enough strength to call again. The same sweet, 'Hello.'

'Sorry to bother you but . . .'

'I am really sorry, but I am still on the other line, international. Call you back later. Byee.'

When Lahya called yet again, an hour later, it was the answering machine.

XIV

It was around eleven the next morning that the phone rang. Lahya did not even try to answer it.

A few rings and a few seconds later Jayshree's reluctant voice rang through the house, 'Lahya, telephone.' Both avoided looking at each other as their paths intersected in the hallway. 'Thanks,' murmured Lahya, hoping she'd understand the thanks were for more than just calling him to the phone. He truly was grateful to her for not snitching, and very sorry for what he had tried to do, but he also knew it was better to keep out of her way than to show puke-inviting gratitude. An overdose of his presence or voice might just tip the balance against him.

His hand trembled as he picked up the receiver, wondering who it could be, refusing even to consider the possibility that it might be Ariel. The disappointment of it not being him would be too much anyway, but crushing if he had a hope.

It was him.

'Hi, Lahya. Sorry I couldn't call you yesterday . . .'

Lahya was in a trance. He could hardly hear the words of Ariel. All he could hear was the magic of his voice.

However, he managed to make out that Ariel wanted him to meet for a quick cup of coffee at 10th and University Place, in half an hour.

Lahya took a bullet shower, greased back his hair like Joost, put on his black jeans and white trainers, and was at University Place and 10th two minutes before time. No Ariel.

Second by second, another ten minutes; second by second, another ten minutes. Still no Ariel, until a soft fleshy palm rubbed tenderly against his neck, making him feel warm as freshly milked milk. Ariel was back in dark hair, this time short, with hazel-brown eyes. That explained why Lahya had missed him coming.

Lahya was dying to *explain* his message, to apologise, but didn't know how to start or what to say. Ariel, too, seemed to have something on his mind which he was having difficulty articulating.

It was a quick cup of coffee.

Twice Lahya tried to speak but couldn't even begin. Twice Ariel began. First, 'You know what I think, I think you are looking for . . . for . . . for someone to . . . never mind. Want a cake or something?'

Then again, 'You know I . . . am fond of you, like you . . . a lot, but not the way you . . . Oh I don't know, maybe I am wrong. Forget it.'

Ariel was off and away in less than twenty minutes. He had to go to a rehearsal. He'd call again.

Lahya knew one thing, and one thing above all. He just had to get out and *do it*. Only when he was a gorgeous white woman, like Mumsy, would Ariel take him seriously; and so would everyone else.

Tonight wouldn't be early enough.

XV

Lahya was walking past the railing of the Jamuna to go back home when Aunt Jamuna waved to him from the restaurant. She was standing in the centre of the doorway, half covering her face by holding on to one end of her sari while beckoning to him with the free hand. The posture and gesture were unmistakable in their intent. She wanted him to go over to her but without making it too obvious. Lahya was not sure *he* wanted to, but he felt he had no choice.

'Come on in, my sweet boy, I have a surprise for you,' she said almost breathlessly, as if she had been running a marathon instead of just moving her podgy hand about for about one hundredth of a thirty-second minute.

'What, another?' thought Lahya, trying to imagine the nature of this surprise. He had still not forgiven her for treating him so unromantically after their night of romance. What could be a more final and humiliating rejection than asking for one's keys back!

Jamuna failed to notice his enormous lack of interest and hurried along towards the kitchen, expecting him to follow, which he dutifully did, but with an enormous lack of enthusiasm.

Once inside the kitchen she continued to move ahead past the cook and, unlocking the pantry door, stood to one side to allow Lahya to go in first. She gave a quick look round before getting in herself and shutting the door behind her.

'Here!' she said, producing a brown paper bag from one of the cupboards with a pride and joy that would have been pride and joy enough had she provided the world with a cure for AIDS.

'What is it?' asked Lahya, having visions of poisoned mushrooms weeping for a lost boy's life in their penultimate agony of being cooked prior to being devoured. *That* could be a more final and humiliating rejection than asking for one's keys back.

'Sheermal!' said Aunt Jamuna triumphantly.

'Sheermal?' he had heard the word, something to do with . . .

'Don't look so surprised. I told you I'd cook you your favourite dish, didn't I? I always keep my promises. Special Mogul delight. All the royal princes loved it, like you.'

How could something he had never eaten in all his life be his favourite? But then faith is never without its mysteries. He thanked Aunt Jamuna and took the brown paper bag off her hands. He dared not open it lest the sheermal took its revenge for his no-cognition of it by making a dish of him. He tried to imagine the headlines back home in the UK. I suggest some here:

BRITISH BOY EATEN BY HIS LUNCH IN NEW YORK

The *Independent* might go. The *Sun* would simplify it to

TEA GULPS BOY.

The *Guardian* might want to say,

PAKI GETS JUST DESSERTS BY MAIN COURSE

but end up saying,

IRONY OF TWELVE-YEAR-OLD IN SHEERMAL CONSPIRACY.

And *Today*,

BLACK MAY NOT BE BEAUTIFUL BUT IT SURE IS TASTY!

'What's the matter? Don't you like it? I thought it was your favourite.'

'It's . . . nice. Thank you.' Lahya did not want to go into any explanations.

But Aunt Jamuna apparently did. 'I am sorry for not talking to you the other day. It's just your Grandma. She imagines things. She imagines we had a . . . had a bath together, the other night. That is why I took my keys back. If she found out I had spares, and gave them to you, she'd think we . . . slept together or something impossible like that. She is old and completely senile, but Dileep won't listen to me. She should be put away. In a Home. A Dog Home. Don't tell her I gave you the sheermal. She will claim I gave you the Taj Mahal, and ask Dileep to charge you rent for it. Completely crazy.'

Lahya softened. The poor woman was only trying to be nice. And she was melty, like a rhino-sized dollop of ice cream, and cuddly and . . . cute. Well, if Andy was cute, who wasn't? The J word was stalking Lahya again. And it wasn't Joost. Nor Jamuna. But it's not easy to admit to jealousy.

He looked at Aunt Jamuna again – did they sleep together, or didn't they? Surely there was a bath involved, somewhere along the line. Perhaps it was all his imagination. That is what Mumsy would say. Or his 'wilful lying', as dadso would put it, succinctly.

But, if it was neither, neither imagination nor wilful lying, then, then, he was *not* such a failure after all. Otherwise Aunt Jamuna would not be nice to him now, would she?

Life sure was like a roller coaster. Either up or down, tearing along at breakneck speed, never letting you be in one place, not with any degree of certitude or peace. But it had its moments.

XVI

On his way out Lahya was stopped by the Bengali waiter and steered towards the Blossom–Burt corner. 'End of story,' he winked. And when Lahya looked blank he winked again and nudged Lahya in the ribs.

Lahya almost stumbled across to Burt as he was saying, 'I am really, really happy that you two are back together again,' looking not half as happy as his words, probably because his shorts had disappeared up his crack, causing acute friction between the cheeks. One would have thought that to be reason for greater joy. Apparently not.

'But, "Only as friends", she said, "nothing more." So I said, "I'm *pleased* to hear it," not at all pleased really, but that's what I said, flapping my arms about like a dying whale, like I do when I'm dreadful. "What's *that* supposed to mean?" she says, irritated more by my flapping arms than words. What I should have said was, "I am pleased that there is someone you are just friends with, everyone else is fucking the hell out of you." That's what I should have said. But I didn't. You know what I did say. You wouldn't believe it. You won't. You know what I said. I said, and listen very carefully, I said . . . NOTHING! Yes. Nothing. That's what I said.'

'You're kidding,' said Burt, quite taken aback.

'No. No kidding. Cross my dick and hope never to be sick so help me God. I tell the truth the whole truth and nothing but the truth. *I said nothing.* That shut her up.'

'Well it would, wouldn't it!'

'Still, I'm happy. I love the slut, you know. Doesn't matter if I can't have her. Just looking at her makes me happy. I don't care who butters her butt, the slut! Well I do, but I'd rather she was

~ 177 ~

there than not, in the next room, having it buttered. After all, I've been slutting ever since I was, what, six foot, six-foot one, I forget, but not fully grown anyway. Yes, I'm happy, in a sad sort of a way. But never, *never* again am I going to let that cat of hers scratch my dick.'

'Jesus Christ! She did?? When? I mean how . . .'

'One minute I am happily sleeping away, dreaming of Jeff Stryker or whoever, not that I like big ones, and the next I am being clawed.'

'She must have seen it move or something. Thought it wanted to play or something. Drrreadful . . . eeyeyee, can't bear to think of it.'

'Telling me.'

'Anyway, I am happy now.'

'And I am happy for you.'

'Yeah. It's good to be happy. Thanks honey. I don't know what I'd have done without you . . .'

Suddenly, and without warning, Burt began to cry with jerky sobs. 'I don't know what I'd do without you. You'll still see me, won't you, now that you two are back together again? Won't you?'

'Of *course*, honey. We could go see *Homo Alone* at the Queer Theater. Or . . . listen. Madonna is in town next week. You know I could kill for her autograph. That girl has done more for us girls than Clinton for lingerie or Hillary for hair. You know there is this absolutely fantastic-looking actor who does the Homo part . . . Well-hung, from what I hear, not that I like well-hung. You know how it is. Some men make a girl come, others make her go. A petite dick does more for me. I've had enough big ones to build a ladder to Heaven. Maybe we can go and see the big guy? How does that sound?'

'I think that sounds fantastic. Absolutely fantastic . . .' Burt's crying hiccoughs turned to screams of squealy laughter, which over, he turned serious again, with a note of questioning hope in his voice. 'But what happened to that faghag she had taken on?' The question was obvious, the hope lay in the return of the faghag, thus releasing Blossom once more to Burt's bosom.

'That core-bore whore . . . Well I must admit she was perfect for that slut in more ways than one. You know, you can do what you like with faghags around, no questions asked, and no demands made. Nothing expected and everything accepted. But, unfortunately, and I say unfortunately but mean fortunately, *unfortunately*, she was the very special hag of the white trash; he got a place of his own and she moved in with him. See!' Burt was disappointed, but there was hope. After all, he and Blossom were going to see *Homo Alone*, together.

And if it could end happily for Blossom and there was hope for Burt; there was hope for the waiter and it could end happily for Lahya.

XVII

That night as Lahya sneaked out of the apartment, he had a sense of destiny. Tonight was going to be the night, the night to change his entire life. He was as sure of it as he was of the fact that his mother was a gorgeous blonde woman.

He was out to stalk his prey, and *get it*, as Kali was his protector, he would. He had stopped thinking in terms of 'prospectives' – too vague. Prey was a much stronger word, more positive. He had also given up the idea of tying skateboards together to bring the body home. It was a dumb idea in the first place. Ideally, it would be best to invite the living prey back to the basement. But if, for some reason, through a stroke of luck or mishap the blow was struck outside the house, a shopping trolley was a much better mode of transportation than a couple of skateboards. An old bum slept just a block away with his belongings in a trolley. It would be easy to steal, or borrow; rent even. He had no doubt the old man would be only too happy to loan it to him for a couple of bucks or less.

He had his flight hand-luggage bag hanging from one arm. It contained a hammer, for close work; a brick, to operate from a distance; and a kitchen knife wrapped in the *Village Voice*. Also in the rucksack were some towels, just in case, in case of blood; a rag for a gag, with a roll of sellotape; and a tiny replica of Kali for luck. It was all heavier than he had anticipated, and he lurched this way and that under its weight, looking more like a drunk midget on a binge than a child on a sacred mission, an impression strengthened by the big baseball cap worn the right way round and drooping down to his forehead, purple sunglasses and a raincoat rubbing against his ankles. All this in the hope of being mistaken for a stunted adult and not a twelve-year-old. Anywhere else in the world it would have badly misfired, and he would have stood out in the crowd like Jeff Koons's penis in the world of art – not very big but very visible – drawing that very attention to him that he (Lahya, not Jeff Koons's penis) wished to avoid. Here in New York it worked, especially in the East Village. He could be any of the crazy characters that walk Manhattan by night, or day for that matter, in all sorts of garbs, or lack thereof. It might still be wise to dart in alcoves at the sight of any policeman, even if not fat and short and bald. The lot of them could tell a bit more than given credit for; whether they cared or not was a different issue.

His other paraphernalia for the occasion included a pocketful of quarters, and two five-dollar bills and five one-dollar bills tucked away in his left sock and an equal number in the right, to tempt and lure a suitable subject. Only as a last resort, as it could be dangerous and rebound. But he was willing to risk the immutable magic of money if and when all else failed.

He was hoping his heavier and deadlier tools and tactics would not be necessary until he got back to the cellar with his prey, but it was best to go fully prepared. The time to dilly-dally and shilly-shally was past.

Kali had kept her promise to Grandma by having Granddad done to death, just the way she wanted it; she would surely honour her word to him, provided he fulfilled his part of the deal. And that's just what he was going to do. Tonight.

The stupid boy's faith was so touching. I couldn't but respond with joy.

XVIII

Lahya had just walked a few yards when he thought he felt a hand unzipping his bag from behind, but dismissed the idea. Then he heard this voice, 'What have you got in there?'

Lahya jumped in the air about as high as the weight of the bag would allow him, and in so doing unintentionally dislodged the hand that was inside it. His instinct to run at the first sign of trouble or when in a situation he felt unable to handle with any degree of competence or rationality was thwarted by the other hand of the owner of the first. It rested on his shoulders and held on to him with a kind of fiery strength. The gaze that met his eyes in the half light of the street lamps was resplendent with the same fiery strength.

The hands, the fire and the gaze belonged to a girl of about seventeen, thin and emaciated to the point of starvation, once white, now of greyish-pale colour, wearing a torn and dirty blouse and a long brownish skirt. Her feet were bare on the broken asphalt, her hair clotted with grease, her skin matted with anguish.

'Books, just some books,' blurted Lahya, not sure what to think or do.

The fire seemed to die out in the girl, and she smiled weakly, showing broken, uneven teeth. 'Oh,' she said, 'I thought it was a baby.'

Before Lahya could even begin to imagine how to respond to that, the girl continued, 'They took her away from me. My baby. I won't stay in the hospital. I can't. Can't you see that?' She brought her ravaged face close to Lahya's, expecting confirmation.

'Why don't you go to your mum? Or phone her?' was the first thing Lahya could think of saying.

The girl was happy to carry on with that strain of conversation. 'I did. I called her. But they took my baby.' Tears started to flow out of her eyes and her body began to shake. She held on to Lahya for support.

Lahya just stood there, letting her hold on to him without knowing what else to do or say. It was the girl who spoke again, 'Let me see your eyes. I want to see your eyes,' and with this she reached out and removed Lahya's purple sunglasses. 'Nice eyes.' She stopped crying and smiled. 'You've got nice eyes. They're kind.' She started crying again, not used to kind eyes.

Lahya stretched out his hand and as gently as he could took his sunglasses out of her hand, trying not to let go of the alleged kindness of his eyes.

'Are you sure you don't have my baby in your bag?' She was a bit suspicious now and once again reached towards his bag.

'I am sure, look.' He quickly let her have a glimpse inside the gap, and then moving away said, 'Look, I have to go now. Mums . . . my mother will be waiting.' He tore his body away from her eyes and started to walk away, feeling both very relieved and very guilty.

The girl's eyes followed him till he was almost at the corner of the next block, then softly she called out, 'Watch out, or they will take your baby away.'

Only when he had crossed over to the other side of the avenue he thought he should have given the girl some money. Although she hadn't asked for any, she looked like she hadn't eaten for days. He turned round to see if she was still there. She was, and he almost went back to give her a couple of quarters or a dollar, but then felt the time had gone; that it would look foolish now. It was too late. Why it was too late he couldn't be sure, just that he felt it was too late.

XIX

Just round the corner an oldish black man with a greying beard blocked his path and waved a chain in front of him. 'Solid gold. Twenty-four carat. You can have it for just twenty dollars.'

Lahya tried to make his way past him but he followed. 'Belonged to my mother. How much can you give? Twenty-four-carat gold.' As Lahya continued to walk ahead, the man got hold of him and thrust the chain into his hand. Before Lahya could respond the man took a cigarette lighter from his pocket and began to burn a section of the chain. 'See, pure gold! Want some food, man. How much've you got? Gimme what you got. Just gimme what you got. Anything, man. Got to eat.' Lahya was about to dip into his socks when the old man quickly withdrew the chain from his hands and turned away. Lahya looked up surprised to confront the surprisingly flat stomach of a tall blond policeman. Lahya's mouth watered. He'd look so good lying dead beneath Kali's feet. Dead, and naked. His eyes blushed and his face became sweatier as his body inadvertently sent his hand to his crotch, but the brain withdrew it with equal speed.

It was past midnight and most roadside sellers were beginning to sort out their wares from the sidewalk and putting them away in black garbage bags for the return journey home, if they had one. One tough-looking man, black and no older than twenty, was still standing by his wordly possessions spread out at his feet. Behind him, on the side of a big brown box, scrawled in white chalk were the words, GOING TO JAIL SALE.

A trendy man in denim shorts and a shoulder bag was kneeling to one side of another man towering above him, trying on a pair of roller blades upon which New Yorkers roll by on the roads at seventy miles an hour, winding their way between cars and death. 'Can you lend me five dollars, please?' The trendy man looked up at Lahya and asked pleadingly, 'He's only asking eight dollars for these. Please.' Lahya ignored the request and hurried on.

Enough time-wasting. He was now in a hurry to get to Avenue A and Tompkins Park. There, among the leather, stud and nose-ring battalion would he get the dissolute but still sturdy and young specimen of white manhood he needed for his sacrifice.

He was well into the end bit of St Mark's Place when another girl ran into him. Also white, this one was plump and well-fed, and in the middle of a nervous breakdown. Crying and screaming hysterically she started mumbling something to Lahya. He could not understand a word of what she was saying, either because she was so overwrought or she was speaking a foreign language. He tried to calm her down, holding her by one shoulder while attempting to put his arm round her. Fortunately, another girl, Indian-looking, came to his rescue, pushed him aside and shouted, 'What the fuck are you doing to the poor girl? Beat it or I'll give you a kick up your ass so hard you'll shit out of your face for a month.' Following that beautiful thought with a threatening look she took the hysterical girl to one side and sat her down on the steps of some apartment building and cuddled her. She had a can of Coke in her hand which she offered to the girl, who began to gulp it down with a violent ferocity rarely associated with plump nubility.

Lahya, not to be outdone by the foul-mouthed Indian girl's offer of liquid refreshment to that out-of-control sample of femininity, and as an act of expiation for not giving anything to the starving girl with the lost baby, dared to go over to the duo, risked shitting through his mouth for at least a month, and took out two dollars from his left sock. 'Here, get her a pizza, or something.'

The foul-mouthed Indian girl looked a little surprised, glowered at him, but took the money without any verbal or silent show of thanks and put it in her blouse. Lahya moved on towards Tompkins Park, now a few steps away, his good deed done.

Even those few steps were not without hazard. He nearly trod on a dying black man. Or what looked like a dying black man. He was holding on to his belly and rolling on the pavement. His feet were swollen and his toes falling off. His face was convoluted with pain and his body reeked with the stench of death and loneliness. A thin white man, young, with absolutely no flesh on his skeleton or teeth in his mouth, came over and tried to help the black man up, but the other succeeded in getting him down. As they both moaned and groaned on the sidewalk, the sound of a live rock band in the café opposite adjusted its rhythm to their oscillations. If Lahya had not been on a life-and-death mission himself, he would have started dancing round the convulsing bodies to the beat of the music. That would have been a way of honouring their suffering, if drink and drugs and nothingness constitute suffering or deserve honouring.

One last look back and he was transfixed.

In the middle of the road, still alive with traffic, in the creepy bloodless glow of the street lights, walked a tall, thin woman. She was nearly naked, her arms were clasped round her breasts, her hands grasping the jutting-out bones of her shoulders. Her head was tilted to one side, indeed her entire body was leaning at a peculiar angle. She continued walking in the middle of the road, regardless of cars or taxis brushing against her near-naked body. Just walked. And leaned. She was going in the opposite direction, westwards, and Lahya followed her with his eyes for as long as he could. She didn't wait for the signal at the crossing and kept walking, straight ahead, in the middle of the road, hugging herself, walking, and leaning, as if in another world, another dimension.

Lahya was brought back to three dimensionality by a rattling cup. 'It's my birthday,' said a tall lanky black man, 'I'm twenty-nine.' He rattled his cup some more and smiled a most endearing and hopeful smile.

Lahya reached into his socks and pulled out his dollar bills. As he handed one to the black man, he heard a voice say, 'He's conning you. He has a birthday every day.'

'I swear it's my birthday. I swear on my mother's life who gave me birth this day twenty-nine years ago. It is.'

Another voice said, 'So what if it isn't. If you die every day you are born every day.'

Still another voice spoke, 'Speaking of mothers, my dick is mother naked. Gimme some of that money for a condom to cover up its shame.'

Lahya looked about him and saw that he was surrounded by about five men of various hues, heights and builds. They had seen through his disguise, and they had seen his dollar bills.

'Leave him alone,' said the birthday boy.

'Or what?' said the naked dick.'Or this . . .' But Lahya didn't have the chance to see what 'this' might have been. A police car rolled alongside with the quietness and stealth of police cars around the Tompkins Park area. In the distance a different sort of police car could be beard roaring past, sirens going full throttle.

The men around Lahya disappeared so quickly they never were, and Lahya dived into the pizza place advertising a pizza slice and a soda for just one dollar fifty, at the corner of 8th and A.

XX

The pizza place turned out to be the best idea of the evening. With large glass windows opening out on both St Mark's Place and Avenue A, Lahya could see a whole array of desirables scattered all over. Tompkins Park was just across the road, and, although closed at that time of the night, its small yet comforting presence was soothing to the weary of mind and body.

Inside the pizza place itself were Mohawks, and ponytails and curlies; green hairs and pink heads and rainbow stripes; nipple rings, nose rings, tongue studs and eyebrow safety-pins; massive hairy chests and necks with 'cut here' instructions, not to mention tattoos of all varieties on sexes of all varieties. Leathers and denims and nothings.

Outside it was rich pickings, some great possibilities ruined by dogs, but nonetheless, no shortage. Just as Lahya was deciding on his prey and the best approach, the choice was virtually made for him by circumstances.

A ringed and studded leather-jacketed girl was busy rummaging in the trash can directly under the window where Lahya was just finishing off his Sicilian. A ringed and studded leather-jacketed young man came and stood behind her, awaiting his turn. The girl felt a presence close by, turned up her head to look, then yelled a hell of a yell and scrammed.

Lahya was surprised. Had there been someone in a grey suit skulking behind the girl he might have better understood her highly pitched consternation; or a copper – though in New York a remarkable indifference was shown towards the greys and blues. But the studded lad, named Angus by Lahya on the evidence of natural red in his upright hair, should have been a kindred spirit, approved and welcomed. But then Lahya saw the reason for the girl's lack of cool. Angus had an enormous rat sitting on his shoulders, proving that even an emancipated young lady with nails on her tongue and a shaved head found some prejudices hard to piss out of her system. That Angus quickly dived into the trash can without any attempt to soothe the frayed nerves of his predecessor showed that liberated men were equally reluctant to surrender their crassness for a touch of sensitive counselling. The rat had an air of intelligent unconcern about him more sophisticated than either of the protagonists of the little drama.

Lahya believed that there was something about the impressive height, broad-shouldered virility and rough good looks of this product of the Almighty's unbridled creativity which would well please the great Kali. Some might have agreed. There were as yet no visible signs of disintegration in the packaging of the said product to cause any affront to the goddess's taste in male meat. Any mental degeneration, however advanced, would only be a source of amusement to her – Kali's sense of humour was well extolled, by me if no one else – while moral decadence was merely a human preoccupation and never bothered the gods anyway, having no place in the higher scheme of things. Spiritual decay was impossible – that which is of the spirit cannot and does not decay.

The Sicilian inside him, Lahya jumped off the high stool and ran out to where Angus was vigorously out to despoil the contents of the overlarge trash can, overlarge, but otherwise of ordinary character and appearance. Angus looked up for a second but went on foraging, quite rightly expecting Lahya to be patient till his turn.

'Looking for something to eat?' said Lahya with great insight but not enough sensitivity.

Angus couldn't believe he heard what he heard but believing what he believed he heard he responded, 'No. I've lost my grandmother.'

'Funny you should say that,' said Lahya, unabashed, stealing and reshaping the birthday boy's story, 'my grandmother died this very day, almost this very hour.'

'Yes, that certainly is funny. I can't stop my sides from splitting.' Angus straightened up to his six foot plus and looked down upon Lahya with crucial concern. For sure this boy was from the ghettos of Wonderland. His oversized raincoat on a dry-as-Reagan's-asshole day, the purple sunglasses . . . Suddenly and disturbingly Angus felt normal by comparison, and it hurt. The boy had already scored one over him just by being, and now he was trying to put one more across on the strength of utter unredeemed stupidity, a formidable weapon at the worst of times, almost unbeatable at one o'clock in the morning on an empty stomach.

At the risk of splitting hairs, not sides, Lahya wanted to say, I meant funny peculiar and not funny ha ha, but not wanting to antagonise his quarry he said instead, 'You see, we have a custom in our family to feed a . . . hungry person on the day, and if possible the time, of a loved one's death. Helps their spirit, along the way, to . . . Nirvana.' He wasn't too keen on the band, but he knew from *Panorama* or *Weekend World* that such terminology was appreciated by white shits.

'So,' said Angus, 'you are offering yourself as food?'

Lahya slapped his thigh and laughed, 'Ha, ha, that was good,' while thinking what a load of crap. 'That was good. No. I mean, if you come with me, I will give you something to eat. In honour of my grandmother. Dead. Normally it is the son who finds a beg . . . the right person. But my father is in Jai . . . hospital. Punctured lung. So I have to . . .'

Angus looked at Lahya sideways, trying to figure out if he really was a kid or really was a midget. Either way he really was a weirdo. Once again he felt upstaged and once again it hurt.

'What's your game, kid? If you *are* a kid and not the creature from the pink lagoon. Are you trying to pick me up or something?'

'Oh no. I couldn't. You are too heavy for me. You'll have to walk I'm afraid.' Lahya smiled his most attractive and naive smile.

'Tall, handsome *and* witty! What next. Where do I have to walk to?'

That hurt where it hurts the most. But things were looking up as far as his mission was concerned. 'Jamuna Restaurant. You know, it's only . . .'

'I know. On the corner . . .'

'Yes. Yes. My father owns it. You can even bring some food back with you. Last you a day or two. Leftovers. Bread and things. We never use anything left over after midnight. It's not bad or anything. Perfect . . . Might even be some money in it for you. Five, ten quid . . . bucks . . . for my Grandma's spirit.' In his desperation Lahya was in danger of overplaying his hand, but he couldn't help it. Angus looked too good to be lost. He resisted the temptation to dive into his sock and bring out a five-dollar bill. Only as a last resort, he reminded himself.

Angus looked more and more puzzled, so much so that for one brief moment he actually felt like telling the weird boy to stuff his food and money but quickly dismissed such unholy thoughts before they polluted his brain cells.

'Let's go,' he said. What could the boy do? He'd strangle him with two fingers if he tried anything.

'Great,' said Lahya, as he felt great. 'You won't regret it. Come, follow me, Angus.'

Angus stopped in mid-step. 'What did you call me?' His nostrils flared and a mixture of fear and rage and something unnamable fought for supremacy in his deep-set eyes.

Lahya immediately realised he had put his foot in it again with his name game. 'Nothing. I called you nothing. Honest.'

'Yes, you did. You called me Angus. How did you know my name? No one has called me that in . . . in . . . months. Everyone here calls me Red. You're a detective aren't you. My Mom sent you . . . Didn't she? Or my dad? Did he? I should have known. The raincoat. Those glasses. How corny can you get. How young are they pulling these days . . . How old are you, fifteen? My God!'

Lahya's heart warmed to Angus. Fifteen! He must be more gaga than he thought. Maybe bad eyes, even the strongest can suffer from those, and no money for glasses. That should help. A semi-blind prey would be easier to tackle.

'No. Honest. No. On my moth . . . on my father's life. I called you Angus because . . . because I had a hamster once, called Angus. Your rat reminded me of him. I called *him* Angus. Not you. I called your rat Angus, because of my rat . . . hamster. Swear. Honest. What a coincidence. You're named after my hamster. No. Not after him. I mean same as . . . Honest . . .'

Curiously, Angus seemed much disappointed instead of appeased. 'So my parents didn't hire you, or your outfit?' His voice trailed off.

'No. I swear not. On my life . . .'

'You're right. They wouldn't bother. Never did before, why should they now? Let's go.'

Lahya was happy beyond belief as they both started walking in step towards the Jamuna. Despite his need for food and his extra-long limbs, Angus was not going too fast for Lahya's diminutive legs. The street teaches you the pointlessness of being in a hurry.

A short way down the road and Angus stopped. 'You said something about money?'

'Yes, but . . .'

'Come on then. I need it. Now. For your grandmother, remember!'

Lahya did not know what to do, but felt he had no choice. Rather reluctantly he bent over, pretending to tie his shoelaces and as surreptitiously as possible took out his dollar bills. His encounter with the birthday boy had taught him not to be too open about dishing out his wealth. He gave Angus five.

'Is that all?'

Lahya gave him another five. 'That's all I have here,' he lied; then, seeing the other's face, dug out a few quarters from his back pocket.

Angus seemed satisfied. Leaving Lahya standing he walked to his right, the wrong end of the avenue as far as Lahya was concerned. I've gone and lost him, he fucked to himself. Angus stopped to talk to one of the many dealers hanging about the corners and some quick exchange took place. Within no time he was back, relaxed and smiling. 'Let's go my friend.' He gave Lahya a 'my friend' pat on the back which sent him rolling across the street. He'd be tough to kill, he fucked to himself, again steadying against a shop front.

Mangoes were temptingly on display among a host of other fruit and goodies. At that time of the night, to a Gravesendian from Britain it was surreal.

A Chinese man smiled at him expectantly. Lahya smiled back, then turned his attention back to Angus. Must keep him in sight. Too much was at stake.

XXI

In the basement Angus looked about him and was impressed by what he saw. Lahya had carefully drawn the curtains across the alcoves containing the shrines to linga and yoni, and placed one of the two Chinese screens in front of Kali's little temple. He had also turned the video boxes around in such a way that the identifying legends were no longer visible. All magazines and other articles of sexual character were hidden away in cupboards. Unlike in the case of Dirk – Patrick – who was specially coming over for sex videos, he wanted this occasion to be simple and homelike and respectable. Granddad would not have approved, but he had had his day, and night/s, by all accounts, and now it was Lahya's turn.

'Neat, man. I like it already. Wow. Even a ceiling fan. Turn it on, man. It's hot.'

Lahya was surprised that he hadn't noticed the ceiling fan until then. Anyway, he turned it on. Cool air swept through the room like kindness.

'What's to eat? Anywhere I can piss?'

Lahya carefully placed his bag in an easily accessible corner, took off his raincoat, put his glasses in one of its pockets and, dumping it next to the bag, pointed towards the bathroom. 'You go piss and I'll get you some food. And beer.'

Angus hurried in. That was the first time Lahya saw Angus hurry, but he came back out in an equal hurry, just as Lahya was about to go into the restaurant through the last door in the basement. That was the second time Lahya saw him hurry.

After seeing Angus hurry for the second time, Lahya saw him embarrassed for the first time.

'Great bathroom in there,' said Angus, looking a bit embarrassed.

He fidgeted a little, crossing and uncrossing his feet. Hope he doesn't wet the floor here, thought Lahya. He can't be thinking the bathroom is too good to piss in, even with a name like Angus he can't be that stupid!

'Can I have a shower? Would your mom, whoever, mind . . . if I . . . I haven't had a shower in . . . years. Well not years . . . seems like years, but . . .' Angus was looking more and more embarrassed.

'Sure, go ahead. Give me time to sort some . . . anything special you like?'

'Fresh hot bread? I guess it's too late for that. But some fresh hot bread . . . I love the smell of fresh hot bread.'

'I am not sure. But I'll see what's there. You go have your shower. I'll be back soon.'

'Thanks. Thanks a million. I'll remember that. Thanks. Christ, it'll be great to have a shower again.' Angus was in danger of becoming maudlin and Lahya excused himself quickly to avoid that nauseating possibility.

There was another possibility Lahya was trying not to confront: coming back with food and finding both Angus and the television gone. Along with a few other friends, such as Mr Video and Ms Stereo and . . .

But still, nothing ventured nothing gained, as his favourite teacher . . .

He couldn't let Angus die without his last meal. And the shower was a great idea. Pity he hadn't thought of it himself. A sacrifice had to be clean in order to be acceptable. Especially when it is flesh you are after. The flesh had better smell fresh, and warm, like newly baked bread.

He could already see himself as a beautiful blonde girl with creamy white skin wearing red court shoes and Mumsy proudly introducing her to her friends, 'Meet Sigourney, my first daughter. Isn't she pretty. Of course my second girl is pretty too, but this one, she is absolutely positively gorgeous, just like me.' And everyone will agree, 'Yes, isn't she, gorgeous, just like you. And Sigourney, what a pretty name too . . .'

Ariel would be so thrilled to meet her, and forget about Joost and Andy and Tone, even his wife, and . . . and . . . what else was there?

XXII

It took Lahya a while to get the food ready. Many of the things were locked, and he was lucky to have Jamuna's keys to get what he wanted. Then he had to heat up some food: stuffed eggplant and pilao rice, bhindi bhujya and nan bread with channa masala. He picked up two bottles of Budweiser, the only name he knew, and also a bottle of red wine. In a brown paper bag he put some bread – no fresh was available, and it made Lahya sad not to be able to fulfil Angus's last wish – and a few cans of beans and sweetcorn and beers. Of course Angus wouldn't be needing all that since he wouldn't be there to need it, but he had to take it down, just to make everything real, so as not to arouse any suspicion. An unsuspecting, well-fed, relaxed Angus he could do away with, taking him by surprise from behind. An alert and suspicious Angus would be beyond his strength and capabilities.

Yes, he would have to get Angus relaxed, drowsy, even asleep. The thought of Angus drowsy began to make him feel drowsy. He had had a good post-sheermal nap in the afternoon – it was OK that sheermal, sent him to sleep anyway. And he had slept from about just after nine to twelve, but still, the last couple of hours had been tense and tiring, and the warm heat of the kitchen was numbing his senses. He might need a shower himself, a cold shower to perk himself up. The biggest night of his life, and he couldn't afford to throw it away because of drooping eyelids.

XXIII

When Lahya came back down there was no Angus. He quickly looked to see if the television was there. It was. At the same time sounds of splashing water in the bathroom accompanied by some near-human shouts of what may have passed for delight indicated that the man was still enjoying his shower.

Lahya pulled the coffee table a little closer to the television, just in case, and began to set out the food and the drinks. He left the bag of goodies next to the table, brought a chair and placed it at the most accessible angle to the food. He was no longer feeling sleepy, and everything appeared under control.

Angus came out, his still wet body inadequately wrapped round the waist in a small pink towel. One of his thighs was bare right to the top where a tight little knot kept the two ends of the towel together, digging in to the man's side. With another small pink towel he was drying his hair and his torso. The rat sat on his shoulders looking eager and alert and happy as Angus.

'You haven't got any clothes you could spare, just to borrow. Only to borrow. Needn't be leather. Anything old would do, as long as it's clean. I'd like to feel clean, at least for as long as it lasts. I couldn't use your shower again, could I? Some day? I mean even if it isn't your grandma's anniversary? I've still got some money left I could use to launder my own clothes tomorrow and return yours.' He was talking fast, as if talking slow might let the moment slip away and he'd wake up dirty and smelly again. There was a mixture of hope, pleading and joy in the voice.

'I don't think so. Nothing that would fit you. My uncle . . . dad is only half your size, if that . . . I can't think of anyone . . .' He felt like telling him he wouldn't need clothes where he was going, but thought it best not to.

'Just thought I'd ask. If you don't ask, you don't get. That's the first lesson you learn on the street. Mind you,' and this was where things began to go wrong, though Lahya did not sense it just then, 'mind you, I didn't ask for any of this. You are an angel, you know that, a little angel. My own little angel. When I get rich and famous I will build you a palace. Just for you, with the biggest, most beautiful bathroom in the whole world.'

There was a degree of buoyancy in Angus's manner which was due to more than just a shower, however wonderful that may have been. Lahya realised this when Angus came forward and carefully laid a syringe on one corner of the table saying, 'Don't touch that, if you know what's good for you . . . Hare Jesus Krishna Lord! That does look good. Amanda Lee would love it.' Angus stared open-mouthed at the food with more delight than Lahya ever thought possible at the sight of mere food. But he didn't start wolfing it down immediately as Lahya had expected. Perhaps his fix had dulled the pain of his hunger. He sat Amanda Lee on the table and picked out large bits of food and put them on a plate in front of her. Amanda Lee walked on to the plate and began eating with sharp jerky nibbles.

Angus himself was about to sit at the table when he turned to Lahya again. 'Not even some underpants? Mine are full of shit and made of cardboard – almost, anyway. I'm sure I'd be able to fit in some underpants. I'm sure I would.'

Lahya inadvertently looked at one of the cupboards. It had underwear. Female, male, unisex. Open-crotch and full of holes where holes ought not to be, not in underwear, though in flesh. Transparent and lace and filly. Leather even, with more holes. And zips, and studs and buckles. Angus would have died for one of those, or not. Lahya couldn't be sure what people died for. It was always a mystery to him how anybody could be willing to die in order to change the name of a country, or to make some man or group of men own a piece of it without in any way improving the lives of those who died, were that possible. But then, he was a stupid little boy and did not understand much.

'You eat your food, and I'll have a look,' said Lahya. He didn't want Angus to start searching through the cupboards himself. That would change the tone of the entire evening, and things were going just perfectly as they were. Any alteration in the ambience and everything could go wrong.

Lahya needn't have worried. Once Angus started on his food he could have brought out the contents of the entire basement and Angus wouldn't have cared what he was up to. Lahya managed to discover a fairly innocuous-looking pair. Plain white jockey shorts of an elasticky material. There was a sort of built-in bulge in the front, but otherwise nothing sensational.

'Hare Jesus Krishna Lord!' exclaimed Angus when he saw the shorts. 'Where did you get those! That is style, man, and expensive. Must have cost what . . . well over fifty bucks or something?' He looked at Lahya with a strange look. 'What is it that you want from me? You can't be doing all this for your dead grandmother or else I am your dead grandmother. What *is* your angle? You want to fuck with me?'

'No. No. I swear not. I'm just a kid. I am doing this for my . . .'

'Yeah, yeah, for your dead . . . I know. As for being a kid, I know that too. I was a kid myself, not that long ago. You said you were fifteen, didn't you? I started at ten. With my neighbour's girl. So don't kid me, kid.' He took the shorts from Lahya and started to put them on. Lahya turned away so as not to look. He wanted to keep his thoughts on his plan. Nothing else mattered, even if there was a curiosity, an excitement even.

'You don't get innocent on me, and I won't get innocent on you. I have done it before, for less. With fat old men and ugly old women. You name it, I have done it, once for just a cup of coffee, when I was new on the streets. You get smarter after a while. So if you want to fuck with me, you're welcome. I've done it for less, much less, and with worse. As I said. Not for a long time though. Anyway, I'm not playing the innocent. Let me have a shower now and then and you can do it when you want, what you want. I won't take a bottle brush. Never again.'

It was Lahya's turn to be embarrassed. The tone of the evening *had* changed, and there was nothing he could do or not do to undo it. He tried to say something but could think of nothing suitable. He opened his mouth, shut it, opened it again, shut it again, and kept it shut. He was not usually at a loss for words, and this inability to speak embarrassed him as much as the cause of it.

'All right, if that's the way you want to play it, that's the way we'll play it,' said Angus, now in sexy white shorts, going back to his food. Or rather, drink. After he had dried up the Budweiser bottles he stretched out his legs and inhaled a deep breath, looking comfortable and satisfied and pleased. Lahya thought the time had come.

Suddenly it wasn't that easy any more. Suddenly he found his limbs freezing with a sort of dread he did not know existed.

What would he do about Amanda Lee? She was back on Angus's naked shoulder.

XXIV

Lahya had yet not plucked up courage enough to go for his bag and the hammer when Angus woke up from a half doze and went back into the bathroom. He returned with his clothes. Putting his hand into one of the pockets of his jacket he brought out a small paper bag. In it was a little glass box. He began to delicately empty its contents out on the table, a white powder. Then out with a razor blade wrapped in cloth. He edged the powder in a straight thin line, took out a little hollow tube and began to inhale. Halfway through he invited Lahya to join in, but Lahya declined, tempted though he was. Angus shrugged his shoulders and continued. Then he produced a thin, rolled-out cigarette and a lighter. Lighting the cigarette, he relaxed back in his chair and began to smoke. He offered that to Lahya as well, but Lahya refused again. 'Open the bottle of wine for us, please,' said Angus.

For a moment Lahya thought, shit, I forgot the bottle opener, will have to go up to the kitchen again, but then he remembered Granddad's drinks cabinet, and there it was. Soon Angus was smoking away the aromatic weed and drinking wine out of the bottle. All that on top of his snorting and needling. He might as well die without any help from me, thought Lahya. Would that count? It should. After all he brought him in, didn't he?

Then, quite without any warning that it was coming, Angus began to cry. His big body shook in childlike spasms and tears poured down his face like winter rain. Lahya instinctively went over to comfort him. That was a mistake.

'My angel,' boohooed Angus. And then, in between sobs and tears, carried on, 'My little angel. I've never met one like you in all my life. And I've been looking. Believe me, I've been looking. My guru taught me we are all gods within, you've just got to know how to look. I've looked, believe me I've looked. But I found no gods. Just shits. All shits. Like me. Maybe that's why. I got shits because I was shit.

'But God must have known that shit though I was, I was seeking. At least I was seeking. And so He sent you. Just to show He exists. *IS*. Understand!' He was slobbering all over Lahya now, calling him 'my angel' and begging his forgiveness for offering him his mortal body when Lahya had given him his eternal soul, for suggesting a fuck when he should have given love. Love, not slove or plove, or blove or lllove, as his guru had explained. His guru said all the problems in the West rose from the fact that the West had no vocabulary for love, and that the same word was used for fucking as for liking a pair of jeans as for worship. He explained to Lahya as his guru had explained to him. Slove was what normally passed for love. Love of a man for a woman and the other way round. It was only slove, sexual love. Demanding, jealous, ungiving, based on ownership, unforgiving, conditional. Anything but love. Just an addiction, like the worst of bad drugs. The complete opposite in fact. For love was non-attachment, undemanding, unconditional, non-ownership. Plove was possessive love, like parents have for children; again demanding, again conditional. Flove was just fancy, like loving potatoes and fluffy dogs and sexy chicks. Lllove was simple lust. And blove was boring love: love that claimed to go on and on simply because it was never there in the first place. All our lovers were slovers or plovers or blovers or flovers. Not lovers at all. He had begun to think love just not was. But then Lahya came along . . .

The big white man was now kneeling at Lahya's feet, kissing his hands, crying all over his knees and begging to wash his feet with his tears.

All the while Amanda Lee was clinging on to his shoulders, adjusting her little paws to maintain her balance as Angus shook and cried and kissed Lahya's hands and touched his feet. Lahya would grow up to be the saviour, the redeemer. It had to be somebody from India, and somebody who knew how to love from an early age. His guru had spoken to him of such a one, and he had said he'd meet him one day. Who'd have believed he'd be chosen to meet him? Just when he had given up all hope. Just when he was going through the dark night of the soul. Amanda Lee. It must have something to do with Amanda Lee. She must be the reincarnation of some true sage, and shown him to the Messiah for being good to her, for loving her. Yes, Amanda Lee was the only person in the world he had truly loved. But that was because nobody had loved him except Amanda Lee. Not even his parents. Especially not his parents. Yes, he owed it all to Amanda Lee. Otherwise he was not fit to look upon Lahya's feet, much less wash them with his tears.

Stupid though Lahya believed it all was, brought about by drugs and drinks and food after a stretch of hunger, yet he could no more kill this man worshipping at his feet than he could Mumsy.

Nothing would have been easier than to kill him in his present state. He would probably bow his head and offer it to be chopped off if Lahya suggested it. But that very ease made it impossible. No. He could no more kill Angus than he could Mumsy. Or Ariel.

And if he couldn't kill Angus, he could not kill anyone else.

But neither was it possible for him to go on as he was. Not any more. His pact with Kali could not just be broken off like that. The goddess had to be appeased. She must have her sacrifice. He had to kill himself. He must. He couldn't risk what she might do to Mumsy, or to anyone else. To Ariel even. But if he killed himself, she would have her sacrifice. It would be a rather poor sacrifice, but then she wouldn't have to do anything in return. Just not do something. That was not asking for much, surely.

He put the question to Kali. I said nothing. He took my silence for assent. As men often do.

A sort of peace descended upon him. A sort of peace he had never known in all his short life.

Of course he had thought of killing himself before. But that was not like this. That was childish fantasy. This was for real. For Mumsy. For Ariel.

He took the big white body of Angus in his arms. He didn't care what white people had done to black people, or to anyone else. A white man was a man same as a black man, same as a white woman or a black woman or a rat called Amanda Lee. Same as dadso. What a revelation that was! It didn't matter if dadso was short and ugly and the colour of dried-up camel shit: he just was. Lahya's heart unfroze, the blood in his veins smiled a warm happy smile and the world was renewed. It did not matter if he was short and ugly and the colour of dried-up camel shit. He just was. Soon he wouldn't be. And then all would be well, for all would be nothing. And nothing mattered. Nothing was all that mattered.

His arms hardly went half round Angus, but he held on to him, and rocked him back and forth, like a baby, like a newborn baby.

He felt sad at the thought of dying. He didn't really want to die. Not any more. But he couldn't live. Not any more. Suddenly life was wonderful and worth living. He must make the most of it, what was left of it. And cherishing Angus was one way of making the most of what was left.

He so wanted to see Mumsy before he died, but he wouldn't be able to. He begged Kali to let him see Mumsy before he died. And Ariel. He must see Ariel too. He would die if he didn't see him and he couldn't die without seeing him.

In the meantime he rocked big Angus in his arms, cuddling his naked body like a baby, like a newborn baby.

PART VI

The Parting

I

Lahya got to sleep at about four in the morning. He was so physically and spiritually exhausted, or exalted, both equally draining, that he didn't wake up until five postmeridian.

When he came down from his room there was an air of death about the place. Understandable. Jayshree was dead.

Savitri told him his parents had been informed. His father was not in a position to take more time off so he would not be coming, but 'Mumsy' would be over in a day or two. She would take Lahya back with her. His school would be opening shortly and she was not happy with the idea of him travelling on his own.

So he *was* going to see Mumsy before he died. Kali had granted his wish, even though it meant killing Jayshree.

He was responsible for her death.

It seemed he was the only one in the house who truly grieved for the poor girl.

II

The next couple of days went if they never were, as if Jayshree never was, her angular, lopsided figure never hobbled its way along the hall for a shit, or across the street for a mango in Tompkins Park; as if her twisted lips never yearned for a kiss from her mother or the boy in apartment 17A. As if she did not know the meaning of pain.

Apart from a visit to the temple and from what might have been a brief but violent stampede of priests, life went on as normal. Savitri had her lunch, and her before- and after-lunch naps; Jamuna spent most of her time down in the restaurant, Dileep minding his taxis and his father's shops and those who were paid to help him with all that.

There were, of course, occasions of comic relief. A couple of times when some visitors arrived, Savitri erupted into wailing and moaning and rocking back and forth in anguish and wringing her hands, crying what a pity it was that her dearly beloved little girl could not find her pills when she had her last attack. How she must have suffered and died in agony and how her poor grandmother suffered and lived in agony.

Uncle Dileep was twice caught laughing out loud with some of his friends and then tried to look sad and repentant and hung his neck low and sighed and moved hesitantly like a sheep on drugs. However, he had to go soon as there was a call on the mobile and his face recovered from sadness and his agility bounced back to prevent him from being late.

During some news on the TV there were reports of a plane crash somewhere and Lahya's heart went into spasms. He rushed to listen, but it was somewhere in Russia or Tibet or something like that and he leaned against the nearest wall in relief and for support. Mumsy couldn't be there.

He needn't have worried. If Kali had arranged for him to see his mother before he died, she was not likely to have her killed on the way. If anything was to happen to her, it would happen after she came here, or on the way back. And only if he broke his pledge to Kali Mata, the second pledge, the new pledge. He had to be ready, ready with his sacrifice, with his life. There was not much time left. The swiftness of Jayshree's death proved that Kali was not one to waste time, or approve of it being wasted. She would not allow herself to be puddinged about.

The moment of weakness when he felt sad at the thought of dying had passed. He was again looking forward to it. Especially now, as he deserved it. He was Jayshree's murderer, if only by proxy, and he deserved to die, as indeed he would. That was his only consolation. But prior to that there were things to be done. It is surprising how impending death clears your mind, makes you see what you never saw before even though it was right beside your bollocks, helps get your priorities straight.

He had to write a letter to dadso, his father. Only a brief one, but he had to. He had to tell him that he no longer blamed him for being short, skinny, black and ugly. He understood that it was not his fault, that it just was. And that he was sorry to have been rude to him several times.

He was not quite sure how he would put all that in words without offending him, especially as the whole purpose of writing was to un-offend him, but he'd think of a way. If not, he'd just say sorry and leave it at that.

He had to reply to Ramesh.

He had to look through Jayshree's things and find something she really cherished – there was a doll, for instance, which she kept on her pillow – and take it to Tompkins Park and bury it close to the bench on which she often sat. It was a silly, stupid thing to do, but he wanted to do it because he was that kind of a boy; a silly, stupid boy.

He had to go look for Angus and see how he was doing, that he hadn't dropped dead with enlightenment. Or drugs and drink.

He had to read another letter for the friendly waiter downstairs.

He might even say goodbye to Blossom and Burt. He would like to have met Petal.

And of course, he had to see Ariel.

He called him. He was busy on the other line and would call back in ten minutes. He didn't.

He called again in half an hour. He was still busy, this time an important international call.

He called again in an hour. He got the answering machine.

He left a message saying he wouldn't be in New York for much longer and would very much like to see him before he left. He wanted to mention the five dollars and *the important phone numbers* that 'he might have forgotten in his room and if he could come and have a look', but decided to leave that till the end.

It was then he remembered something. Something he had forgotten which he shouldn't have forgotten.

He had Ariel's keys.

He would ring again, and, if he wasn't in, as the answering machine would prove, he would sneak in and wait for him, surprise him. He wouldn't be angry, especially if he told him about Jayshree's death, and that he would be going away himself. He might even tell him the truth, that he was going to die. He couldn't be angry with him after that, could he?

He had to see him; and there wasn't much time.

III

Lahya spent the night dreaming of Jayshree and Angus and Jamuna and Ariel and porn stars and the many severed heads of Kali and sobbing and whimpering and masturbating and feeling more and more guilty after each ejaculation. He felt so rotten by the morning that he could have died, pact with Kali Mata or no pact. The palms of his hands were greasy with sweat and semen and fear, and so were the bedclothes. Since there had been no planning, and indeed no desire on his part for the night's sex sessions with himself – and no pleasure either, except perhaps negatively through a release of pain – he had not arranged for any rags or an old shirt to be handy, and all was a big sticky mess. He quickly rolled everything up and hid it away under the bed. Later, at some stage, he would take it to the laundromat and wash and dry it for the night.

However, as the day developed, he realised the importance of it. It was one of the few at his disposal. He took hold of himself and came up with some positive things to do which would honour the day; things that were essential, prior to his departure from Manhattan on a no-return basis.

Mumsy telephoned, and that cheered him up greatly. She was coming over the following morning, and he wanted to be ready for her by feeling good, really good, which he would, after he had done the very important things he planned.

He was going to bury Jayshree's doll and one of her shoes in the park.

He was going to see if he could find Angus.

And most exciting of all, he was going to 'surprise' Ariel in his room.

He could hardly wait for dinner.

IV

Lahya was down in the park by about nine o'clock. It was still light, not a good time to be seen burying anything, but a good time to 'case the joint'. But he'd have to be careful otherwise he might end up in the joint himself. He didn't normally bother to be with it when it came to US-speak, but he thought he might give it a try, in honour of Hillary, whom Jayshree admired. He had a feeling that she secretly harboured the desire to be the First Lady of the United States of America one day. After all, anything was possible in that land of opportunities. She might even have hoped to be the first woman President of the same said land. Who knows what she really wanted, or hoped. Who will ever know. Or care.

At first sight his undergrounding of Jayshree's relics seemed an impossible task. All areas, especially around the benches, were full of all sorts, and the ground was hard or concreted or tarmaced or whatever. The dog enclosure was the only place where something could be easily buried, and he did not think it quite appropriate for Jayshree's favourite doll and one of her walking shoes she wore to the park to be stuffed under whatever it was resembling wood-shavings, spread around to absorb dog shit. But then he saw some soft earth beneath the trees within the grassy plots. Lack of sunlight around the trunks had not allowed grass to grow, and moisture and shade had prevented the ground from hardening. Obvious, but this was the first time Lahya had occasion to observe this simple fact.

It would work beautifully. He could sit with his back resting against a tree, in apparent innocence, while digging away with a hand behind his back. He was lucky in finding a tree not far from Jayshree's favourite bench, facing the south half-moon where boys kicked ball and where a stage was constructed for crazy concerts and suchlike when crazy concerts and suchlike took place in the park every other Saturday or whenever.

It seemed so easy that he didn't even deem it necessary to wait for darkness. He went over to the tree, sat against it, produced out of his shoulder bag a sharp-edged ladle purloined from the restaurant kitchen and began dishing out the earth between his back and the tree. The earth was quite soft, softer even than he had imagined as someone had only just watered it with copious piss and prepared the soil for easy digging. Although Tompkins Park was one of the two places in the entire United States of America which provided a Ladies and a Gentlemen for its citizens, a visit to the 'convenience' was a greater health hazard than naked dalliance in a pit of snakes, more morally mortifying than naked dalliance in a pulpit on Good Friday; and the more life-affirming of the sick and dying of Tompkins Park could be forgiven for preferring outdoor facilities. Be that as it may, all would have gone well had the stupid boy not started to cry.

'What's the matter, son?' A piss-soaked, puke-splattered candidate for the cold slab came and began ruffling Lahya's hair with black fingers which would have washed out white with soap and water. The shit under his fingernails had ceased to smell some time ago, the rest of him had not.

Lahya was not in a mood to cope with kindness, not without breaking down. A deluge of sob-suffocated words poured out of his mouth as if they were to be the last words ever spoken on planet Earth. He told the walking toilet everything there was to tell about his life and impending death. The other did not or could not understand what it was all about, but he knew pain when he saw pain.

He helped Lahya dig under the tree and bury Jayshree's doll and shoe. Then he began telling Lahya the story of his life.

Halfway through Lahya asked him if he knew Angus, Red.

'You mean the big guy with the big rat?'

'Yes, him,' said Lahya, quite excited. He would love to meet him again – though he wasn't sure if Angus would consider that to be the correct use of the word love – and having a little heart-to-heart. After all, he had never been so appreciated in all his life.

'He went back home this morning. Said he was going to make a new start. He met this bodhi sattwa or something, a little angel or a redeemer. Don't know what he was talking about. Anyway, this sattwa or what changed his whole life, he was born again, and starting again. Crazy. Never works, going back. I tried. Never works.'

Lahya felt flattered, confused, sad. He hoped it would work for Angus, hoped he was going back only to go forward. Either way he'd never see him again. Which reminded him. He had to see Ariel. Thanking the puke-punting, aesthetically challenged piss-pot and refusing his offer of a much valued cigarette-end, he hurried away. He must go home for a shower and change before 'calling on' Ariel.

Burying Jayshree's doll and shoe, talking to piss-pot, learning about Angus and having a good cry had made him feel very much better. He was ready to tackle the world, for as long as. The prospect of meeting Ariel was the diamond in the gold. He would meet him for sure, after all he would have to come back home some time, and Lahya would stay on until he did.

V

Freshly washed and reclothed, Lahya rang Ariel. It was strange, unnatural, to hope that he wasn't in, but that's what he hoped. It was not much after ten; chances were he would be out gallivanting somewhere with one of his many . . . whoever and whatever they were. The J word prevented him from being any kinder, the L word from any unkinder. Jealousy and love had their boundaries.

Luck was on Lahya's side. Ariel was out, Savitri in bed, Jamuna still in the restaurant and Dileep away as usual. He did not even have to explain to anyone where he was going.

Just outside the Hare Krishna House, Lahya called once more, just to make sure Ariel hadn't come in in the meantime. No. It was still the answering machine.

Outside the main door of the House Lahya hesitated. He could see into the hall and as far as he could tell no one was about. Quickly yet stealthily he turned the key in the lock. The door opened with surprising ease. He stepped inside and tried to look as if he belonged. If anyone asked, he would say he was there to see Ariel. Some of the residents had seen him the morning of his first and last visit here and that should help. Anyway, no one saw him.

As boldly as he could, he walked up the stairs, then on to Ariel's room. After standing outside it for a few seconds that moved slower than minutes, he gently tried the handle to see if it was locked. It was.

Out came the keys again. With his heart beating inside his skull he rapidly turned the keys and entered the room.

'What the fuck,' jumped a voice which sounded vaguely familiar, followed by Ariel's voice sounding quite unfamiliar, 'Oh my God!'

On the huge bed, big enough to accommodate three, in the light of two enormous red candles lit at the foot of the bed, were two intertwined bodies untwining themselves, the creamy white of Ariel, the ink-black of Benjamin.

Benjamin, thought Lahya, as if not there, as if gone back to one of last night's erotically sickening nightmares. In the strange way in which children expect certain things they know little of, without knowing why they expected them, he might have expected Andy, or Joost, Tone even – though he was greatly grateful it wasn't Tone, somehow that would have been too, too . . . too something or the other – but Benjamin he had not expected at all! Ariel had hardly seemed to know the guy the other day they were together.

As he stood calcified where he was, Ariel came towards him holding his underwear in front of his genitals. Ben had slunk under a sheet.

'What *are* you doing here Lahya? How did you get in? I think you better go now unless you have a very good explanation.' Ariel's voice was rising until it was very nearly angry in the end. Lahya had never thought Ariel could ever be angry with anyone. But he had a reason to. He had reasons too. 'A very good explanation' as Ariel had put it. Jayshree was dead, he was going to die . . . but he wasn't going to tell him. Not then. He couldn't. He was still trying to come to terms with what he had barged into.

'Come, I'll take you out,' said Ariel turning round to put his shorts on. As he did so he swayed his naked buttocks with an ever-so-slight a hint of a sexy swagger. It was certainly not the time or the occasion to have been a deliberate gesture. It just came naturally. Sexuality was a way of life for Ariel which couldn't be turned off just like that, no matter what. But to Lahya, at the time, Ariel's naked buttocks were just naked buttocks. They could have been anybody's. They didn't mean anything special. And they should have. Or should they have? But then, nothing seemed to mean anything at the time. His mind was frozen as if not intended to thaw out until a century hence.

Shorts on, Ariel caught Lahya by the arm and led him out of the room, then down the stairs and out of the building.

'Can you go home or do you want me to call you a taxi?'

'I can go . . . Listen. I am sorry, Ariel, please. I didn't mean to. It won't happen again, I swear . . .'

'You are damn right it won't. The keys. Give me the keys. If I had any sense I should . . . forget it.'

'Please, there is something I want to . . . can I see you tomorrow, please????' He made his voice at once as pleading and as contrite as possible.

'I don't think that is a very good idea. The keys now, please.'

'Here. Here are your fucking keys. And you are a slut.' He remembered the Blossom–Petal episode and the vocabulary that came with it. 'Just a common slut. You and your black trash. I never want to see you again for as long as I live, never, never, never . . .' That was the last thing in the world he wanted; that was the last thing in the world he wanted to say, but he said it again, 'Never again. Not for as long as I live, which is only a few days, thank God.'

And with that he flung the keys on the ground and ran out of the situation like even he had not run before.

VI

The next day Mumsy arrived and Lahya tried hard not to cry, but he did. She was worried for him. He looked pale and ill and not at all like his usual assertively snidey self. She would never have thought he would take Jayshree's death so badly. They never got along together. Were they treating him all right here? She never did like Savitri, nor was she overly fond of Dileep. Raj may have his faults, but he was honest and faithful, and quite fond of her in his own inelegant sort of a way.

· Lahya was grateful to poor Jayshree yet again. At least he could be miserable without having to invent lies to explain why. He couldn't tell Mumsy he was about to die, for her sake, at least in part. Nor could he tell her about Ariel. But he could say he was upset about Jayshree dying, which wasn't a lie anyway, even though it was far from being the whole truth. It was enough to satisfy Mumsy, at least to a point, and he wasn't cross-examined any further.

However, once Lahya's own pain was a bit dulled by tears and the joy of seeing Mumsy, he noticed that *she* didn't seem on top of the world either. Forgetting his own problems for the time being he asked if she was all right. She was not. She was having a 'difficult time' and had had a few tests to determine if everything was all right with the baby, and herself. She did not really want to talk about it, and she did not give many details, because she was not sure herself, but she was due to get the results of her tests soon and would find out what, if anything, was the matter.

Lahya was terrified. Was Kali preparing the grounds for her vengeance upon Mumsy?

Once again he called out to me and begged to know if the sacrifice of his life would be enough to spare his precious Mumsy. Once again he took my silence for a yes; when my silence resulted from the very suggestion that vengeance was my way, which it isn't. But I was not to be put in a position of justifying myself to stupid little boys.

VII

After the way he had behaved: more or less breaking into Ariel's room, violating his privacy and his right to live his life his way, infringing upon the life and privacy of a friend of his; and then, to top it all, calling him names and insulting him, it was not surprising that Lahya could not bring himself to call Ariel.

On the other hand, his sense of mounting urgency and his preception of time in terms that denied him time was compelling him that he must contact him if he was to die in peace; that they meet one last time, as friends, with affection and kindness, if not love, as Angus would have it.

Just not seeing him at least once before he died would have been bad enough, but living his last hours with the pain of their last meeting was quite simply unbearable. Living with the consciousness that the last words he said to him were lies, and angry lies at that, and, worst of all, that Ariel had seen him off with angry eyes, eyes which appeared to regret they ever saw him. And they were such beautiful eyes too, gentle eyes, eyes that cared. As was his voice. Such a beautiful voice. A gentle voice, a voice that cared. And yet, the last his eyes looked upon him, they did not care, the last his voice spoke to him, it did not care. How could he die with those eyes and that voice freezing the marrow of his soul! And yet die he must. How could he talk to Ariel after that night! And yet talk he must.

And then he thought of Andy. Cute Andy. Cute or not, he had been quite friendly with him and had even given him his telephone number to call him if he wanted to meet some deep-throat artists, vocally speaking, though some of them were reputed to excel otherwise. Anyway, calling Andy could be a way out. From Kali

Mata to the Virgin Mother. From grandmother to mother. Mumsy was supposed to believe in mediation, intercession, especially by the Virgin. The virginity of Andy may have been a matter of minor doubt, but his intercessionary capacities could well exist, and could therefore be exploitable. It was worth a try.

He rang Andy.

'Who's that? Lahya??? Who, when . . . Ariel. Ah, yes. Yes yes yes yes. Look, I'm busy now, the other line. Call you back later. OK.'

He didn't.

Lahya tried later.

'Is that Lah . . . ya? Have I got the name right? Look, I'm with a client now. Can I call you later? What time is it now. Three-thirty? I'll call you at about five, five-thirty. Take care. Bye.'

The next morning Lahya made another try.

'Look, I really can't talk to you now. What time is it? Ten-thirty . . .'

Lahya decided if he had to take that kind of shit he might as well call Ariel and take it from him than from cuter-than-shit Andy.

He called Ariel.

'Listen, I can't talk to you now. I'm busy. What . . . Well, I can't. I'm doing something now. No, I can't. I'm moving to my own apartment and I have a lot of packing to do. No, I can't. *I'm doing something.*'

'Don't you mean *someone* is doing *you*?' laughed Ben as Ariel put the phone down and stretched like a cat.

'I don't know what to do about that kid,' said Ariel, disengaging himself.

'He has put you off your food. That is certainly one for labelling and storing. Just tell him to fuck off, man. Simple. That's what I'd do. I'd have kicked the shit out of him the other night if he had crept up on me like that. Well he did, but not in my pad.'

'I can't do that. I . . . like him. Feel sorry for him . . .'

'Feeling sorry never gets dinner on the table. It's not the same as liking someone. Don't tell me you are going cradle robbing!'

'Shut up. Of course not. It's just that . . . Oh . . . I don't know. He's had a tough deal in life . . .'

'Don't you go believing every sob story you . . . I thought you didn't go for that charity stuff.'

'Well, I don't. That's why I know there is some trouble there. Some pain. I can feel it.'

'How long have you known him? All of ten days, so what's the big . . .'

'More than that. But that's not the point, is it? Some people you know all your life and they mean nothing. Others you see once and they are important. How long have I known you . . .'

'So it *is* like that, then.'

'Don't be so stupid. How can you even . . .'

'Well *you* may not be, darling, but I'm sure the kid's wet for you. That's all there is to it. And the sooner you tell him to push off the kinder for him.'

'I suppose you're right. But the trouble is, and now, listen to me carefully . . .' Ariel laughed his laugh before resuming what he was going to say. 'Don't go getting ideas and I do *not* mean it like that, but I sort of love him too. *Don't* you dare. I mean, like a child. He's warm and affectionate and laughs with me and is . . . different. Real. I don't know. You know I like children . . .'

'You can sure do better than him, man, if you *are* going underage . . .'

'Shut up. It's not that at all, and you know it. My wife was Indian – you didn't know that, did you, you didn't know I *had* a wife – and if we'd had our child . . . Of course he'd only be . . . I just don't know what to do. Sometimes I think it *is* best to tell him to beat it once and for all, and that . . .'

'Well I'm fucked. *You* married! But, you live and learn. Still, I think you give him the push. The harder the better. Gently won't do it, he'll only keep hoping. It's best for him. Why string out his, whatever. *You* may think of him as a child, but I'll be fucked if he thinks of you as a father.'

'Maybe he does. His father has . . . does it to him, I think.'

'This is getting crazier and crazier. The sooner you get rid of him the better. He'll get you in trouble, you just remember that.'

'He's only a kid. And I . . . like . . . being with him. He's fun. Different. I can be myself with him. Play around. Be a child . . . I don't know what I am talking about . . . Wait, now you'll think I am very stupid, but I will consult the oracle!'

'Consult whaaat!'

'I know you'll think I'm stupid. But when I have doubts I consult the oracle. Here, I'll show you.'

Ariel jumped off the bed, dived into his jeans pocket, came out with his wallet and took out two bits of paper folded tightly into tiny little squares. He opened them out and showed them to Ben. One had 'yes' written on it, the other 'no'.

'Whenever I am not sure about something, especially something important, I roll these on the floor, and pick up the nearest to me. If it says "yes", it's yes, and if "no", it's no.'

'I don't believe I'm hearing this,' said Ben.

'No, it's true. I swear. Sometimes there is an important meeting and a serious decision to be made. And I excuse myself and go into the toilet and consult the oracle.'

'You mean there are ten people waiting for you to make a big decision and you are in the bathroom rolling two bits of paper with "yes" and "no" written on them? That's . . . that's crazy, man.'

'I know, isn't it?'

Suddenly, getting very serious, Ariel shook the pieces of paper in the palms of both his hands, shut his eyes and looked up for a while, then cast them reverently on the floor and picked up the one closest to him. It said 'no'.

'I'll try again. Three times,' he said.

He tried again. And then again. Each time it said 'no'.

'What did I tell you,' said Ben looking pleased with himself, 'even your oracle is telling you not to see the kid again. So just drop him, will you, unless your brains have fallen through your asshole. Drop him.'

VIII

Lahya woke up looking and feeling like an overdone fried egg. But good news was soon to cheer him up.

dadso called. Mumsy's tests had all come out fine and there was no problem with either the mother or the child. Lahya had a moment where he could have wished otherwise for 'the child', but he cursed himself for such a thought. Soon Mumsy would be losing her first born and would need another one to take her love; now more than ever.

He also spoke to his father. Raj was surprised to hear him talk with something approaching affection and it almost moved him to tears. Lahya could sense his father's emotions and felt like crying himself. It was good; good to be reconciled any time, but especially when one's time was over.

It was not to be so with Ariel. Lahya had given up. He couldn't take the hurt of another 'busy on the other line', or 'ring you later', while any mention of an 'international call' and he would have been back to his murdering days again. The nicest rebuff of all had been having the phone put down on him. At least it was more honest. So, when all was said and done, reconciliation with Ariel was not to be. Lahya had given up. Playing the wallet card, as he had often thought, looked like such a pathetic idea. Who cared. Still, you win some, you lose some, as his favourite teacher in his first comprehensive etcetera etcetera.

However, it meant the time to go had come, before Kali changed her mind about Mumsy. Also, the longer it went on, the longer would linger the hurt of Ariel.

Tonight would be the night.

He thought of various ways to go about it. The easiest would be to take a whole load of Jayshree's pills – an overdose was supposed to be deadly even if you needed them, more especially if you did not – go to sleep and never wake up again. So peaceful, so tempting, so inviting. Bottles and bottles of Jayshree's pills had suddenly sprouted all over the place. When she was alive it was hard to find one.

Quicker and more exciting would be to jump under a car, or a Subway train. But then you would be away from home. He had to be home, in front of Kali's shrine. She had to have her sacrifice in front of her. He could take the pills in the basement and go to sleep there, but the very advantage of that method was its disadvantage. It was too peaceful. Perhaps too much so for Kali's appetite.

In the circumstances it would be right to hang himself. Dramatic, definitive, and violent enough to satisfy Kali. He'd try to make his tongue loll by sticking it out before kicking the chair or whatever. Neck broken, tongue hanging out, especially if bloodied – he might give it a cut beforehand – would be just perfect for Kali. Perfect enough for her to forswear vengeance on anybody else. He had already begun to feel secure that Mumsy was safe, and if Ariel hated him now, as he surely must, there would be no point in hurting him. So it turned out for the best that they broke up like that. Not that there was ever anything between them to break up. Best for Ariel. And that was what mattered. Nothing mattered for him, not personally. He would be out of it.

There were bits and pieces of rope lying about in one of the cupboards in the basement, probably used to cart video boxes in. He went down to the cellar after lunch to make preparations for the night. He found one piece of rope strong enough and long enough to be quite suitable. The ceiling fan hook was an ideal place to hang it from. He wished someone could turn the fan on after he had croaked. It would be quite an impressive sight to see his dead, convulsed body, tongue lolling out, dripping with still-warm blood, rotating above the room with the blades of the fan. Yes, that would be the perfect touch, though he wasn't sure how he could manage it.

He placed the coffee table under the fan, a straight-backed chair upon it, and tested if he could reach the centre point of the fan. He could. Climbing down he got the rope, tied a hanging knot on its one end, then took the other end and began to knot it round the hook. He wanted everything to be properly set up. He didn't want to come down in the middle of the night and start from scratch. He would have it all in readiness, just waiting to climb up and into the noose, kick the chair, and Dileep is your uncle. Simple.

With Jayshree gone no one was likely to come down to the cellar, not in the determinate future, so no one was likely to find out.

IX

When Lahya got back up Mumsy looked at him in surprise, 'Where have you been? There was a call for you just now, I thought you were in but when . . .'

'Who, who was it? Who called?' Lahya was finding it hard to breathe.

'Someone from a very stormy weather . . .' and when Lahya looked blank, she added, 'Didn't I take you to see *The Tempest*? No. You had the mumps then. I was quite, quite annoyed. I really did want to see that production. Right funny you looked. We saw the other one, *A Midsummer Night's Dream*, remember. I think it was Ariel, Michael Clarke, or was he Caliban, or was that a film . . .'

But Lahya wasn't listening. He ran to the phone almost brushing Mumsy aside. Marilyn, though used to Lahya's escape dashes, found this one a little strange as it seemed quite uncalled for, even by the standards of his unpredictability.

Praying to God and Jesus and Kali all in one go he dialled Ariel's number.

A professional-sounding voice informed him that the number he dialled had been changed to . . . giving another number. Lahya's breathing finally stopped. He didn't have a pen handy. He rushed around trying to find a pen and as it happens on such occasions there was none to be found. He had to approach Mumsy again, who went into her room, got her handbag, searched through it and gave Lahya a pen and a look. On another occasion the look, demanding an explanation, would have got one. Today Lahya barely noticed it.

He dialled the old number again, got the new number, wrote it down, then started pushing the right buttons. He couldn't believe his ears when Ariel's voice answered.

'Hi, Lahya, I called you just a minute ago. First you were in, then you were out, and now you are in again. Some news for you; I've moved into my own apartment I was telling you about, and this time you are not getting anywhere near the keys, I'll see to that. I don't know how you got them last time, but I'll have to . . . anyway, I am so happy. I've been looking forward to it for such a long time. It's only small, but it's mine, and I'm so, so happy. But look, when packing my things I found this little wallet. It had your name and some . . .'

'Oh thanks. Yes, that's mine. I thought I dropped it in the park somewhere.'

'Well you didn't. You must have left it in my room, during *one* of your *visits*.' There was more meaning than mere words in his rainbow voice. 'Look, I've got to run now. But I am coming down your way to see a friend of mine this evening. I can bring the wallet with me, and come and see you, if you like?'

Would he? Would Madonna like an Oscar? Would Blossom want Petal? Or Reagan a stiff dick?

So it was settled. He would be there around nine. He was going to some party at the USA later that night, and he was seeing a friend in the Village to check if their names were on the list, and if not, to take on names that were.

Lahya didn't follow it all, but who cared. Ariel was coming to see him and all was well with the world. Proof that Kali was happy, happy that he was doing the right thing, happy that he was going about it the right way. He knew the idea of him hanging himself from the ceiling fan in front of her altar would appeal to her. His sacrifice would be accepted.

Lahya told him he would meet him outside the restaurant and then 'smuggle' him into the basement as he had something to show him – his excuse to get him somewhere private, to himself – and the house would not be 'the right place since Jayshree was dead'.

Jayshree, his cousin who was . . . well, not quite . . . well . . . Ariel wasn't sure if the boy was telling the truth or not, but he didn't push it. He'd be there at nine.

It meant about half past, at least, thought Lahya, but he didn't care. He'd be happy to wait for a lifetime if he knew he was coming. For Lahya it was a lifetime.

X

Lahya had six hours and thirty-nine minutes before Ariel was due. He had to make the most of those six hours and thirty-nine minutes. Make the most of his life.

First he'd go out and buy a present for Ariel, something he could remember him by. Then he would take a walk around the streets and avenues that had provided him with entertainment over the past many days. Entertainment, and friends, even a wisdom of sorts. And then on to Tompkins Park and see for the last time all the strange and wonderful people that sheltered within its gates. He might even check to see if Dirk – Patrick – was back, albeit in plaster, or not. Then he would go home and spend time with Mumsy until just before nine. Ariel was sure to be late, but Lahya would be there on time, just in case. It was good to have his whole life mapped out so clearly, and so full of things and people he had learnt to love and enjoy.

It would be nice if he could say goodbye to Blossom and Burt, and great if he could meet Petal; lucky Petal to be loved so much. An encounter with Guppy and Puppy wouldn't be a bad idea either. His mind then retreated to Gravesend, and he remembered Ramesh, as if in another world, another time, neither real.

He wanted to buy Ariel a beautiful new apartment, a huge apartment, the best in the entire city of New York, in the entire State of New York, in the whole wide world. That should make him happy and he'd remember him for it, always. Maybe not always, but for a long time. Quite some time.

But he would have to settle for about fifty dollars'-worth instead. That's what was left of his money. He could have asked Mumsy for more, but he didn't want to. He did not want to say or do anything that might lead to questions. As for his present to Mumsy, he would cut off his hair for her. Hair never dies, he had heard on some television programme. So he would leave Mumsy a part of him that never dies, like love. Love and hair, what a silly combination. He tried to imagine what Angus would make of it. He hoped he was all right. He liked Angus. Big Angus, and his big rat. Amanda Lee. He wondered if that was the name of someone Angus knew. A girlfriend? A favourite aunt? Lahya smiled to himself as he thought of Aunt Jamuna and their night together. He was happy. Happy that Ariel had got his new apartment. Happy that Mumsy and her baby were fine. Happy that Mumsy was here. Happy. Just happy. Happy that his rope and noose and table and chair were all ready and waiting. Happy that Ariel was coming over to see him. Happy. Just happy.

XI

It was after he had decided on a present for Ariel and was in the process of buying it, waiting to pay at the counter, that his happiness got tarnished with something quite unpleasant, more so as he felt ashamed of it, and of himself because of it.

Up until then he had felt so guilty about his escapade with Ariel that night, and since the afternoon so elated about his call that he had blocked out of his mind what he *actually saw* in Ariel's room. Unexpectedly and without warning it hit him between the legs with a steel-capped boot.

The coiled naked bodies of Ariel and Benjamin, in the flickering light of the giant candles which caused them to undulate suggestively even when, for a long split second, they were motionless with shock, rose and fell before his eyes, as if in the very act at that very moment in that very shop for all to see, openly, boldly and without shame.

How could he . . . How could he . . . the voice of unreason swelled within him as he felt a swelling begin to manifest itself in the shameful regions of his body. *How could he . . . How could he . . .* this time meaning himself.

If only it was someone *deserving* of Ariel he could have forgiven, at least understood. The anger and jealousy that he had felt his entire life in the belief that dadso did not deserve Mumsy was compressed into brief passionate seconds and he could feel the sweat from his forehead seeping down to his toes with searing speed.

But then, who deserved Mumsy!

And who deserved Ariel? Certainly not any that he had seen, certainly not among his friends. At least it wasn't Tone, that seemed to be his only consolation. But again, it wasn't Tone *that* night. Who was to say he wasn't the one on another night?

Like a jealous lover who wasn't allowed his share of love, his brain was about to explode with the enormous possibilities of Ariel's unlimited sexual encounters opened up by that one encounter when the kind old lady at the counter spoke, 'And what have you got there, young sir?'

He tried not to look between his thighs and offered his intended purchase to be boxed while he got his money out.

Just as he was about to leave the shop he saw Ariel's naked buttocks. That night, in his state of numbed shock they had meant nothing. Suddenly they were more important than the whole world. Unable to cope with the vision, he turned Ariel around and saw the underwear he held in front of his genitals. His head went dizzy and he had to steady himself against the nearest wall. There was a poster with a picture of one of the candidates in the local elections pasted at the lower end of the wall. On top of the picture it said PISS HERE. Many people had obligingly obeyed. Lahya hurried away to avoid the stench, carefully stepping over the avant-garde patterns of urine splattered across the pavement, sidewalk if you like.

XII

There was a concert going on in Tompkins Park.

On a makeshift yet surprisingly spacious stage a band comprising and technically assisted by blacks, whites, Hispanics, and one Native American was blasting forth some kind of rock music. In the arena in front and all around the park people, comprising blacks, whites, Hispanics and several other types whose origins Lahya could not even try to guess at, were sitting, standing, clapping, head-banging, dancing, or just passing by. From leather to denim to gingham and skin, and a lot beside, was on free and abundant display. Living and alive faces were reflecting the brilliance of the sun under the sun or the trees or each other.

Lahya was lucky to find a place on Jayshree's favourite bench. After squirming his backside about he managed to settle himself down in a comfortable position from where to watch both the players and the spectators. From his bag he took out the box containing his present for Ariel. It was a happy-looking crystal cat.

He remembered seeing it in the little curio shop the day he had bought the figurines of Kali. He loved all crystals, especially the clear quartz ones that split light into rainbow colours. While looking into different shop windows trying to think what best to get Ariel, he saw a big fat cat looking out of a shop window at people looking into the shop window. Her eyes shone with such green intensity from a shamelessly ginger head. That and the quiet patience with which she sat eyeing those who eyed her curiously reminded him of Ariel. If only she was a rainbow-coloured cat instead of ginger, thought Lahya, she would just sum up Ariel, in as much as it is possible to sum up any human being, however outwardly simple, not to speak of Ariel. And then he remembered the crystal cat.

A crystal with mutating rainbow colours, appearing, disappearing, merging, fragmenting . . . like Ariel's rainbow voice, like Ariel's rainbow eyes, like Ariel's rainbow presence.

And now, sitting in Jayshree's place, watching the rainbow panorama of human existence dancing its dance of energy and matter and light, playing its music of exultant joy and boisterous suffering, he saw Ben as one of the fragments of Ariel's rainbow life; as indeed was Andy, or Joost, even Tone. Beautiful Tone, whose limbs and eyes and voice and walk were of a snake. A graceful snake. A cool and smooth roll of vibrant life packaged in silk and splattered with gold and diamonds on its skin, gold and diamonds that weren't sold in shops. An utterly, utterly wonderful creature from the creative repertoire of an utterly, utterly wonderful creator.

How could he possibly have grudged Ariel his pleasure, his happiness? Whether or not he similarly enjoyed the pleasure of Andy or Joost or Tone, or half the men and women of New York city, was quite, quite irrelevant, had nothing to do with his essential purity and beauty, or theirs.

Lahya's vocabulary may have been different from mine, but words, like age and experience, are not only not necessary for truth, they are an obstacle, often an insurmountable obstacle.

All he knew was that he loved Ariel, and that was all he needed to know. And it had nothing to do with the inflammation of emotions or body parts.

XIII

Mumsy was getting a bit fed up with Lahya almost literally hanging around her neck for the entire evening, asking her if she wanted anything, offering to make her coffee, or something to eat, or get her a glass of wine, so she was more relieved than curious or angry when he looked at his watch, exclaimed, 'Shit, it's ten past nine,' and ran out of the house. Five seconds and he was back, running up to his room and stomping down with a bag across his shoulder, then to Mumsy again, gave her a big, strong, lingering hug and dashed out once more.

Only after the door had banged shut she felt her cheeks were wet. Had the stupid boy been crying? For the first time she looked worried and a strange foreboding clutched at her guts with rusty fingers. It must be the pregnancy and the pills, she thought, but the answer did not satisfy her entirely. She wished Lahya was back with her again. Strange, ten minutes ago she was praying he would leave her alone to get on with Margaret Atwood.

XIV

Surprisingly, Ariel was already waiting for Lahya on the street outside the restaurant. 'Where have you been? Where have you been?' he said, showing his teeth, a green glint in his eyes, head cocked slightly to one side like a mischievous teal.

Lahya suggested they had better go into the restaurant for a coffee or something. The waiters were hanging about close to the windows and he didn't want to be spotted going into the basement from the outside trap door. It would be easier to sneak down through the restaurant on the pretext of going to the toilets which were close to the stairs leading to the basement.

There was so much Lahya had wanted to say to Ariel, but now he was there he didn't know what or how. All he could do was repeatedly apologise for behaving like an idiot, a criminally inclined idiot, and for saying all those mean things he did not at all mean, and if Ariel would please please forgive him. Ariel kept responding that it didn't matter, that he was not an idiot, that we all do the best we know how at any given time, and that there was nothing to forgive. 'I've been through it myself. When I was six. I know what it's like.' Lahya was happy to hear that, but he would have been happier to hear Ariel say that he forgave him rather than saying that there was nothing to forgive.

Anyway, after a while the apologies and their acceptance got a bit boring for both concerned and Ariel changed the subject by suggesting they should go to see *Jurassic Park* soon.

Lahya went quiet at that, and said he would have loved to, but he'd be going away. Mumsy had come over after Jayshree's death and she would be taking him back as his school was soon reopening.

Ariel was disappointed to hear that he was leaving, and thought he would probably miss the little blighter. More than that, there was something in the tone of Lahya's voice and the way he spoke which made him feel uneasy. Perhaps it was Jayshree's death. The boy seemed different, more mature, and something else besides. Ariel couldn't give it a name, but whatever it was, it certainly made him apprehensive and concerned about the boy in a way not in keeping with his usual positive and optimistic approach to life and living.

The talk of going, and Lahya brought out his crystal cat, his present, or what he called his 'parting gift' for Ariel. Ariel was touched. He rose from his chair and went over to Lahya to give him a hug. 'Don't call it a parting gift, we'll see each other, soon. I'm sure you'll come back to New York; your relatives are here. And I certainly keep going over to England. I have lots of friends there, and some business clients. So don't look so down. We'll meet again, sooner than you might think.'

They had had a cup of coffee and a cola by then, and Lahya insisted on paying. Then he suggested they go down to the basement. 'You'll like it there. It's nice. Also, Granddad's camera is there. I'd like to take a picture of you, of us together, before I . . . go. Please.'

'All right,' Ariel responded, 'I haven't much time, though . . . No more than fifteen minutes.'

Lahya had expected Ariel wouldn't be staying long, but was still depressed to hear him say so. However, as cheerfully as he could, he said, 'That's fine. You can go whenever you feel like it.'

He asked Ariel to go towards the toilets about a minute after him. 'I'll wait for you by the basement stairs with the door unlocked. As soon as you get there, just run down and I'll follow.' Ariel was amused by all the mystery, but agreed.

That settled, away went Lahya, and Ariel followed shortly behind.

XV

As Lahya entered the basement, half a second later than Ariel, he heard Ariel draw in his breath and exclaim, 'Oh my God!' for once forgetting to put sex in his voice.

It took Lahya another half a second before he realised that it wasn't Ariel's sense of wonder at the elegance of the basement that prompted his overawed amazement, but the noose hanging from the ceiling with a chair upon a coffee table beneath it.

In his excitement at Ariel's arrival, and before that his desire to be with his Mumsy for his last night among the living, and with all the other little things he had had on his mind, he had forgotten about his exit arrangements.

In different circumstances he would have tried to lie his way out of it, coming up with a million implausible explanations to divert his attention from the obvious, but the unexpectedness of it, and the thought that Ariel might think it was a macabre joke on him made Lahya blurt the truth. 'It's for me, not for you. Honest. I told you I . . . won't be here, that I was . . . going, didn't I? Didn't I? Honest. Honest to God.' His whole body was trembling and he started to cry, softly and noiselessly. 'I forgot to take it down. I am sorry, I should have taken it down. It's just that when I set it up I didn't know you were coming. I got your call afterwards, and I forgot to . . . I thought I'd save myself the trouble of setting it up at night. I didn't know you were coming. And when I did, I was so happy I didn't think . . . Honest. I was so happy . . .'

He was speaking through silent sobs, so softly even he could hardly hear himself.

Ariel stood listening to him as if immobilised in a nightmare. Then pulling himself out of it he looked at Lahya, still in a half-daze, and said, 'Poor boy, my poor boy, what has the world done to you so early on in life? You are still a child, you have your whole life in front of you . . .' He walked up to Lahya and put his arms round him and held him close. 'It is very selfish to . . . to . . . do this, you know. Think of what your mother will feel. What I will feel. I do care for you, you know. Love you. Not in the way . . . like a friend, a brother. I will be really hurt if you ki . . . do this. You don't want to hurt me, do you? And you certainly don't want to hurt your mother, now do you?'

Lahya snuggled as close against Ariel as he could, wishing his body would devour his, leaving behind nothing but emptiness. No one had ever cared for him so much, loved him so much. He had to die while it still lasted. Before Ariel discovered what a stupid little creature he was and learned to hate him, or mock him, like everybody at school, and the wise of Gravesend.

'I don't want to hurt Mumsy. Or you. In fact, that's why I must die, otherwise something bad will happen to her, or to you.'

Ariel released Lahya, moved a step back and looked at him again. 'How do you mean?'

It was Lahya's day to speak the truth. No point in lying when you are about to die. He told Ariel everything. Beginning, most embarrassingly, about wanting to be a gorgeous white woman, like Mumsy; his pact with Kali, his change of mind and the new pact demanding his life instead.

Ariel was relieved beyond measure. He laughed his happy, happy laugh and said, 'Is that all? How stupid can you get. Of course . . .'

It was the wrong thing to say. 'I know I am stupid. Everybody knows I am stupid. You don't have to go on about . . .'

'I didn't mean it like that. You should know I didn't. Look, take me to this Kali of yours and I will talk her out of it.' His eyes twinkled with merriment and he nudged Lahya in the ribs. 'Go on.'

Knowing in his heart that it wasn't really a very good idea, he obeyed, almost robotically. Going to the Chinese screen, he moved it to one side to reveal the little shrine of Kali.

Ariel tried to look serious, 'Now listen, Kali Mat . . . what did you call her?'

'Kali Mata, it means Mother Kali.'

'Now listen, Kali Mata,' and with this he reached forward and lifted the figurine with his hand and, pointing the finger of his other hand at her nose, began to say, 'Now you listen, Mata dear, you leave this boy alo . . .'

'No don't. Don't,' Lahya screamed, 'don't make her angry. She killed Jayshree. She had Granddad killed. She is powerful. All-powerful. You cannot . . .'

'Oh yes I can,' said Ariel as he began to dance around the room with Kali in the palm of his hand. 'Oh yes I can, oh yes I can . . .' He turned around on his toes and still pointing a finger at her continued, 'Now you leave my friend here alone, otherwise, you, Mata, are for the trash can along with . . .'

'No. No, please, Ariel, don't, don't . . .' He got in the way of Ariel's dance steps, trying to get Kali out of his hand. Ariel raised his hand with Kali up in the air to prevent Lahya from getting at it. Lahya jumped high to reach, but as he did so, his foot tripped up Ariel who fell forward on to the standard lamp, taking it down with him, smashing its globe-like bulb.

Lahya laughed a nervous laugh. 'See, serves you right for messing about with Kali.' He lunged to the floor and snatched Kali out of Ariel's hand.

To his surprise Ariel did not react, made no attempt to hold on to Kali, or make a verbal protest or laugh or joke or say anything or do anything.

'Come on, get up now,' said Lahya, squatting on the floor beside Ariel, 'get up you stupid man.' He would get even with him for calling him stupid.

Ariel did not stir. A cold dread began to creep up Lahya's spine. He knelt beside Ariel and tried to move him, at first gently, then with a force born out of desperate fear. He managed to turn Ariel's body over. His tank top had slipped low, revealing his left nipple. Just below it a sharp piece of glass from the lamp had gone straight into his heart. One tiny drop of blood marked the spot.

Ariel was dead.

PART VII

Realisation

(once upon a long long ahead)

(or not)

'You killed him, you killed him, why did you kill him? Couldn't you have waited just another hour? You'd have had me by then. Couldn't you have waited for just a little while longer, just a little while longer . . .' Surprisingly, the voice was soft and gentle; sad, but not angry or aggressive as a little boy's at the abrupt croaking of his one and only true love should have been.

'I didn't kill him, You did, Sigourney,' Sigourney heard my voice say. '*You* wanted to be a woman. *You* accepted the deal. *You* brought him here. *You* told him about me. *You* tripped him up. *You* killed him. Not me. Besides, you should be happy. You've got what you wanted. I am honouring my part of the bargain, now that you have yours.'

Sigourney had difficulty seeing what had happened. Sigourney had difficulty seeing. Slowly she rose to her feet where she had been kneeling beside Ariel's body. She tottered on the red court shoes with the very high heels and nearly stumbled and fell. Her legs were so weak she could barely walk.

'What have you done to me?' she asked, quite bewildered. 'I cannot see properly. I cannot walk properly.'

'You have got what you wanted, like I said before. In return for offering the young man's white body . . .'

'But that was an accident. An accident . . .'

'Do not worry. There was no accident. There *is* no accident. There are no accidents. Ariel is the one I chose for you, *and* the one you chose. Once you have made your choice, or it's made for you, the rest follows. You have done well. He is beautiful, and good. Now you have your reward. Be happy.'

'I don't want to be happy. Not like this. Can't you change

~ 243 ~

everything back? Please,' she begged. 'You are all-powerful, you know everything, you can do everything. Can you not please change it all back? Can't you? Can you?'

'Can I change back time? I cannot, because I never created it. Time is your illusion. I can change what I create. I cannot change what you make. I can change reality, I cannot change illusion, because there is nothing there to change. I cannot undo what hasn't happened, cannot happen. It is your illusion. Only you can change it. It is up to you.'

Sigourney's head spun around. I was too clever for her. Or rather, she was too stupid for me, but then, isn't everyone? She stretched out one long, bony hand in front of her and tried to find something to lean against, to steady herself. It was a white hand. A spectacularly white hand. Old and wrinkled and veined, but white. Unlike some old hands that go greyish-brown, hers was stark, pasty white.

She saw her hand, old, wrinkled, veined, spectacularly white; and was more bewildered than ever. 'What have you done to me?' she asked again, in too much pain to scream or cry.

'You wanted to be like your mother. You are,' Sigourney heard me explain.

'But my mother, Mumsy . . . her hands are beautiful, so soft, so smooth.' She sounded like a commercial for her mother's hands.

My patience was wearing thin. 'Go upstairs and *look*. She is in your room. Waiting for you.'

Sigourney slowly made her way to the stairs and began to climb up, step by step, minute by minute, step by step. Up to the apartment, and another set of stairs. Sheer strength of will carried her as she started the second climb. She got to the door of her room and pushed it open with all her withered might.

Inside, on a rocking chair, sat a very old woman, rocking, mouth open and dry.

Sigourney could not make out the details, but she saw enough to see what she saw. 'Mumsy?' she whispered. Marilyn looked up and a half-crazy smile of recognition played on her love-starved lips. She stretched out a hand to greet her; it was wrinkled, veined, spectacularly white. Sigourney could see her face in her, as in a mirror.

But she was still not satisfied. She wanted more answers. First she thought of going down back again, but then remembered my temple in the room opposite. She started that way. After all, it was there that our little pact was first made.

My door was unlocked. She came and stood in front of me as boldly and strongly as she could, as I stood on the dying body of my pretty victim.

'But I am supposed to be young.' She was beginning to get a little assertive. 'Yes, young. You have not kept your word. Not really.' Her half-blind eyes were reddening with a rage of sorts.

'Youth was never part of the deal. Never mentioned.'

'But gorgeous. I surely said gorgeous. Heaven knows I said gorgeous often enough.'

'But you *are* gorgeous. What's this about you mortals that you can see no beauty in age! In your terms I am millions of years old, and I am gorgeous. So are you. If you can't see it, it is not my fault. I can see it.'

Sigourney looked out the window. She could almost make out people running about their nightly business, laughing, talking, gesticulating . . .

'My life,' she finally cried out in agony. 'Whatever happened to my life?'

'Life wasn't a part of the deal either. Life never is.'

Sigourney knew when she was beaten. Bowing her head, she was about to leave when she thought of one more question. 'And Ariel. What about Ariel?'

'He is where you left him. He is lonely.'

Sigourney smiled. Best get back to Ariel. But before going she wanted see Mumsy once more. Hold her in her arms. Tell her that she loved her. She went into her room again. It was empty. No Mumsy. No rocking chair.

She started walking down the stairs. Who would have thought that the high-heeled red shoes she so longed to wear could be so painful to wear, so difficult to walk in, but she'd be damned if she took them off now!

Step by step by hurtful step she went down one flight to the main apartment, and then down again into the basement. It seemed it would take the rest of her life to do that, and all her energy, but she managed.

Ariel was lying on his back, one arm stretched above his head, one by his side, as young and as beautiful as ever.

Sigourney shambled to where he lay, then, lowering herself slowly and painfully, lay down by his side, nestled cosily against his chest, and, lifting his outstretched arm, wound it round her body. Then, resting her head on the fleshy part of his shoulder, she buried her nose in his still-warm armpit. And as she did so she knew the ecstasy of the realisation of love. The ecstasy of realisation.

Lahya knew then that red court shoes were not for him. Nor Ariel. He wanted life. Life that was denied Jayshree.

Ugly and crippled and ignored and unwanted though she was, she loved to live. Ugly and short and skinny and black that he was, he should love to live. And he could. And he would. Even if he grew up to be a mere man.

Like dadso.

Like his father.

After all, his wonderful and beautiful and gorgeous Mumsy married him. So he couldn't be all that bad. Or all that ugly.

Neither was he.

Ariel liked him.

He jumped to his feet, grateful for his seamy sneakers, all eager to help Ariel up and to thank him for making him see sense. But he was not there. He must have left. He had said he was in a hurry.

Lahya was sad. But only for a moment. There was so much to do. A life to live. Watch some dirty videos, for a start. He was happy.

So was I. I had succeeded.